Spellbound

&

Hellhounds

By: Nia Rose

SPELLBOUND & HELLHOUNDS

Poisoned Apple Publishing, L.L.C.

Printed in the United States of America

Coven Chronicles series by
Nia Rose & Octavia J. Riley
SPELLBOUND & HELLHOUNDS

Stand Alone Novels by
Nia Rose
SONS OF STARS

Dedicated to: my mother.
You were the queen of glitter, my beacon of hope, and my magical inspiration. The world didn't lose you; you just became more than a person. You became a memory, a feeling, and a spirit that will forever - now and always - inspire me to never give up.
I love you mommy.

Chapter 1:

Swirling snow swept through the air as two figures moved with haste down the sidewalk. One was a giant in size, and his form was gawked at by all those that the couple passed. His shadow alone blocked the sun from the girl's path who trudged with purpose in front of him.

He had two sharp horns, two rows of jagged teeth nestled into a square jaw with two large bottom teeth jutting up ever so slightly from his lower gums. The creature had several hundred pounds of muscle packed away under deep gray skin that was modestly covered up by a well-pressed navy shaded suit, and it was accompanied by a snappy sapphire-blue tie swirled with gold designs and dangled from around his neck. The being's height was bordering a monstrous seven feet, and in his gargantuan paw, he clasped a tiny – in comparison – book. A small, silvery set of circular framed glasses were resting on the bridge of his nose as he flipped another page and followed diligently behind the young girl as he was lost within the leather-bound tome.

The girl was an average of five feet and six inches and looked like a dwarf next to the creature behind her. Her night dipped locks were tucked snugly under the hood of her mauve-colored garment in a tightly woven plait that spilled out from under her hood. On the front of her raven shaded cloak that draped over her shoulders was a dim, bronze emblem of a proud phoenix with its wings outspread over its head. It glinted dully in the bright buttery rays of the early morning sun.

The emblem was a well-known mark of any respected Coven member, no matter their ranking. Wearing it proudly, she prowled the streets with little regard for those they were passing. In one hand, she bore a knotted, rich mahogany staff that she used to aid in her quickened steps, and the other was shoved into the pocket of her tightly wrapped robe. Around her hip was a thick, sash-like belt that an assortment of multicolored bags dangled from by bronze hooks. They swayed from side to side with a soft jingle as she strode along the sidewalk. Her favorite, worn, buckled boots crunched over the little snow that was packed on the walkway as they headed down the crowded streets.

"I really don't see the point in all of this." The voice held a bit of a sophisticated lilt to it, and it came awkwardly rolling from the mouth of the giant moseying behind the girl.

"When there is chaos, you can swipe just about anything, and we might as well get something out of the deal since the Coven sent us out on this job. Besides, explosions and sirens equal fun, Bobo," the girl responded, her deep russet eyes shifting from side to side as they passed more people that had their jaws slack with amazement at the demon ogre behind her.

The creature flicked his ocean blue eyes from the pages to the witch before summarily returning his gaze to his engaging read. "Why must you insist on calling me that? It's Botobolbilian," he corrected his master.

The girl aggressively threaded a stray strand of jet black hair behind her ear with an annoyed expression before answering with, "Too hard to say in the middle of a battle."

"Clearly as well in casual daily conversation," the beast said, licking the pads of his rather large fingers and flipping another page of his book.

"It's easier to shorten it, okay?" Vanessa snapped back.

"Yet, you decline my thoughts on addressing you as Nessy," Bobo grumbled.

"It would be an insult to my people to shorten my name," she said, raising her chin proudly.

Bobo let the book fall from his face, and he narrowed his gaze at the back of his master's head. "*Your people...?* Aren't you an orphan?" His inquiring tone insinuated that she didn't know if she even had a "people" to speak of.

"Shhh," she snipped. "We are here."

"Oh... how convenient," Bobo replied with a roll of his eyes and marked the place in his book with a thin strip of ribbon before placing it carefully, along with his glasses, in a small satchel at his hip. Oddly enough, a large battle-ax was dangling from the belt as well. Bobo's massive hand went to cup the top of the blade as his eyes searched the rubble piled outside of the building they stood in front of.

It was the largest academy in Tolvade, Runerite, Academy of Wizardry and Arcane. Naturally, it was one for magic and basic apothecary training. If you passed the classes, you went on to the next level of training and – if you were lucky – you could progress beyond that to be part of the Coven. If not, you were stuck doing basic love spells, curses, and making luck charms for the general public. Not such a bad gig, but most aspire to do more than your run-of-the-mill jobs in these times. Though, that was not to say there weren't those that attended that didn't love the jobs offered outside of the Coven. It was just that those jobs weren't what *Vanessa* wanted. She dreamed of being in the Coven ever since she knew she had magic coursing through her tiny body.

Vanessa was one of the lucky ones. She graduated top of her class, even though she slept through most of them. Two years into combat spells and verbal enchants classes at the Runerite Academy and she was picked up by Coven scouts and taken to their ritual grounds for an interview. Being an orphan, she was lucky that her orphanage even had the money to put the kids through school that first year. Excelling at her studies only broadened her horizons and made the orphanage more compelled to pay for the next year's school fees. When she was picked up by the Coven scouts, the orphanage was compensated by the government for aiding in the advancement of the parent-less youth. This was the norm in Vanessa's world.

Even though Vanessa had been raised within the walls of the orphanage that resembled a worn-down hovel on its good days, she hadn't been mistreated like some kids in other orphanages. She was lucky; she always seemed to have the touch of the blessed on her side. Whenever she asked her caretakers what her parents were like when they dropped her off, they seemed nervous when they replied that it was because of her magic capabilities that they gave her up.

Strange as it sounded, magicless parents giving birth to a magical child was not completely uncommon. Sadly, if it was too frightening or too much responsibility, a child would be given up if they showed signs of magical capabilities. Even though orphanages were plenty, money to run them was not. Vanessa never lost hope, though. She became a touch cynical and had a sharp tongue, but she never abandoned her dreams of becoming more than what she was. If her magic was the reason she was given up, she'd make it her defining quality.

Often she would daydream about joining the Coven ranks. Tracking down those that abandoned the 'white ways' and took on darker magics. Those that raised the dead, summoned feral demons, and practiced the black magics were of the 'dark ways,' and it was up to the authorities to track them down and bind their magic.

The Coven was the police force and government of this world and anyone associated with the 'dark ways' were the criminals. Witches, warlocks, mages, sorcerers, and priests were all expected to practice safely and respectfully the 'white ways.' Those that did not were branded as outcasts – dark witches or dark way followers – and hunted down immediately before they unleashed evil or harmed innocents.

Shortly after the interview, Vanessa was informed that she had passed, and the Coven would accept her as a low-ranking officer until she brought in twenty-four dark witches for proper magic binding. As standard procedure, she was given one talisman, one weapon of her choosing, and one summoning stone upon being brought into the Coven.

A talisman was a charm necklace that held the fragmented piece of a Celestial soul. It would bring good luck to the user during battles. The talisman also came with its own incantation that could be spoken and bring forth a magical shield for a short period of time. The spell usually only lasted a few minutes and took some time to recharge. The weapon of choice was a government-issued – and magically marked – item, and far more powerful than anything a standard magic-user could get their hands on.

Finally, the summoning stone. It was an enchanted artifact that would allow the user to open the gates to the underworld and call upon one spirit within the domain to be the Coven member's pet or hired footman. Depending on that witch or wizard's magical capabilities, the level of the pet would vary. Vanessa got an ogre, the foot-soldiers and guards of the demons in the underworld.

Though, Bobo was one of the most sophisticated foot-soldiers she had ever met. They were usually a barbaric, nasty creature with an attitude that matched their hunger for human flesh. That is, of course, unless your ogre gets blasted with two intelligence spells by your superior officers accidentally and at the same time. Bobo was a perfectly timed mistake. If the spells hadn't been timed just right, he would have exploded on the spot … or worse. In Vanessa's case, the spell worked a little *too* well on Bobo, and she suffered from his constant nagging and correcting daily.

Still, having a well-mannered ogre that could punch through a brick wall was a far better companion than a succubus/incubus trying to seduce everything with two feet, or an untrained hellcat that would light your apartment on fire every time it needed to relieve itself. So, Vanessa took the highly intelligent ogre, which had manners that far exceeded her own, with a smile and his insults with a grain of salt.

With how bad some of the missions could get, she was silently thankful that she had a strong companion on her side that could also think for himself when the situation got tough. More often than not, Bobo's presence paid off. Because of him, she was sitting at nineteen successful take-downs of dark witches and counting down until the magical number twenty-four. Today's mission would mark number twenty if successful.

Little did Vanessa know that it would mark more than that.

 *Chapter 2:*

Vanessa sniffed at the air and crinkled her nose. "Do you smell that?" she asked in a hushed tone as she scanned the walls of the building. The whole east side of the academy looked like it had a bomb go off inside it.

Bobo cupped his nose with his free hand and spoke softly in reply, "Unfortunately, I do."

The air that leaked out from the still smoldering holes of the academy's walls reeked of sulfur and ash. Trademark scents that something from the underworld had recently come through a summoning portal. Every now and again, it could be blamed on the occasional inexperienced student trying out a high-class alchemy spell, but, judging by the amount of widespread damage that surrounded the area, Vanessa and Bobo doubted that being the case.

They carefully found sound footing between the piles of stone and rubble while keeping their eyes peeled to the silent confines of the school's open rooms ahead. Once they were inside, Vanessa pointed out a black marking, staining the far wall next to Bobo that appeared as though the area had been hit with a fireball. He narrowed his gaze at the destruction and inched his way closer to inspect the damage.

Meanwhile, Vanessa circled the room and made way to the classroom entrance that would open into the empty halls. She slowly opened the door, wiggling her head through the small crack she had made, to see out into the dark and silent space beyond. Without warning, the door creaked and then fell from its half-melted hinges, landing on the floor with a loud *thwack!*

Vanessa jumped at the sound after she had watched the dense chunk of wood plummet, unable to stop it from falling to the floor. Dust clouds billowed around the edges of the thick, wooden door. Slowly, Vanessa looked from the door on the ground over to Bobo, who was staring at her with an extremely exasperated expression tugging at every line and crease on his ogre face.

"*Sorry,*" Vanessa mouthed with a light shrug of her shoulders.

"Oh, no. I'm the one that is sorry. I didn't realize we were going to invite the enemy to a tea party. How foolish of me, I didn't bring the kettle. But you brought the biscuits, didn't you? Please tell me you brought the biscuits," Bobo teased in a quiet, incensed tone.

Vanessa found no humor in his jab at her honest mistake, and she glowered with a hard frown at her pet. "I wish the Coven supplied us with muzzles," she hissed under her breath.

Bobo let his large paw reach up and gently touch the black soot on the wall. "And I wish we could have a trial period with our masters," he stated with a touch of sass in his voice.

Vanessa rolled her eyes and peered out into the hall again, holding her wooden staff close to her chest with both her hands as she did so. "Nothing," she whispered.

"Surely, you are *not* to thank for that," Bobo taunted again.

"What did you find?" she growled back.

Bobo grunted in response and quickly got back to work. Leaning forward, the ogre sniffed at the wall, his eyes screwed shut and face contorted as he concentrated on the deep-rooted scents left behind. After opening his eyes, Bobo replied, "Scorch marks. It appears to be hellfire in nature." He then raced a thick, clawed finger over the area. Rubbing his index and middle finger together with his thumb in front of his eyes, the ogre inspected the soot on his digits the way an alchemist would a new magic dust with a questioning mind. "Looks like we are dealing with a tier two classified demon," he snorted and shook his head. "Maybe even a guard," he added with a sigh of displeasure.

"What?" Vanessa almost forgot to keep her voice down and had to regain her composure before speaking again. "How in the hex did that high of a level demon get through?"

"I can't really say. I think we should check out the surroundings a bit more. See if we can find any signs that will give us some hints as to what happened here," Bobo advised, and then looked over his shoulder to the open streets beyond.

Most of the pedestrians steered clear of the crumbled academy walls. They knew that this much damage to such a high classed school meant that there was danger afoot, which was a good thing. The last thing that Vanessa and Bobo needed was to try and keep rubbernecking civilians safe while bagging a possible dark witch, or worse, a high-level demon.

Vanessa didn't like the idea that they might be dealing with a tier-two demon or third-tier demon with hellfire abilities. Demons ranked at that level and having that kind of power usually required a group in order to take them down. The hellfire abilities were reserved for special kinds of demons. Hellcats, demon princes, and – you guessed it – hellhounds.

Of the three, Vanessa would prefer to not deal with the hellhounds. Unlike hellcats and demon princes, they had the worst attitude, and they usually traveled in small groupings. However, just because the packs were small, did not mean that the damage that they could inflict was not off the charts. In fact, the only hellhound encounter documented was from two hundred years ago and took an entire city's section Coven to take them down. Most professors told the story of the de-summoning as an inspirational story to teach new Coven members about the importance of teamwork. But no one had since then dealt with feral demons.

Knowing that the marks were caused by hellfire was unnerving. Hellfire was one of the most damage inflicting powers that the underworld beings had to offer aside from fear ingesting and soul collecting creatures like devils and reapers, which were tier-three demons and the most powerful. Needless to say, hellfire wasn't caused by a group of inexperienced students making a training whoopsie. This was the product of a large and calculated summoning spell.

Now, back to the scorch marks…

Bobo let out a long drawn out sigh and shook his head at the wall. "I think this is at least a Class A or even an S, Vanessa. You won't like what I'm going to say, but we are going to need to report it to the Coven."

"What? The Coven? No, this is my case. We've got this, Bobo,

I know it. There is no way I'm pulling my hand out of the cookie jar when I'm this far in—"

As she ranted, Bobo sighed again and rolled his eyes. "See, I knew you weren't going to like what I had to say."

"—We are seeing this case through," Vanessa huffed.

"Ah, and my fearless master makes yet another well-thought-out and intelligent decision. Aren't I a lucky ogre?" Bobo grumbled glumly.

Vanessa groaned and poked her unwilling servant with her staff. "Come on. Stop pouting. You know yoouu waaant tooo," she changed up her attitude and spoke in a sing-song tone.

"No. I really don't," Bobo mumbled.

"Oh… come on now, Bobo. I know you do. Look, if things look even a teensy bit bad," she paused to show the measurement with her thumb and pointer finger and then continued, "…we'll pack it up and go tell the Coven."

Bobo took in a deep breath, straightened up to his full height, and inspected Vanessa as though she were a girl scout and he was trying to choose between ordering nothing and waaay too many boxes of cookies. Would it really kill him to take the risk? Only time would tell.

Finally, after a long moment of silence – and Vanessa wearing her most convincing and innocent smile to the point that her cheeks were starting to ache as she waited, complete with bright, hopeful eyes – Bobo huffed and flailed his massive paws over his head. "D'all right! You are such a spoiled child. But the moment there is trouble—"

Vanessa held up a hand, palm out, and closed her eyes, solemnly nodding to her partner in crime. "We leave and go straight to the Coven."

Bobo's eyes glazed over, and he sighed again. "Why do I not believe you?"

"Come on!" She whispered excitedly, ignoring his question and hopped over the door that had previously fallen.

With amazingly little effort, Bobo managed to be quieter than Vanessa as he followed slowly after her through the door and down the hall. "This spells trouble. Capital 'T.'" He watched her practically skipping down the main hall as he bickered to himself. "All capitals," he continued to furiously mutter under his breath.

 *Chapter 3:*

The further into the destroyed building that they went, the thicker the scent of sulfur and ash became. While Bobo looked like something was going to leap out, yell surprise, and *then* eat their faces clean off, Vanessa looked like a kid in a candy store with a pocket full of coin.

In the academy's main hall, the place looked like an abandoned war zone. Just past the massive entrance to the head offices and main doors, there were scattered pebbles that were speckled over the once spotless floors below. Wreckage that once made up the left-hand side of the staircase that led to the second floor was stacked in a heap below the base of the stairs. Carefully, they rounded the right-hand side.

Bobo looked up the stairs and shook his head *no* at Vanessa, silently telling her that the coast was clear above them. She nodded before turning to peer into the office door's window. There was nothing to see but papers that appeared as though they had been met with tornado winds and office supplies that were littering the floor of the empty room.

She sighed. This was nowhere near the level of excitement she had been hoping for. She hadn't been greeted with screaming students or frazzled faculty staff. Just silent, rubble-filled halls and the soft sound of her and Bobo's footwork disturbing the debris cluttering the academy's tiled flooring. She pursed her lips to the side and gave a short, nasally sigh, and the air from her nostrils lightly fogged the glass inches from her face before the haze disappeared without a trace.

Bobo spared a look at her and instantly rolled his eyes at his owner. "They evacuated the place long before you were heading this way," he told her quietly, only furthering the sour taste in her mouth from the lack of the desired atmosphere.

Vanessa turned on heel and leaned against the office door as she aggressively blew stray strands of hair away from her face. There was something that caught her eye across the way. Ending her pouting fit and perking up a bit, Vanessa locked in on the new scorch mark on the wall. There was a silver nameplate mounted next to the door under a thick layer of soot that had almost been hidden from sight under the shadowy film.

Noticing her interest being caught by something, Bobo came up behind his owner and looked over her shoulder.

"What did you find?"

"Another scorch mark," she said in a hushed tone as she inspected the area surrounding the wall and then focused on the blast mark again.

"What does the nameplate say?"

Vanessa shrugged as she searched around her for something to clean off the plaque. Feeling Bobo's tie resting on her shoulder, she grabbed it and yanked on the clothing, forcing Bobo forward as she used the tip of it to rub off the black ashen blemish from the surface of the nameplate.

Instantly, he yanked the tie from her grasp and eyed over the item. The ogre sucked at his teeth and inspected his dirty tie. "I just had this dry cleaned. Do you know how hard it is to find a decent, good-looking tie these days?"

"Oh, hush. You know Big & Troll will be more than happy to see me walking in with you and waving around my Quarts Card at them."

The beast raised a single brow over a disbelieving eye, "You mean the store we got banned from because you made fun of the pixie working at the service desk?" He hopelessly scrubbed at the blotted tie to no avail.

"It's not my fault that I found it hilarious that she was working there. She was so … tiny." She strained the last word and then added, "And, yes, that store."

There was a bit of silence as Vanessa read the sign, finally. "Hey, Bobo, look here," she said, thumbing to the sign as she reached over and grabbed the cracked open door that led down to the underground level of the building.

"Curious," he remarked, noticing the words 'boiler room' etched into the silver nameplate. The door made a sound as though it was trying to object to being peeled open. The witch cared little for the door's protests and had managed to open the heavy door enough to give room for her and … *Well, he could fit if he sucked in his gullet,* Vanessa thought as she looked the ogre up and down and let her eyes rest on his tummy region.

He held his stomach defensively and grunted at her, "I've been dieting lately." He gave a wheezing cough and tried to change the topic. "Is that the door?" he gaped.

"Yeah," she said ignoring the worries of his belly and comments of dieting.

"A bit much for a boiler room, don't you think?" Bobo inspected the thick metal door that looked like it was more like two doors rather than one. On one side it was a regular looking, thick wooden door. But upon opening it, you'd see that the opposing side wasn't wood but another few inches of reinforced steel with a layer of patchwork metal magically nailed to it. He furrowed his brow at the curious door. "Hold the crystal ball… is that iron?" Bobo gulped after inspection.

Vanessa only nodded in reply and then swiped her hand over the wall. After repeatedly hitting nothing, she sucked in air with a hiss-like sound and whispered, "Blast it all." She dusted off her hand after noticing cobwebs and a thin sheet of gray dust caking her hand.

She reached into her pocket, dipped her thumb and middle finger into a golden, shimmery dust and snapped her fingers together. A spark leaped from her fingers, and an orb of light danced and bobbed around her before stopping in front of her face. "Light switch, please." The orb gave a jingling sound like it was a floating bell, and the bell was giggling or answering her in a series of high-pitched rings. It sped away in a flash and went spinning in dizzy spirals down the staircase. A moment passed and then the florescent lights overhead blinked on and occasionally dimmed in and out as they struggled to stay lit.

"Did you really need to use Tinker Bell's Spirit to find a light switch?" the ogre asked in a disbelieving tone.

"What? I couldn't find the—"

Her words were cut short by Bobo jutting a massive digit at the switch under the nameplate, and she defensively shrugged. "Never hurts to practice magic…" she said with a carefree expression.

Rolling his eyes, Bobo squeezed in through the opening enough to look downstairs. The light barely touched the floor at the foot of the steps, and there seemed to be a lot of cobwebs, dust, and dirt indicating that the space was rarely used.

"Interesting," he whispered.

Interesting indeed.

Why did the academy need such a massive door? A door like that was built to keep things in, not out. The iron was on the other side, the …the wrong side. That meant, whatever they were trying to keep at bay was contained in the confines of the basement level of the academy. Why on Raen would they need that?

Good questions, but there wasn't anyone there to interrogate at the moment. Information to log away and come back to later. But, for now, it had both Bobo and Vanessa enquiring what was going on in the building. That wasn't normal.

Normal or not, nothing was stopping Vanessa from venturing further into the lower region of the building to find answers, adventure, and fun. Bobo, on the other hand, felt like he was forced to babysit the most reckless preteen the world had to offer. Though, Vanessa was an adult – or so she claimed ardently and often – because she was old enough to smoke from a pipe, drink the hottest on tap ale from a local tavern, live on her own, and pay her own bills. Though she did those all respectfully, she had a destructive streak in her that put her younger counterparts to shame.

Vanessa was practically skipping down the steps. "Come on, Bobo!" she called up to her companion, and the beast had to inspect every crack in the paint before he looked down at her as she descended.

"You know, most of us get a say in the matter. Nooo. Not with you. *Come on, Bobo. Let's inspect the dark basement, Bobo. What could possibly go wrong, Bobo?*" he mocked the whole way down the narrow decline into the practically black abyss. All the while, Vanessa ignored any slight upset chatter that she might have overheard coming from the demon.

She dipped her fingers into the Tinker Bell's Spirit again and then into a pouch to its side, but hanging a few inches lower, and then rubbed her finger, thumb, and pointer together in front of her face while breathing on the collected powders. A slight chant, though it was whispered on an exhaled breath, hardly audible in any realm, escaped her lips and touched upon the dust. Instantly, a soft tangerine glow rose around her hand, and she used her appendage as a flashlight, pointing it in the directions that light was needed, as they trudged through the tight space of the lower building's halls.

There was a hushed, almost strained whisper coming from Bobo as he followed behind his master. "Be on your guard," he advised, his eyes darting through the blackness like arrows searching for a mark. A worry was growing in the pit of his being, and it screamed through his every limb to be on alert, so much so that his ax was pulled and ready to swing at any threat that dared to approach the pair. The cold steel in his grasp did not alleviate this gnawing excitement that nipped at every fiber of his being. Somewhere down there, something was bound to leap out at them. He was sure of it.

Traveling deeper into the boiler room, they started to stumble upon things less basement-like of an academy and things more akin to a spot that was not safe for any person of Aeristria. Bleach white candles, hanging bundled bunches of lavender, and thick charcoal smudges slowly crept over the edges of the cold concrete flooring and walls that led to a small hall. The hall was also lined with the large, dove feather shades of candles. It gave way after a short distance, opening into a room holding darker colored candles of azure, plum, crimson, and obsidian.

Bobo stopped just before the opening into a new room and saw it ablaze in a burnt sienna glow of collected candlelight. He turned in the hall, looking back from the eggshell washed room laced in dry lavender bundles and white candles and … *banish a banshee* … was that salt? He spun on heel and called for his master in a strained voice, "Vanessa." She heard him, but she was too busy eyeing the room with her jaw slack in awe and inspecting every detail in an unbelieving and sluggish manner.

"Bobo," she breathed his name as she started to tremble, and then the light that she had called upon went out, along with the teeming assortment of candles in the basement. "They're here ..." her voice sounded panicked and scratchy.

What had these people done?

Chapter 4:

If there had been a shred of light in the basement, Vanessa would have been able to see her breath. Desperately clinging to the air in frosted puffs that moved so slowly, one could hardly tell they were drifting before disappearing inches from her frightened face. A sudden chill had gripped the world around them, and the silence that bled into the room was as thick as a dragon's hide. "Bobo," Vanessa whispered.

"I'm here," he breathed back.

She waited with bated breath for something to emerge from the unforgiving abyss beyond her strained vision and solidify the fact that, indeed, things were not right within the academy. Vanessa was too scared to try to use a spell to light the room again. She feared that, in doing so, whatever horrors were lurking about the murky oblivion of the halls would spot them and rip them limb from limb before she and Bobo could think of a counterattack.

As time ticked by, the anxiety that had been swelling within Vanessa's chest had started to die off. She was beginning to find her nerve once more when she started to reach for her pouches, hands attempting to locate the proper sacks to create a light spell from memory alone. Her courage dissipated like an insomniac's hope for a full night's sleep when the sound scratched over her nerves, giving birth to new terrors that devoured her heartbeat like a ravenous beast. She suppressed the urge to gulp when from the dreaded dead silence there came the sound of long claws clicking over the cold concrete floor.

Tick-tick. Tick-tick. Tick-tick.

Each sound of the paws, with sinfully lengthy claws resounding in the small confines of the room, made poor Vanessa's heart stop for a brief moment before restarting with a quickened tempo. The painful heartbeat was forever on the rise like the muscle had become a savage animal, and it threw itself against her chest franticly before trying to scale her tightening throat. The terror was as copious as the darkness and almost as pungent as the stench of brimstone and sulfur.

Banish a banshee! She couldn't swallow. She couldn't move. The fear had reached out from behind her and hugged her close to it. She was lost in the darkened room and all she could think of was how the creature was inching closer and closer to her. There wasn't an escape.

"... No..." It was a barely audible whisper when the word was squeaked out of Vanessa's dry mouth. This wasn't some tricky imp or feral succubus. The dead giveaway was the growl that had risen and washed through the ink drenched room. It started off low and almost unnoticeable, but it soon rose in pitch, and there was a heat that flowed with the sound as if you could reach out and grab the sound itself and yank its source toward you. Within that growl, though, were the sounds of Hell. Screams and wails and booming dark laughter entangled the guttural noise until it seemed to be one fluid sound, and you couldn't tell where one began and the other ended.

This was not a normal trait of any animal or being. No standard puppy was this threatening. This was ... a hellhound.

Well, double-dip a candlestick. If she could just get to her —

Vanessa's thoughts were cut short by a flame igniting across from her, and the light of the fire cast a glow over the horrifying beast that was snarling in her direction.

A lion-like tail with a flaming puffed tip connected to a massive, burly body. Its lower half was hairless and was covered in obsidian skin so pronounced one could mistake it for a pocket of a deep, endless void. The black, leathery skin stretched over a hulking frame and strained to conceal ripples of bone that rolled up its spine. There was matted, knotted, and greasy hair lining its neck and the contours of its face like a lion's mane. Around the chest, stomach, and throat there was an ember-like glow that emitted from the creature as if a campfire was its soul, and all that looked upon it could see the raging fire that rested just beneath the flesh. But a campfire smelled far better than this beast.

The face was made up of harsh, sharp bones lacking both

skin and fur. Two twisting, weathered horns spiraled back from the posterior of its skull-like antelope horns. Great billowing clouds of smoke thinned out from its face like the whole beast was about to become engulfed in flames. For the brief moment that the room was alight with the hellhound's tail tip, it made a growling hiss at her, and the glowing throat of the demon rattled with the low gurgling sound. Sharp-as-talon claws chipped the concrete under its paws effortlessly, and Vanessa's breath hitched at the sight.

The tail flame dimmed down slowly, and the hellhound's eyes brightened like two radiating rubies right before the comfort of light left the room. Only the sound of the growling exuding its final warning filled the space until that too faded from the scenes, and silence resumed its role around them.

She knew it was coming. The lunge that the beast had calculated when it had gotten Vanessa's placement in the room after igniting its tail. She could do little to stop it. Without a sound, the hellhound's jaws were suddenly inches from her face, and she screamed as she threw herself back, only to hit the wall a second later. Pain blossomed over the back of her skull and shoulders, only dulling down when her will to live switched from an apprehensive coil in the pit of her stomach to clutching her mind like a vicious demon possessing a being. Her whole body tried to melt into the wall, attempting to recoil from the second attack. There was no time to react, no time to whisper a spell or dip her fingers into a powder to buy herself some time, or dust to save her soul.

Onyx claws sank deep into her clothing, the threads fraying at the curved touch and slitting the garment as they curled into Vanessa's arms. She felt the harsh points jabbing into her, threatening to tear more than just clothing. It was on that fine, aching line between bruising and drawing blood. Her gloved hands kept their steady hold on the staff that was aiding in keeping the beast at bay, but the wood was sizzling and faint cracks could be heard as the creature twisted and threw its weight about the weapon in an attempt to overpower her.

Pain flared as the heat of the hellhound poured over her, and she felt her visible skin start to burn on the verge of bubbling, causing her to shriek in deafening agony. Scents of slow charring flesh assaulted her nostrils. She could smell her own body roasting from the heat that the hellhound emitted. The burn started to scorch through layers of clothes and caress the meat underneath with scalding waves of heat.

Her stomach churned in a nauseating fashion with fear as she accepted the fate that was to befall her. Only … it never did. A roar that would put a tiger to shame caused Vanessa to rip her lids open and search the darkness. A torch pushed the black at bay, and the one wielding it was Bobo! One hand clutched the blazing baton while the other was balled into a fist that mercilessly slammed into the boney head of the hellhound and resounded with a sickening crack upon impact.

A yelp snapped through the air as Bobo's fist connected with the creature and sent it flying into the opposing wall, the dent of its massive body imprinting the cobblestone made Vanessa's eyes bulge in amazement. Quickly, she snapped her gaze from the crumpled hell-pup to Bobo. Her mouth unhinged, and she drew in a breath but couldn't speak fast enough. Bobo grabbed her wrist and yanked her toward him and, ultimately, toward the exit. "Thank me later," he hastily sputtered.

As Vanessa and Bobo peeled around the corner, she stole a glance back at the hellhound on the floor. She could see the core flame almost gone, dying, and then it suddenly erupted to life, the fire consuming the coal colored body in a burst of garnet and tangerine flames. The broken bones seemed to mend on the spot and just before the sight was hidden behind the wall, Vanessa saw two more boney heads enter the room near the fallen hellhound and sniff the ground before giving a shrieking howl that carried eerily through the basement.

"Bobo, more of them showed up," Vanessa warned in a half-whine as she ran behind her pet.

"Why do those foul things have more friends than you?" Bobo groaned.

"I have friends," she barked back.

"Just because I save your suicidal hide on a regular basis doesn't mean we can start having luncheons," Bobo rebutted.

"I wasn't referring to you," she snipped.

"Wonderful news. The best I've heard all day. Tell you what, let's get out of here in one piece, and I'll throw you a party for not considering me as a bosom buddy, and you can invite all your friends to it," as Bobo spoke, his breath began to sound labored, and he dare not chuckle at his own joke as air was more important than laughter. They flew through the dusty halls with purpose as they tried to find their way to the basement exit.

"Let's focus on getting out of here!" she yelled as they heard the pounding paws of the hellhounds fast on their heels. The sounds of the beasts tripping over candles and slamming into walls were giving Vanessa the most unnerving distance check. "The purifying room won't hold them off for long, they're too powerful to be held back by those wards and spells!" she explained as they ran.

"The door will surely keep them at bay if we can make it there," her pet reminded her breathlessly.

A snarl too close for comfort startled them both, and Bobo turned to look behind them. Stumbling over his footwork, he fell, and the torch was sent flipping head over end and sliding to a halt a couple of yards out of reach. Vanessa promptly found his backside with her face and groaned as she landed on top of him. The pair both looked up to see the torch in the distance, lighting up the foot of the stairs with its lapping flames.

Talk about stumbling at the finish line...

Vanessa rolled over as she heard the paws slow in their approach. Horrifically, they watched as the luminosity of the dogs dimmed down until it was just night shaded bodies and burning rubicund eyes edging their way toward her and Bobo. Sharp teeth snapped at the air victoriously as they encroached upon their helpless prey.

 *Chapter 5:*

As if fearing for your life wasn't painful enough, waiting for the hellhounds to descend upon them was a whole new level of excruciating anticipation. As their assailants inched closer, Bobo protectively pulled Vanessa close to his chest in a tight hold, almost constricting air from her burning lungs. He slowly drew his ax from his hip while his eyes stayed transfixed on the imposing threat dead ahead.

"Bobo… I'm so sorry. I never should have dragged you down here," Vanessa admitted in a child-like whimper.

The ogre only replied by hugging her closer and brandishing the weapon in front of his body, ready to ward off the beasts with it as long as he could.

Leaping with their boney jaws gaping open, the hellhounds pounced at them ready to feast. Vanessa gave a shrill cry and pushed her face into the hulking chest of her pet. Bobo growled and pulled back his ax arm, the tension in the length of his appendage building for a blow that would promise a head to roll.

From behind them a voice quickly bellowed out, piercing through the howling hounds, "In prayer to the goddess, I ask for power, in prayer to the spirits, I ask for protection, bless them with a barrier from evil!"

Golden light twinkled overhead as a dome appeared and slammed down around the ogre and Hunter. Smashing against the glittering barrier, the hellhounds came to a halt as the magic popped and sizzled with each impact the creatures made. Zaps of protective magic held the creatures in suspended animation before flinging them to the ground below. The pain it had caused sent them yelping back down through the basement halls.

Bobo and Vanessa were firmly hugging each other, as they had expected to be consumed by ravenous demon dogs and were now stunned in a silent stupor. They gradually averted their gaze from the withdrawing pups and looked to the stairwell behind them. There stood the well-known Coven member Leon, poised with a talisman spell in his hand and two fingers raised to his forehead. His eyes narrowed in on the hellhounds as they stumbled over one another in their fast-paced retreat.

Once the man was sure that the threat was gone, he rose to his full height and glowered down to Vanessa, who instantly flashed a toothy grin at the man. "Oh, *hi*, Leon," Vanessa nervously giggled.

"F-fancy meeting you here, good fellow," Bobo stumbled, trying to remain calm and refined, but failing.

Leon was a Spellweaver, the Coven rank that Vanessa was striving so hard to achieve. Under most common circumstances, it was rather pleasant to know Leon. However, Vanessa rarely ever met him under common circumstances. Thusly leaving their level of friendship in a stagnant pool that neighbored the sea of chastising and placed under the skies of rank looming. As she chewed nervously at her bottom lip, he remained glowering over her like she was a petulant child. Which, of course, she was... to some degree, but it certainly didn't make her feel like she wanted to go out of her way to be nice to him, and it most definitely put a strain on his own social acceptance of her.

To make matters worse, he wasn't just a rank higher than Vanessa, he also had a few years in his ranking and hardly a year older than her! Hex, the man was a shoe in the door of a promotion to Summoner status.

She hung her head in shame as he continued to list all the things she had done wrong as they promptly made way for the exit and bolted the door shut behind them before heading outside to contact the Coven about the unfortunate, horrible find in the boiler room of the academy. Paying more attention to how she was going to dig herself out of trouble this time than his growing list of her wrongdoings, Vanessa dragged her feet as they headed out to the main entrance.

It wouldn't have been such a horrible fate if the man didn't look dashing even on a bad day and had a set of dreamy eyes that put Aeristria's magnificent crystal blue Lake Lorvo to shame. Long, sandy strands of hair dangled just past his shoulders and made the blue of his eyes painfully bluer. His thin, athletic build could often be seen pressing through the button-up shirts and made most of the girls, and a few of the guys, go a bit dreamy-eyed upon introduction. At an even six feet, he – like Bobo – towered over poor Vanessa. Attractive? More like salt in an open wound. The goddess had to love how she made him because he was honestly perfection manifest. But the real rotten cherry on top of it all was his smooth-as-silk, deep voice. It rode on the cusp of too deep and just perfect. And he was a well-respected member of the Coven. Hex it all, it just wasn't fair!

"Blast it all, Vanessa. I had the High Priest Council contact me with your whereabouts because you hadn't checked in with them yet. You are *so* well-known for your ability to get into trouble that they didn't even bother trying to contact you and went straight to me to hunt you down," Leon griped.

"Oh, come on. I wasn't gone *that* long…" she huffed.

"That's my point!" Leon yelled, exasperated. "Could you at least *attempt* to stay out of trouble? Just once?" he pleaded.

Her retort was silence and a long, hard eye roll that ended with them outside the entrance to the main building, and Leon pointing at the ground before him. "Don't move from that spot. I'm going to contact the Coven," he informed before pulling out a small crystal orb and walking a few steps away to make the call. His glare peering over his shoulder in a paranoid fashion.

"Oh, go make the call. There is no way I can get into trouble just standing here," she muttered.

"Are you sure about that? I'm willing to wager next month's rent on your ability to do so," Bobo snickered.

Vanessa ignored her pet and tried to focus on the call Leon was making. She could barely see the glass sphere softly glow as the call was made. Bewildered after his frantic spiel mentioning hellhounds, the Coven immediately patched him through directly to the High Priest Council. Their cross faces stared out from the crystal orb at the Spellweaver. Leon spoke in a hushed and quick fashion, debriefing them before requesting more Spellweavers to assist him in a sweep of the basement level of the building and giving them the dreaded news of the hellhounds personally.

While Leon chatted away, Vanessa leaned against the railing of the steps at the peak and looked down to the crowds of people collecting and swiftly shuffling away from the scene like calm waves that would wash up on the shores of the beach, lapping on the edge of land before receding to its home.

Bobo sighed loud enough to catch her attention.   "I need to mark this day on a calendar," the ogre gasped, suddenly realizing something.

"Why is that?" Vanessa asked, looking up to him with a puzzled look.

"Because, you apologized to me," he remarked with a wide, toothy grin.

Instantly, Vanessa's face warped into regret, and she huffed as she shook her head. "I did not. Besides, even if I did, *you* hugged me," she said with a twisted chortle and a mock grin plastered to her face.

Bobo instantly coughed, choking on nothing as he nervously looked around him. "How preposterous. I did nothing of the sort. I was merely holding you close to use as a meat shield from those brutes' attacks," he said as he straightened the cuffs of his jacket and the collar of his – now soot blotched and dilapidated – button-up shirt.

Vanessa rolled her eyes hard and kept the wicked grin on her lips as she said, "Whatever you say, Bobo."

"Vixen," he hissed back at her. They both turned their back on one another. She went on to busy herself with dusting off while Bobo reached for today's most recent reading material.

Moments passed and the two stood on opposite ends of Raen while they waited for Leon to be done with his call. Leon walked back over to them, slipping the tennis ball-sized crystal orb into his pocket pouch that was dangling from his belt. "Well, we are going to finish up here with a sweep of the boiler room, as soon as backup arrives, and then we have to go back to the Coven to make a report before those blasted blue cloaks want to have a private audience with the three of us," he said with a tired gaze.

Bobo peered over his shoulder as he slid the ribbon back into the book and sealed it shut. "I take it we will be part of the venturing crew?" He didn't sound delighted at the idea in the slightest.

"Afraid so, big guy. We should keep an eye peeled for the team. They should be arriving shortly. I want to get this over with as soon as possible. I didn't expect to be doing this with my afternoon," Leon sighed.

"Aye. Me too. Me too." Bobo joined in on the sighing.

"Hey, I didn't want to be—" the two instantly glared at her, daring her to deny her desire to do anything dangerous or risky, and she pursed her lips to one side and crossed her arms over her chest. Staring at anything but the two leering gazes of those in company, she pouted at being cut off with the synchronizing glares. Her foot found a stray piece of rubble, and she kicked it down the steps, the stone bouncing chaotically all the way down before the quiet took over once more.

Barely an hour passed before the Spellweaver squad had shown up on the scene and started to speak with Leon about the tasks needing to be taken care of and what sort of matters had already taken place. Vanessa couldn't really say much, being a low-level Hunter within the Coven ranks. She was the furthest down the chain of command and had to sit patiently and prettily until they started to line up to make way down to the boiler room in an orderly fashion.

Vanessa was far from a happy Hunter when they finally started to head back into the building. For one, this had been her case and now she had to diligently follow Leon's orders simply because he was a higher-ranked Coven member on the scene. Not to mention, she really wasn't keen on traipsing through the hellhound riddled halls. A swarm of Coven members in tow, or not.

Briefly, they stopped just in front of the boiler room door. Leon turned to face the Coven members. "All right, everyone, be on your guard. This is a high ranked assignment. We have a confirmed hellhound pack reported, and you need to be prepared for a lot of unknowns. What we do know is they can eat flame, so try to use light magic, and stay away from torches if you can. They travel in packs; if you see one then, rest assured, there are more in the area. They can be harmed by barrier and protective spells, but long-lasting damage has not yet been confirmed. For now, keep in mind that we may have to bind them and bring them into a holding cell. In the meantime, buddy up into groups of three and let's sweep the area diligently and thoroughly." He motioned over his head for everyone to get closer. "Let's go, light spells up and barrier spells at the ready!" Leon tugged the door open and a gush of cold, stale air rushed through the hall and crashed over everyone with the dying aroma of brimstone.

Ominous much?

Vanessa had been there before and now she feared going back to it. Bobo looked over to her and coughed into his fist before nudging her with his elbow, causing her to shudder, and she broke away from the black hole that mocked her from the bottom of those stairs. She managed to catch a small smile on Bobo's lips before he turned away.

"Are you ready?" Leon asked in a low voice to Vanessa as the light spells ignited in a wave behind her like a massive pool of candles being lit in a darkened room.

Vanessa searched the bright lights and then looked at Leon with a smile that split her face in two. "I was born ready," she said, and her own light spell was created before she hastily brushed past Leon and descended the steps into the boiler room with false confidence.

Bobo cleared his throat into his massive paw and leaned over to the Spellweaver as he spoke in a hushed tone, "You should stay close to that one. If that girl was born ready, I was born an incubus."

For a moment, Leon's eyes widened and then his brow bent in confusion. His gaze followed the line of the massive door and fixed on the mauve robes of the Hunter in question. Nodding once, he wordlessly stated he'd keep watch of her. Then, he too descended into the depths of the academy's underbelly. The pool of Coven members following after their fearless leader.

 *Chapter 6:*

Shuffling footwork consumed the halls and once empty rooms down below, as spills of light radiated into every nook and cranny and eradicated the darkness with a spell all its own. Carefully placed steps took the Coven members deeper into the boiler room and eventually down the hall that held the lavender and the white candles. It wasn't until they reached the summoning room that the muted murmurs of the group came to an abrupt hush.

It was around this time that Vanessa started to get twitchy. Every awkward placement of steps or occasional stumble over an unlit piece of raised or off-kilter concrete slab by one of the many Coven members would cause her to jerk her gaze in every direction. Frantically inspecting the source of the sounds like she was a mouse trying to cross a field guarded by an army of hungry owls. She placed a hand over the scald marks that traced her arms under her garbs as the memory of the burning sensation flooded her mind.

Leon came to her side and put a hand on her shoulder and when she jolted from the touch, he dug his fingers into her clothing, biting into the skin below. It didn't hurt, but it did tear her wild eyes from the darkened hall and made her swiftly turn her gaze to him. His eyes held a softness to them like a worried expression that was hidden behind his usual cold and confident appearance.

"Keep behind me, we need the experienced spell casters in the lead," he said and put enough pressure on her shoulder to keep her in place, not hurt, but the pressure was like a boulder to Vanessa. Perhaps it was because of the sting that came with his words. She wasn't *weak*. How dare he tell her to stay back! She scowled at the back of his head as he motioned for a few of the more skilled Spellweavers to come to the front with him, and the rest of the Coven members followed thereafter.

"Jerk," Vanessa grumbled. "*Keep behind me,*" she mocked him in a low tone and sucked at her teeth before kicking a nearby candle and sending it rolling into the wall.

She intersected her arms over her chest with a huff and meandered over to the back of the group leading the way through the halls that went deeper into the boiler room. Just because she couldn't be at the front of the group didn't mean she was going to be the little-depressed-witch-caboose at the back of the scouting crowd.

Vanessa squared her shoulders and tried to hide her deep sulk as she squeezed into the crowd when they went further into the boiler room. The air started to smell like mildew, and it lost the remaining tints of freshness that lingered from the previous floor. Harsh undertones of burnt trash filled the stale air; the remaining foul scents were more than likely caused by the pack of hellhounds that had dived deep into the musty, dark confines of the academy's underbelly.

A few moments had passed when the pace of the group stilled. Vanessa went on her tiptoes to look over the throng of Coven members to see them all inspecting wearily the mouth of a harshly carved opening that stretched beyond the walls of the academy. She wiggled through the throng of casters to a better spot, hoping to hear and see what exactly was going on.

Leon motioned for two members to come next to the opening with him. "Let's check it for barriers, wards, curses, and the like. I don't want any more surprises if it can be helped," he said, waving at the foreboding entrance. He pointed the light spell into the opening and glanced around while the other two worked. Soft blue lights emitting from their hands as they traced the opening with their spells.

Turning, Leon spoke to the rest of the group, "It would seem that whoever is responsible for this has constructed a healthy stretch of tunnels. We are unsure of how deep these tunnels will be or what will be lurking within them. Keep your protective and battle spells at the ready. Move on my mark." Leon turned to face the two examining the hole in the boiler room wall.

"Sir, it would appear there is no threatening or curious magic. However..." the male Spellweaver trailed off.

"However, what?" Leon hoarsely urged the man to finish.

"The opening was made recently, perhaps only months ago, but the tunnels beyond are far older," the female Spellweaver said softly.

Leon looked between the two and then stared off into the tunnels. "What have we walked into?" he whispered, but only a slow stream of air replied. "Let's go," Leon yelled out, and the crowd of Coven members took the first steps through the threshold.

They delved deep into the tunnels, and Vanessa was awestruck as she inspected the curved lines of the wall and the winding side passageways that snaked through the depths deep below the capital of Aeristria, Tolvade.

The walls were aged with time, and it was hard to tell if magic or tool had made them. The newfound catacombs twisted deeper beyond the academy walls that any had anticipated. Splitting up into teams, the sweeping group got lost inside the burrows as they searched for foe or culprit or dreaded hellhound. Only, nothing appeared to be inside the winding span of warrens.

Empty echoes of slinking footwork and soft chatter from the Coven members reverberated off the walls, but not a whisper of danger or a hint at the fact that there was a creature to be captured was found within the elongated carved halls. There were just endless spirals of rock and dirt. Vanessa sighed and peered down one of the side passageways and looked to Leon for confirmation that it was all right to move on down that way with a few of the others when she heard the twinkling of bells. It seemed someone had a crystal ball call. To Vanessa's surprise, suddenly, there were many crystal ball twinklings happening at the same time only seconds after the first soft jingles of a crystal ball call.

What was going on?

Leon was the closest to her, and she craned her neck as she nosily twisted out of normal stance to see who the culprit of the call was. A blue hooded shadow peered back from Leon's crystal ball. Bless her spell! All the calls were made to Spellweavers. It was a mass call from the blue cloaks… but why?

She tried to lean in without seeming interested in what was

being said and bumped into Bobo as she leaned a tad bit too far. He too was straining to hear what was being said, and they only traded a glance before resuming their curious eavesdropping.

The voice of the High Priest could barely be heard on Leon's orb. His call was private, unlike the others that had received a mass call from the High Priest Council to address the issue at hand. "It would seem that this mission has exceeded our expectations, and we feel that the Summoners would best be fit to take over the current task. Report back to headquarters to file a report and have Council with us. Oh, and bring the Hunter with you," the blue cloak stated, waiting for the compliant nod of Leon before letting the orb wink out. The crystal ball became plain picture-less glass once more.

"What?" Vanessa griped, not even hiding the fact that she had been eavesdropping.

"You heard him, Vanessa. We are to report back to the Coven headquarters," Leon sounded tired as he slipped the orb into the pouch once more.

"What a load of imp poo!" She shot back without blinking an eye. "Who knows how many more miles of uncharted tunnels there are, and those hellhounds—"

"Are no longer our problem. The High Priest Council has spoken, Vanessa. We have no grounds to defy them or their orders. We report back and that is *final!*" Leon's voice boomed back at her, his tone alone daring her to challenge the blue cloak's decision a second time. In a frustrated flurry of rippling cape and with a hard scowl screwed in place, Leon turned to address the Coven members. "This mission has been officially decreed out of our expertise, Summoners will now take over this duty and we are *all*," he fixed his gaze for a split second to Vanessa behind him before carrying on, "…to report back to headquarters. Call in the remaining groups that have divided down side passages, and let's make our way for the surface."

The lines of Coven members started to form and flow for the exit. Meanwhile, Vanessa tried not to look like she was a sulking child as she tried to get her rattled emotions in check. The Coven was making the right choice, but Vanessa wasn't happy with it at all. This was supposed to be her case. If she had bagged a pack of hellhounds she'd be a Spellweaver by day's end. Instead, she was tucking her tail between her legs, hanging her head in defeat, and clamping her mouth shut before she said something that got her put in the stocks for a week…

"Well, that was rather anti-climactic," Bobo mumbled to his companion.

She nodded in reply before drawing her gaze up the mammoth-sized creature at her side. Bobo's gaze was locked dead ahead, his eyes lost in something beyond the stretch of tunnel. Vanessa had to actually take pause and make sure that there wasn't something at the end of the burrow before she turned to him and asked, "What are you thinking?"

His furrowed brow deepened with crease marks. "I'm not sure. It just … something feels off…" he admitted, and she agreed. But there wasn't much that the two of them, or the small group of slow retreating Coven members, could do to change the minds of the High Priest Council.

 *Chapter 7:*

Outside, droves of Coven members split up, this way and that. Taking on new cases or taking lunch or simply going home at the end of their shift. Vanessa pulled her hood up and drew her cloak around her body like a blanket right as a blast of flurry filled air slammed against her with a howl. The fabric saved her skin from most of the wintery bite, but she hissed as the blistered skin beneath her robes found the chill to be more than her burnt coating underneath had anticipated. After a moment or two, the cold was welcomed, and the charred skin found reprieve in it.

Snow whined under the weight of Leon's glossy, black boots as he beelined it for her and Bobo. She groaned and didn't even mask her displeasure for the man heading her way. "Stop being a brat, Vanessa. I didn't yell at you because I liked it. I did it because you were about to get into trouble with your tongue again."

She rolled her eyes. "I'm sure a part of you enjoyed it, Leon."

To that he flashed a quick, blazing-white smile, and, for whatever reason, Vanessa laughed. She knew that if he didn't speak up, she was going to speak out against the Council, and not all members of the Coven were as lax as Leon when it came down to reporting minor offenses. He was saving her hide in the long run, though, it did nothing for her pride in the present.

"Say, where is your pet?" Vanessa inquired.

Bobo visibly cringed and whirled around with wild squirrely eyes. Anxiously searching the snow mounds and rubble piles for the vixen in question, Bobo's bulbous eyes combed high and low meticulously. Leon laughed at the spectacle and patted Bobo's shoulder.

"Calm down, big guy. She's at the spa and won't be back until this evening," he informed, and Bobo practically exhaled so dramatically that Vanessa swore he'd be making snow angels on the ground as a victorious ritual of sorts. A pall of air became a whitened puff in front of Vanessa's mouth as it escaped.

"Come on, we should teleport to headquarters," Leon said, motioning for her to come closer for the spell.

Vanessa visibly poked her lip out as she pouted with no restraint, and Leon flicked her jutted bottom lip. With a cat-like mewl, she recoiled and rubbed her gloved fingers over the inflicted area. Leon laughed, and she shook her head. "No, I don't want to race back there. I just want to take a carriage," she admitted.

Leon rubbed his chin in thought and nodded. "Very well then, I shall join you."

She raised a brow and cut him an inquisitive glare. "Oh?"

"Yes. It's been a long day, and a nice relaxing ride would do my mind some good before filing a report and speaking before the Council," he proclaimed.

Vanessa eyed him over while in thought. "Fine then." She smirked and swiftly added, "But you're paying."

He opened his mouth and then closed it realizing that he'd been defeated. "Very well, Vanessa," he sighed the reply while searching his pockets for his white cloth gloves. Withdrawing them, Vanessa eyed over the burning phoenix emblem sewn into the back of them. Slipping his hands into the gloves, he waved one hand and a flare emitted from his appendage and burst overhead in a small, yet brilliantly colored, firework detonation.

The melody of prancing footwork and jingling reigns soon came dancing closer to them before slowing to a halt. "Mundane Magic transportation services ... at your, well, service," the man holding the reigns called out to them with an awkward smile.

"Catchy name...." Bobo jested.

"We get ya there," the man added with a nod and forced the smile a touch more.

Vanessa stood there staring at the man, waiting for him to tie up his catchphrase, or whatever it was, and he did a double-take from the partially frozen roads to her deadpan face. "What?"

"Is... is there more?" she asked.

"What?" He looked perplexed.

"That's it?" Vanessa corked a brow over one eye.

He nodded, seeming sure of himself for the first time in their brief meeting. "Yes, ma'am. We get ya there."

She blinked a few times at the driver before Leon laid a hand on the small of her back and ushered her closer to the carriage. "Come on. Let's let the nice man drive the pretty ponies where we need to go." He glanced up at the driver. "Coven headquarters, please."

Bobo piled in after Vanessa and one could hardly hear him speaking under his breath over the creaking of the carriage in response to his weight, "Teleportation would have been easier on the horses."

"The horses will be fine, Bobo," Vanessa tried to soothe the ogre's worries, but by the strained whinnies of the animals, there was little room to dispute the claim.

"All in a day's work, Bobo. Try not to worry. I'll tip the driver and, hopefully, my generosity earns the beasts a bit of rest and well-deserved treat," Leon said with a grin.

Bobo nodded, though, it was clear as the deep lines on the creature's face that he was still concerned for the horses.

Trying to divert her pet's attention, Vanessa changed the subject. "What do you think the blue cloaks want to see me about?"

Leon groaned while taking a moment to *really* think about how to respond to that question. "I'm not really sure, Vanessa." He rubbed the back of his neck, and his long sandy strands started to sway to the same rhythm of the carriages rocking motion, and Vanessa got lost in their golden glow as rays of the sun played in his mane. Slowly, silence took over the conversation for a short while. "It's probably nothing more than them wanting a face to face report of what you saw. After all, Vanessa, it's been two hundred years since anyone has seen a hellhound."

Now that made sense. She was not only the first being to come into contact with them and come out alive, but the first person to do so in over a century. That was nothing to shake a wand at. Perhaps they just wanted to be brought up to date and not have to wait for the report to make it through the inner webbings of the Coven before it graced their podiums. "I suppose that is the most logical answer," she said, feeling a little less sick to her stomach when she let the comment sink in.

The worry that had gnawed at her nerves had been the cause for her lack of desire to use a teleportation spell. First of all, she didn't want to yak in front of Leon, and teleporting on a queasy tummy was sure to make her lose what little of her morning meal that remained in her belly. Plus, Leon would never let her live it down if she did. She didn't want an extra reason for the handsome and annoying Spellweaver to tease her every day. The other reason was the dread that came from knowing that she'd have those powerful and stoic judgmental eyes cast down on her. They were ruthless, pragmatic, and cold... Or so the stories told from those select few that had been before the High Priest Council. She hadn't been in front of them yet and she didn't want to be today. She wanted to fly under the radar and become a highly respected Spellweaver, yet, she constantly got into trouble and regularly issued clean up jobs by the Council as punishment.

The High Priest Council, or blue cloaks – as most called them – were thirteen elder members of the Coven that were well versed in many magics and respected for their achievements as well as their vast amounts of power. Six females and six males made up the Council. The thirteenth member, however, was neither a seasoned Coven member nor a magic-less being ... it was a Celestial. And all thirteen members made up the rules and laws that all of Aeristria's society followed.

Nothing to worry about, right? She was only seeing the primary leaders of their society ... She started to feel queasy again.

"Calm down. You're turning pale. It's nothing, I'm sure of it," Leon spoke softly with a slight smile playing on the corners of his lips.

Vanessa nodded a few times and audibly gulped after she drew in a deep breath and looked out the carriage window. The rhythmic *click, clack, click, clack* of the horses' hooves prancing over the cobblestone was relaxing and an easy sound to try to have her heartbeat mimic. The cool air howled outside the glass window and sent snowflakes twirling through the sky like dancing ballroom lovers. The gentle sound of parchment paper rubbing against parchment paper rode through the air as Bobo turned another page in his book.

Moments passed in a sublime silence. Finally, through the carriage windows, the familiar shops that surrounded the Coven headquarters came into view. Apothecary Herbs & Beyond, Tarot & Fortune Telling Works, and Crystal Ball Emporium were a few of the most popular. They drifted from view as the carriage, much to Vanessa's dismay, didn't slow in its approach of the Coven headquarters that was nestled into the capital of Tolvade.

The stretch of cobblestone wall topped with spear-tipped, rot-iron fencing was a cold and uninviting barrier. Its ends were quickly consumed by the harsh slate face of the building's forward-facing side, where the stone skyrocketed up three floors high and loomed over the streets below with a foreboding presence. The only color to the construction that wasn't painted in hues of gray were the bushes that had been perfectly planted in a uniformed manner around the base of the structure. Yet, even these lively organic ornaments lacked a warm and cozy feel to them, as if the very blade that cut and shaped them were cursed and had snipped each twig with pure hate. The other was the ornate stain glass window that glittered brightly under the rays of the sun like a rainbow on fire had been trapped within the glass. The picture held a burning phoenix inside its nest. It had many of the same characteristics of the Coven member's seal. The burning eyes of the flaming bird seemed to be judging all those that passed by the main entrance.

On either side of the main entrance were two intricately carved – but now weathered with time – statues were leering out from their home. Parallel to them were two columns that rolled up to a flat overhang at the top, just below the stain glass phoenix. Below the overhang, a stone plaque with "Coven" etched in olden tongue rested above the immense black-as-the-bottom-of-an-inkwell opening that led to the large wooden double doors of the front entrance inside.

Each statue mirrored the other. They were long, cloaked, bearded figures that stood erect, holding a staff with an orb perched at the top. One hand positioned at the neck of the long wooden stick, the other was suspended, almost laying completely flat, over the round surface of the cane's sphere. Soulless stone eyes stared into the capital that lay beyond the face of the Coven headquarters.

The carriage rolled to a stop, and Leon was the first to

remove himself from inside and went to pay the driver. Bobo didn't look thrilled or upset, he seemed rather neutral, but his head craned over to view the horses as he exited, checking to make sure none of them collapsed from exertion caused by lugging around the mammoth-sized demon. Vanessa drew in a rather reluctant breath and exhaled it aggressively as she forced herself out of the carriage and onto the sidewalk outside.

She could hear Leon in the background. "Look, just take the money," he urged. "I insist," he added before dropping a small satchel into the driver's open palm. "Just promise to give those poor beasts a rest, all right?" Leon said, patting the neck of one of the horses in passing.

"Of course, sir!" the driver exclaimed as he opened the bag and poked his index finger around the tiny borders of the small sack, stirring the gold coins therein with a rather awestruck expression displayed across his features.

Pouting at the heavily breathing horses, Bobo slowly turned from them and looked at the main entrance. He brushed off the one shoulder of his tattered and dirty suit just as Leon came to stand next to him and Vanessa. "Well," he said with a sudden sigh, "let's get this over with."

"Please," Vanessa groaned. "I want to go home and get lost in a pint of ice cream after this," she admitted.

The trio made way into the building. The dark entryway gave way into a most unexpectedly illuminated and massive open space. The main room of Coven HQ was walled off into the shape of a large circle. On either side there were halls stretching out to each side that led to multiple rooms, most of which that were for training, learning new spells, team debriefing, and storage. A few were selected for medical needs or cleansers. In the far back, past the spiraling staircase that led up to the other floors, there was a line of arched doorways that lead down a long stretch of stairs. Each arched door had runes marked overhead, a way to know which part of the colossal and extensive library you were about to delve deep into, that made up the basement level of the building.

The floors were sun touched gold and blazing white marble with the Coven phoenix emblem dead center of the room. There were three large, curved, red oak desks that were in the main room. One was straight ahead and two were off to the right and left. Leon, Vanessa, and Bobo headed for the main desk at the far end of the room.

A head popped up from behind the desk, and the bright yellow-blonde locks that were pulled back in a sloppy bun had stray curls poking out in different directions as if the woman had done her hair, stuck a fork in a light socket, and then drenched her tresses in hairspray afterward. She had wild freckles kissing her cheeks and nose and a set of large, bright green eyes.

"Hey, Ell," Vanessa said, waving to the kind girl.

"Hmmm?" Ell replied looking up from the desk, her hands rummaging about and moving piles of paper and looking under and through stacks of folders and peering under cups of pens and containers brimming with paperclips.

"Lose something again?" Bobo asked, though his expression wasn't surprised when she nodded in reply to him.

"Whatcha lookin' for?" Leon asked.

She inhaled deeply and let her shoulders sink in defeat as she sighed with a pouting lip. "My pen," she said sadly.

Leon blinked at the girl and, after they were completely to the desk, reached over to the side of the frazzled woman's head. Ell flinched and looked at Leon in a rather odd way right before he plucked the pen from its perch behind her ear.

"Oh," Ell whispered with a bright flush racing over her soft pale skin. She reached out and retracted her hand slightly before regaining the confidence that she had briefly lost and retrieved the pen from Leon's grasp. "Thank you," she said meekly.

Suppressing a giggle at the poor thing, Vanessa cleared her throat and gained Ell's attention before saying, "Do you have any blank standard report forms?"

She blinked rapidly as she stared Vanessa down. "You need to file *another* incident?" Ell asked.

Now, it was Vanessa's turn to turn red. Sheepishly, she nodded and visibly looked as though she were shrinking in size like she was trying to slink away inside her own skin when Leon suddenly choked on his own laughter.

"Yes, please. If you wouldn't mind, my dear, we need to seek audience with the Council once the matter is attended to here," Bobo's thick, gentleman-monster voice rolled out and caused Ell to peel her half-amazed stare at Vanessa and turn to the rather large ogre.

Nodding a few times, again, the girl went to shuffling about the desk. As she did so, she shoved stray golden hairs behind her ear, only for them to defy her a second later and branch out in hostile rebellion to being tucked away.

The sound of parchment paper rustling as scrolls rolled aimlessly about before leaping off the edge of the large desk and bouncing off the marbled floor below filled the library-like silence of the main room. Although it was the main entrance to the Coven, it was a rather quiet place. Each room spelled with silence barriers to keep noises both in and out, and the main room and spreading halls each held hushed tones, chatty whispers, and the clicks of boots or heels against the hard, polished floors below.

She huffed and bent down on the floor to send her fingers flying over the files tucked away in the cabinet below, and a few scrolls rolled under the ledge of the desk. Ell reached over and snagged them just as she found the form Vanessa and the others needed. "Ahha-oow!" Ell's victorious cry swiftly turned into one of agony as she slammed her head on the bottom side of the desk. Rubbing her throbbing head in the area a knot promised to show up, she grimaced in pain and handed the form to Vanessa.

The trio looked at the freckle-faced, messy-haired lass and smiled warmly, though they looked completely sympathetic to her discomfort.

"Get some ice on that, dear," Bobo advised with a worried look.

She nodded and quickly retrieved an icepack from the mini fridge's freezer space and held it up to wave it from side to side with a nervous laugh. "I will," she exclaimed as they walked off. Only to make a high-pitched sound as she realized her skirt had become caught in the door of the mini icebox, and she tumbled back to the floor with a thud followed by the hollow sounds of scrolls pit pattering on the floor around her. Neighboring workers gathered to make sure she was all right, only to have an icepack raise high in the air, and her tiny voice reassuring everyone with, "I'm fine."

 *Chapter 8:*

They filled out the paperwork, and Leon went to file it with Ell while Vanessa and Bobo waited at the foot of the spiraling staircase. Bobo looked up the circling railing of the staircase and into the deep blackness that took up the space between floors.

"Suddenly afraid of heights?" Vanessa teased.

"No more than you," he shot back, but it lacked the usual bite. It felt bland and after a pause, he added, "I'm suddenly afraid of that third floor, though."

Vanessa now, too, was staring up into the void and seemed to become drained of color for a moment. There were two more floors to the Coven building, and the last was the least desired to be traveled to.

Leon came back and brushed past them. "Come on, then. The blue cloaks know that we are here and wish to have us put all other matters on hold until we've seen them."

"Great," Vanessa groaned as she watched any hopes of procrastination fly out the window.

"Move it, Vanessa," Leon called after her, and she made a whining groan.

Bobo motioned for her to go first. "Ladies first," he said with a grin.

She narrowed her eyes, "You're an evil pet."

"I know, dear, I know. Born in Hell and all that. Enough with the lip and get to climbing those steps," Bobo snipped back with a quick slap to her backside. She yipped and turned to face the stairs. With a solemn expression, she followed Leon up.

As they scaled onwards, they passed by the wide-open mouth of the second floor that greeted them between the first and third floors. White-washed rooms so crisp in color and floors so thickly lacquered that they looked like the Coven members that shuffled about upon them were walking on a massive mirror. The wide entrance gave way to a giant crystal ball that hovered in the farthest reaches of the room and stood a good fifteen feet in height. Twenty-two members of the Coven stood around the orb, tiny pictures in view in various points around the globe that thrummed with power. The Coven members would tap on the images, use their hands to spread out or zoom in to a particular area and make note of the incident that had caused the black magic detection warning to go off. After a quick inspection, the picture was balled up with the Coven member's fist and swiped off the crystal ball to the right or left room as a floating sphere of dim yellow light that would weave and bob until it reached an open crystal ball in the room that it was directed to. Behind the bleached walls were two separate rooms. Both completely identical in setup, with rows and rows of desks with medium-sized orbs placed on the top of a small desk that a rank four Coven member sat at. One room was dispatch for Spellweavers, like Leon, and the other was the dispatch room for Hunters, like Vanessa.

Despite the pure-white appearance of the room, that floor always disturbed Vanessa. Perhaps it was the constant hum of power that rolled out of the ginormous orb or the fact that the room was so white that it felt empty and lacking life, but it bothered her nonetheless.

As she took a moment to realize where she was, she hissed under her breath as she reached the top of the winding stairs, "Double-dip a candlestick."

"Try not to say that in front of the High Priest Council, Vanessa," Leon warned in a pleading fashion.

She cut him a look but said nothing in retort as she didn't exactly want to speak on this floor. The halls were a mesh of gold, black, and white. The ebony paint on the sidewalls made the wide hall leading to the ominous double doors at the far end seem smaller, and the gold sponged on paint that dusted over the onyx color made it feel regal. Regal and deadly. The white baseboards were almost blinding in comparison to the dark coal color above. The only light came from oil lamps that lined the walls from end to end. Vanessa's eyes hurt in the dim, orange glow that the oil lamps provided. As they walked, she looked down the left and right skinny halls that seemed to have a plethora of doors covering the gloomy and abysmal stretch of space.

Those doors led to the small offices of the Summoners and, eventually, it led to the few offices of the Second Chosen. Summoners were a rank above Leon and Second Chosen were promising members appointed to replace members of the Council. Spellweavers were the third rank, Hunters were the fourth, and at the same ranking – but with alternate titles – were various other Coven members with jobs less exciting than that of Vanessa's, in her opinion. The first tier, however, was the Council and as that thought boomed in her mind so did that massive knock that Leon lay upon the double doors.

"Enter," a very deep and threatening voice called out from the other side of the wooden barrier.

"Breathe, Nessy," Bobo whispered to his owner.

"I will end you in front of the Council if you call me that again, Bobo," she seethed.

"That's my girl," he chuckled huskily and then fell silent as the spell Leon weaved opened the doors and let a blinding light spill out into the dusky hall and wash over them all in a way that made Vanessa feel like she was on some terrible ride and unable to get off. She hadn't realized that she had shielded her eyes from the light until she noticed the dark shadow that lay over her face, protecting her eyes from the torment of the sudden light that poured out from the High Priest Council's room.

Thirteen high-backed, throne-like chairs were spread out over a half-circle rise at the far end of the large room. A set of three steep, but stubby, steps rose up to the placement of chairs that lined the room before Leon, Vanessa, and Bobo.

The doors slammed shut behind them, and Vanessa jumped and looked back to her only escape in horror. Slowly, her gaze returned to the front, and the cold eyes that peered down at her from behind blue cloaks. There was a cherry wood podium nestled dead center of the stage and all the seats.

Blue cloaks wore just that, blue cloaks, with golden emblems of the Coven's insignia over the breast of the garment. The cloaks were not so much a status symbol as much as they were spelled relics to keep the magic that the High Priest Council possessed from emitting out of them in choking waves.

She couldn't even begin to fathom what it would be like to be in their presence if one of them was de-cloaked, much less all thirteen. And the Celestial? She might as well lie down and die on the spot. The one known as the Celestial had no name and her cloak had rays of white dashing out from behind the veil, glimpses of golden spun hair and mother-of-pearl colored eyes were the only features that could be distinguished.

"Spellweaver Zvěrokruh," the blue cloak on the far right spoke; it was male, and the High Priest known as Ronan.

That's a mouthful, Vanessa thought as Leon bowed to the Council. "Greetings, High Council," he said in a loud and formal fashion.

Ronan's surprisingly soft gray eyes glided over the room and rested on Vanessa's form. "And this is Hunter Peterson?" Instantly, Leon masked a laugh with a cough and hid his monstrously large grin behind his hand that he skillfully brought up to his face before the Council could take notice of his ear-splitting smile.

For a quick moment, she stole a look to Leon with daggers darting in his direction before she too bowed before the Council saying, "Yes. Greetings, High Council."

"Do you know why you are faced before us?" This time the voice belonged to a woman, Mia.

As Vanessa rose to her full height, she shook her head at Mia and the other Council members. "I do not," Vanessa replied, unsure of whether or not they desired her to speak. Not being met with backlash toward her reply made her ease up just a smidgen.

"We have heard word of your encounter at the academy. Could you tell us what you saw?" Mia asked with a gentle smile.

Blessed be the goddess that looked down upon Vanessa in that moment, for Leon had been right in his assumption for why the Council had wished to speak with them. This caused the stiffness in her body to melt away before she spoke clearly to the Council of the happenings back at the academy.

"Yes, ma'am," Vanessa confirmed and drew in a slow calming breath before weaving the tale to the Council. As she explained her and Bobo's findings, the members leaned into one another and folded forward to whisper to other blue cloaks a few seats away from their own placement.

Once she was finished with her story, the next one that spoke was another male, Dmitri. "And that is when Spellweaver Zvěrokruh came to your rescue?" he asked with a single brow raised over one of his dark blue eyes that almost seemed black.

Vanessa looked to Leon and then Bobo before facing the Council once more and nodding slowly. The Council members again fell silent as Dmitri turned his attention to Leon. "And you saw the hellhounds?"

"Yes, High Priest Dmitri, there is no denying it," Leon boldly spoke to the blue cloaks.

Hushed whispers ensued as Dmitri held up a hand for silence, his bottomless, glacier gaze burrowing deep into the three that stood before the Council. "How would you explain your relationship with Hunter Peterson?" he asked without a shred of guilt.

Leon stuttered for a moment before announcing proudly to the Council, "Annoying ... sir..."

Dmitri and Isolde (a female blue cloak) cracked a grin at the comment, and it was Isolde that leaned over and whispered to Mia, who nodded, and after a few traded words between the Council members, Mia announced, "Due to the severity of the situation and Hunter Peterson's uncanny habit of getting into trouble, we decree that you shall be partners until further notice and reside within her home for the next two weeks to help keep her in line."

Vanessa's stomach hit the floor at the same time that her mouth became unhinged, and her eyes bulged to the point that her sockets pinged with pain.

"Wait, what?" Leon gasped.

"This is effective immediately!" Mia proclaimed in a booming voice.

"This. Isn't. Happening," Vanessa stated quietly, feeling like she was going to be sick.

The Celestial stood and clapped her hands in front of her chest, and it was like thunder had exploded around them. "And so, it shall be!"

"Wait..." Vanessa and Leon tried to reason with them as they all removed their hoods and the power became overwhelming. The Celestial was the last to remove her hood, and nothing but hot light pierced their vision. Vanessa could feel the bonding of the spell that would tie her and Leon together for the next two weeks. *No, please!* But her mental plea was ignored.

Her chest felt like stones were resting atop it as she was stuck at the bottom of a river. Sound was consumed by the power that flowed out of the High Priest Council and made Vanessa feel as though she was drifting out of her body for a moment before it was all sucked back in and the hoods were replaced over the Council's heads.

Sweet air!

Gasping to draw in as much oxygen as she could, Vanessa doubled over and held her head as she tried to catch her breath. Bobo was groaning as he knelt low to the ground, and Leon seemed to be in a similar pose as she while he, too, tried to regain consciousness. However, Bobo seemed in a bit more pain, and his arm shook as he struggled visibly to keep himself from falling face down on the ground right there in the Council room. Vanessa hated seeing him like that but was rendered motionless by the immense power that had recently flooded the room.

The Celestial looked like she was hugging herself, and then the ivory beams of light radiated from her blazingly as she opened her arms and reached far out in front of her. "May the light be with you," the voice was almost song-like, and at the stretch of the Celestial's arms, Leon, Bobo, and Vanessa were all sliding back out of the room and past the open doors. They watched as the Celestial replaced her hood and sat down just before the double doors slammed shut in the trio's faces.

 *Chapter 9:*

There was a long, silent, and unbelieving moment that Leon and Vanessa shared while staring at the deep brown, wooden door that was between them and the Council members. Bobo was straightening his soot-covered tie and smoothing out the wrinkles in the once well-pressed suit. Vanessa rubbed her temples and groaned, "What have I done wrong to deserve this?"

"Shhh…" Leon hissed as he stared hard at the sealed entrance.

She turned and blinked at him. "What?"

"This is all a bad dream. I had a horrible vision just now. I'm waiting for them to open the doors," he said in a rather convinced tone.

Bobo walked up and clapped a massive paw over Leon's shoulder, and it made the Spellweaver jerk, not expecting the touch from the massive beast. "Give it up, you're looking less collected than her," Bobo said, thumbing over to Vanessa.

Leon grumbled under his breath and let his forehead fall onto the door in front of him. "I'm in hell," he whined.

"Probably," Bobo agreed. Slowly turning to face the ogre, but keeping his head connected with the door, Leon stared at the creature. Dramatically, Bobo leaned in with a grin, "And that is saying a lot coming from me," he said.

For whatever reason, perhaps the man finally snapped, Leon laughed so hard that his belly hurt, and he had to fold in half as he chuckled through the pain. Once the laughter had subsided, he had to wipe a tear from the corner of his eye.

"I suppose if you've survived as long as you have with her, then two weeks should be nothing for me," Leon sounded like his old self again, and that seemed to satisfy Bobo, but Vanessa seemed too angry to care about his minor fit over the Council's decision.

She had stormed off down the hall without even bothering to call after Bobo. "Well, she's going to be a delight the whole way home," the ogre griped.

"How lovely, my first night will be such a cheerful one," Leon sighed sarcastically.

"I'll have the gin and tonic at the ready," Bobo remarked before sauntering down the hall to catch up with his owner.

Leon had let Vanessa carry on with her aggressive march through the Coven building. She wasn't happy with what had just transpired, and he needed to use a quick teleportation spell to go home and gather a few things before he'd catch back up with her and Bobo back at headquarters later. Bobo assured Leon before he had left that he would ensure Vanessa would stay at the Coven headquarters until the end of her shift.

On the way downstairs, Bobo was a bit too hasty in his attempt to catch up with Vanessa. His final steps being bumbled near the end, and he elegantly caught himself just before he reached her.

"Oof!" Bobo grunted as he connected, and hard, with Vanessa's back.

She screeched in return and caught herself on the railing, her back leg extended trying to balance herself as her head lunged forward and hands clamped down on the wooden railing like tiny vices. Her foot jutting backward to aid in gaining her balance contacted Bobo's lower stomach, and he roared in pain. To the roar, both to Bobo and Vanessa's surprise, there was a sound of a mousy yelp and then the sound of papers flying, and they turned their awkwardly twisted bodies in the direction of the tiny girl that had made the sound. They twisted just in time to catch a glimpse of wild blonde hair and a long navy blue pleated skirt fling backward and then tumble, head over feet, down the staircase.

"Double-dip a candlestick!" Vanessa seethed. She pivoted her one good foot, saddled the railing and slid down as her hand reached into three different dust pouches on her hip. Squeezing the dust into her hand, she channeled energy for a second and then flung her hand out behind her yelling, "Feather fall!"

Blue light erupted from her hand and skyrocketed faster than eyesight could keep up with before spiraling down after the plummeting maiden. A gentle squeak was heard right after the light left Vanessa's hand. She slowed her ride down the railing when she saw Ell floating in mid-air. Her tiny hands were gripping her skirt in a fashion that would keep it from rising up and showing the world all her wonders as she tucked her legs under her bum and blinked, looking around her and then blushing madly when she saw Vanessa. "O-oh, h-hi again, Vanessa," she squeaked and then looked behind her to see how far she had to go before she'd reach the bottom of the staircase. Which was only a few steps, but with the feather fall spell upon her, she'd take a minute or two to reach the comforts of the solid floor below.

"Blast it all with hellfire, Ell!" Vanessa remarked with concern glinting in her eyes. She dismounted from the railing and walked next to the slow falling girl. "Are you all right?"

Ell took a moment to smooth her hands over her body and attempt but fail miserably, to fix her hair. "I-I think I'm all right," she said with a nod.

"Still..." Vanessa sighed, "I'll want to sweep over you with a quick recovery spell just in case. Don't need you waking up sore tomorrow and running up a bill at a clinic because of my bluster."

Ell bit her lower lip and looked down at her hands folded on her lap, "I don't want to be a bother. I'm sure that I'm fine."

"What a load of imp poo. I'll mend you and that's that," Vanessa said, stomping her foot on the ground at the foot of the steps.

As she started to float up upside down, Ell squeaked and flapped her arms wildly trying to turn herself upright again just as she came within inches of the ground and the spell broke, causing her to fall the minor distance to the floor with a soft groan. Ell rubbed her backside and looked to Vanessa. "I suppose if you insist."

Vanessa put her hands up on her hips and puffed her chest out proudly. "I do."

Just as Vanessa started to search her pouches for a quick spell, Bobo came racing down the stairs with sloppily stacked papers and filing folders in his massive arms. "Is she al—" he called out huffing and puffing.

"She's fine," Vanessa said, and Ell nodded with a warm smile. "I'm going to give her a quick recovery spell just to be sure," she added.

"Oh, blessed be," Bobo said, almost melting into the steps as he went to sit down and catch his breath on the foot of the staircase.

"Are those… Oh, they are! Bobo, you wondrous beast, you gathered my files for me. I for sure thought I'd have a terrible time trying to recollect them all," Ell exclaimed with a bright, cheerful grin.

Bobo couldn't help but smile back at her. He rubbed the back of his neck and started to flush as he spoke, "Oh, it was the least I could do. After all, it was my bluster that caused you to fall."

He hung his head low and she waved in front of herself frantically saying, "No, no. Really. I'm fine. Don't worry so much over a silly accident, please, Bobo."

"We are both sorry, Ell. You could have been hurt really bad if I hadn't cast that spell in time…" Vanessa admitted, and that was when Ell went silent, her tiny hands plucking at the fabric of her skirt in nervous frustration.

Vanessa's hands reached out and hovered in front of Ell's chest, and she started to whisper a chant for minor healing. A soft, spearmint green light started to pulse out of Vanessa's hands as she closed her eyes, slowed her breath, and focused on channeling the spell to heal Ell's minor bumps and bruises. As Vanessa worked, Ell watched in partial amazement.

It was no secret that some of the record keepers that worked at the Coven were magicless or possessed such low-level magic that they couldn't get promoted to a Hunter class or more. A lot of magicless people were hired on at the Coven to be record keepers. There was always a place for people, magic or not, in this world. About seventy-seven percent of Aeristria's population was made up of magical beings. The rest was magicless, but still had a place just as much as those that possessed it. Discrimination against magicless beings did happen and was highly frowned upon when it did, but it was still a rarity in Aeristria.

Not to say that the mass majority of magical beings didn't

have it all easy in and out of the work field because of magic and spells. There were things that magical beings had to endure that magicless folk would never have to face, like Medusa's Kiss. A magic eating disease that slowly eats away at the magic a being possesses, and this is called withering. Once all the magic in the body is consumed the carrier turns to stone and dies.

But, still, on occasion, you'd stumble upon those people that cannot perform spells on the level that Hunters, Spellweavers, and Summoners could, and you'd find their eyes twinkling with a sort of cheer that was full of wonder and innocence. Ell was not able to perform much magic past calling someone on a crystal ball, but she was always fascinated when her peers did a spell in front of her or, in this case, on her.

"There," Vanessa said before sighing heavily and slumping her posture a bit. "That should be enough."

Ell twisted and turned her body, patting at it here and there but focusing on her hips, bum, and one of her upper arms. "I must say I'm glad that you insisted on that spell. I feel so much better now," she said with a grin. "And not all that you repaired was from my tumble down the stairs," she added with an embarrassed look upon her delicate features.

Bobo and Vanessa both couldn't help but find the act and statement both painfully truthful and adorable and burst out laughing after trying to hold in the side-splitting cackles for a few seconds. Ell turned redder than a cooked apple and fidgeted with her fingers a bit and nervously giggled along with the two of them.

Bobo was the first to break free from his laughing fit. "Worry not, dear. You are just so precious. Just too precious," he said, standing and holding out the files after tapping them on a step to straighten them all out. "I believe you need these back."

"Oh. Yes. Of course," Ell fumbled over her words as she retrieved the folders from the ogre. "Thank you. I need to file these down in the library," she said, flicking her fingers through the files to make sure that they were all in order.

"Do you need some help?" Bobo asked.

"It is the least we could do," Vanessa chimed in before Ell could politely reject the request.

She blinked at the two before her lips curved into a wide smile. "Actually, a light spell would help me a bunch! Those torches down there sometimes don't light the bookcases that we need to use, and it makes filing these records even harder," she confessed.

Bobo motioned for Ell to lead the way and then for Vanessa to follow close behind with her light spell. Straightening out her pouch belt hanging on her mauve robes and pushing her ashen black cloak behind her shoulders so she could better see each pouch, Vanessa poked around until she had the powders she needed and summoned a light orb.

"That took longer than usual," Bobo said.

Vanessa nodded with a half-pout, "I'm running low on golden dust," she said, sounding less thrilled than usual. "We'll need to stop by a supply shop to pick up some more on the way home."

"Hmm… is there a place on the way home?" Bobo asked as they stopped in front of a dark doorway with baby blue glowing runes above the entrance. Ell seemed to study the markings for a moment while the other two spoke.

"Honestly, Bobo, I forget you're an ogre some days," Vanessa sighed.

"Well, thank you, but I don't see what that has to do with what I asked," he tightened his half-singed tie and stood tall and proud. If anyone could make a tattered suit look good, it was Bobo.

She rolled her eyes. "Spellvana, the dust shop that is right next to your favorite book shop," she explained in a tone that was attempting to rattle his memory.

He looked lost for a brief second before gasping and saying, "Oooh, that one place next to The Dragon's Tale."

Her deadpan glare was bordering a mix of un-amused and annoyed. "Yes, Bobo. *That* bookstore. And the store next to it is Spellvana. Stay with me on this…" She sounded as exasperated as she looked in that moment.

"Right. We'll stop by Spellvana on the way home then, Vanessa," he assured.

"This is it!" Ell sounded delighted that she found the proper door and pointed at it energetically while Vanessa and Bobo came closer to aid her in her descent down the dark steps and file the stack of folders she had.

The ivory washed walls swiftly turned into smooth cobblestone and held a blue-gray hue to its aged, rocky skin. As Ell had explained, there were torches that filled the descent into the library. Torches were also fastened to the edges of the bookshelves and even along the walls and pillars that lined the library halls, but their light was dim, and they were scattered so scarcely around the halls that it was hard to see between their outer edges, and there were patches of encroaching darkness between the firelight. Someone really should tell Being Resources about this. It was a safety hazard for sure. But, one needed a touch more courage than what Vanessa possessed now because it was run by boogeymen. No, really. All the Being Resources in Aeristria were run by boogeymen.

Vanessa used the light spell to look down one of the isles. "I never knew how big this place was." Astonished, she peered down a few narrower passages.

"Over here," Ell called out to her and started to shimmy between the bookshelves.

The ogre looked around them and grumbled while looking at the small birth between the shelving units, "Didn't exactly make these with … larger beings in mind."

"This place is about a hundred years old, they didn't really build it thinking that it would last this long…" Ell informed.

"What do you mean?" Vanessa asked. She knew a lot about spells and sorcery, but she was sort of bad with history and never paid that much attention to it while attending the academy.

"Well, the first Coven built was much older than this one, but it burned down a hundred years ago. We lost a lot of scrolls, records, spells, and knowledge because of that fire. My family was one of the three that provided extra documents and literature for the new library the Coven erected years later." As Ell spoke, she went about her work and the other two followed her as she educated them. "About a hundred years before that was the last demon sighting."

"You mean the hellhounds?" Vanessa asked.

Ell nodded. "Yes."

"But, how did the other Coven headquarters burn down?" Bobo inquired.

Ell stopped shelving her folders and looked around to make sure that they were all alone. She hooked her finger and motioned for the two to come closer as she whispered in an ominous tone, "No one knows, but some say…" as she said those magical words that seem to start every horror story, Bobo and Vanessa leaned in closely to listen. "…that it was caused by elven folk that came from the Black Forest. But no one is for certain, or why they would have done it."

"Elves?" Bobo whispered, perplexed. "I thought they had died out long before that."

"Yeah, the last sighting of an elf was around the time that the last demon was sighted," Vanessa whispered right after Bobo.

Ell gave them a look that didn't match her nature, it was almost dark and gave both Vanessa and Bobo the shivers. "They say that the elves didn't die, that they all went into hiding after the elven war. To hide from each other so they wouldn't die out completely." She stared at them a bit longer and they were all silent until Ell straightened back up and fanned at them while laughing into her free hand. "But that's all just Coven tales that the seniors tell the rookies. Could you imagine elves actually still being alive?"

Bobo grumbled something under his breath and turned to venture off through the library while Vanessa continued to help Ell. "It would be pretty cool if they were…" Vanessa sighed and looked up the thirteen-foot-tall shelf as Ell shelved another folder.

She looked over her shoulder to Vanessa. "What would be?"

"If the elves were just in hiding."

"Oh, yes. Well, all of us magic beings were sort of created by them, or by the humans and elves mating," Ell said and let her hand caress the top of the manila folder. "Imagine the spells they could teach, the stories they could tell, and the knowledge they would have. They were not only the creators of everything we hold dear now but the ones that taught us how to control and use magic from the very start." The mousey blonde seemed struck with wonder and daydreams for a moment.

"Yeah, but it's been so long since anyone has even heard the re-telling of a sighting. Surely, they have all passed," Vanessa sounded sad, and she slumped her shoulders. Even the light spell she was controlling dimmed as her demeanor turned sullen.

Slowly, Ell stopped shelving the files and turned to face Vanessa. Opening her mouth to draw in a breath and speak, Ell was prepared to attempt to lift the Hunter's spirits only to have a scream erupt from her as a jumbled collection of loud clattering clashes echoed through the library.

Vanessa jumped at the scream and the several sudden crashes that resounded through the basement level of the Coven. *Thwack, thwack, thwack.* The thick wooden sounds of the massive bookshelves as they slammed into one another in a booming domino effect rumbled through the shadowed library.

Both of the girls turned just in time to see Bobo standing with three shelves in front and three behind him. All of them toppled over and only hindered from causing more damage by the pillars that were placed between every six cases, to halt such an occurrence from transpiring past a few bookcases instead of the whole section.

Coughing, Bobo waved away gray clouds of dust that billowed around him like he was in the middle of a sandstorm. The echoing sounds of the fallen bookcases subsided, and Ell and Vanessa had run to the edge of the shelving unit they were at in order to catch a better glimpse of the pouting ogre standing above the wreckage as the billowing clouds of dirt was slowly dissipating.

Nothing was said. The ogre simply finished the movement that had caused the accident (his elbow had slammed into one of the bookcases and sent them toppling over, and when his large form turned to catch it, the other side toppled over). He pulled out his spectacles from his pouch, placed them atop the bridge of his nose and blinked rapidly, letting his eyes focus before bending over the fallen shelf in front of him. A large digit raced over the spine of the books and stopped when he came across a title that had caught his eye.

"Ah-ha!" he cheered victoriously and plucked the book from the shelf and started to open the book and skim through the introduction pages. Glancing over at the ladies, he grinned wide with an obvious blush growing on his cheeks as he waved the book from side to side and pointed at it with his other hand. "It's the complete works of Darion Black, the famous epic poet who wrote about the elven wars," he exclaimed.

At that point, it was too much, and Ell laughed hysterically, and Vanessa looked embarrassed to have Bobo as her pet while trying to slink into her own body like a turtle slipping away into its shell.

 *Chapter 10:*

The trio picked up the mess, which was rather easy considering that Bobo could lift each of the bookcases on his own, which left the three of them to pick up the scattered books and scrolls to re-file onto the shelves. Ell being the quick-handed filer that she was, made the task go by even faster.

After the spill of scrolls, files, and books were cleaned and put away, Bobo and Vanessa walked Ell back to the front desk on their way out of the Coven. Vanessa had a smile on her face and had forgotten all about the woes of her day, that is until she bumped into Leon. He was lazily leaning against the grand entrance with a duffle bag at his feet as he waited for her and Bobo to arrive. Then, the nightmare that was her life now resumed its rightful spot in the front of her mind. Her smile curdled on her face and she frowned while staring at the man that was now her temporary roommate and partner.

"Ah, that's the lovely face I look forward to coming home to each and every night," Leon teased.

Vanessa blushed angrily while Bobo snickered, and she brushed past them while saying, "I hate you."

"Who?" Bobo and Leon asked in perfect unison.

"Both of you!" Vanessa snapped in a half-yell as she stormed off – while carefully watching for snow patches that would injure her backside and pride – at a slower pace than she desired.

A teleportation spell would have been wonderful, but it required her to hold hands with Leon and Bobo and, at the moment, she was not up to the task. It didn't help that those things cost a pretty coin that her current earnings wouldn't allow her to frivolously cast without thought or care. Besides, the cold was actually bringing her critically high anger down a notch or two as she had to focus on keeping her cloak and hood wrapped around her to fight off the winter chill more than her tenacious desire to list off reasons for said anger.

"Stubborn thing," Leon mumbled.

"Preaching to the choir," Bobo sung as he took notice of the growing distance between his owner and himself.

With a groan, Leon hoisted up his bagged belongings, throwing them over his capable shoulder before they both headed off to catch up with the angry witch that was storming through Tolvade's busy streets. The usual chatter of the capital's center market rolled through the air like a familiar melody that brought comfort and disappeared deep into the normal hustle and bustle of the city life as a welcomed background noise. Local vendors filled the streets while many workers stood outside their shops calling out the day's sales.

The men lingered behind Vanessa, who was fuming with rage and trying to keep her mind off the day's events that had turned from sweet and hopeful to sour and nightmarish. She marched with purpose and hunched in on herself as she muttered angrily on her way to Spellvana. Giggling children paused when they took notice of her and quickly removed themselves from her path, whispering that she was a madwoman and that they should steer clear of the obviously *tainted* witch.

The term 'tainted' reached Vanessa's ears, and she rose slightly from her forward fold and slowed her stride while blinking her scorching anger from her eyes. It was true, if not for the polished bronze insignia on her cloak, she probably looked the part of a tainted witch, a sorceress drunk on black magic. The horribly addictive stuff that turned good witches, mages, warlocks, and worse with just a simple spell.

If you were lucky and had enough will power to reject it, you could do black magic and walk away from it just fine. But, most, sadly, could not. Even those that could reject the urge to dive deeper into the black arts didn't go beyond simple curses. Go beyond that and you were lost. Black magic becomes a scratch you can't itch, a thirst you cannot quench, and you slowly fall into madness and turn into something even darker than a demon. Some invited this into their lives, others fall into it unknowingly, but no matter the case, it was because tainting could consume a magical being so quickly that she and the others fought so hard to stop it from spreading and to bring down the dark witches before they hurt or killed innocent people.

While deep in thought, Vanessa hadn't realized that she had arrived at the shop she was so urgently trying to get to and had stopped just outside its doors. An old man peered through the window with a deep, sullen expression until he saw the familiar robes Vanessa usually wore. He beamed at the sight of her and raced to open the door.

The pealing of the silver bell woke Vanessa from her thoughts, and she saw old man Wit'ticker holding open the door with one hand and churning the air with the other as he grinned from ear to ear. "Come in child, come in! It's frightfully cold out there!" he urged, and she couldn't help but smile at his contagious upbeat attitude and shook off the snow from her shoulders as she stepped into the warmth of the shop.

Her boots made a thick sound over the worn wooden shop floors. She removed her hood as his short white hair and bright blue eyes came into view. "Needing anything today?" he asked with a hopeful gleam to his old gaze.

Nodding, she admitted, "Gold dust." She opened the pouch to show that there was more bottom to her bag than powder. "I'm running low."

He looked grave for a moment and hummed. "I see, I see. Follow me, I just received a shipment yesterday. Anything else?"

She smiled. "Maybe some nightingale feathers." They were mainly useful in veiled magic and sleep spells as well as several other uses.

Her eyes glided over the many bottles of various shapes and sizes and colors. Fading sun from the day poured in through the large glass windows in the front of the shop and splashed over the contents of the tiny bottles therein. As if spring had bloomed within the shop, rainbows and glittering light bouncing off the bodies of the flasks and vials painted the room in a colorful and magnificent enchanting glow. Sandalwood and clove, lavender and sage, rose and dragon's blood, frankincense, and myrrh, scents that she had tied to comfort and filled her youth when she first started practicing, rolled through the senses and ignited a deep-seated excitement for magic that resided inside of her as if the smells and sights of the store rekindled a dying flame.

"How's business been?" she asked, looking at a jar of dried rattlesnake tails.

"Slow, but not unusual this time of year. Folks are more focused on presents and preparing for the snowstorms rather than spell casting," Wit'ticker admitted as he climbed up a ladder at the back of the shop near the register and opened a few drawers before finding what he was looking for. Using a small wooden scoop, he gathered a helping from the box and dumped it into a small pouch before sliding the container back and climbing down a step or two and grabbing the feathers she had requested. "Been a lot more healing herbs purchased lately, but those are a dime a dozen and usually don't bring in much of a profit," he continued as he shuffled over to the counter and rung up the purchase at the register. "Thirty-five gold and seven silver," he claimed, looking up at her still as happy as when he first opened the door.

"I wonder why that is…" she fished for her money and paid him.

"It is cold season," he announced. "Nothing you should be worried about." He smiled warmly as he took the money and handed her the paper bag.

"I suppose you're right." She retrieved her items and bid him farewell.

The cold rushed back to steal the little warmth her body had collected inside the shop as she opened the door. Shivering from the cold, she turned to face the others as she pocketed her dust. Both Bobo and Leon looked pitiful huddled close to one another in an attempt to stay warm. All of a sudden, Vanessa realized that it wasn't Leon's fault that the Council had made the choice that they had, and that he didn't want to be in this situation any more than her. And Bobo? He had ruined another good suit because of her innate ability to get into trouble without really trying … most of the time… sometimes… Okay, all the time.

"Sorry for the wait," she muttered in a soft voice to them.

They turned to look at her and then to each other. Leon spoke first, "It's about time. It's freezing out here!"

Why? Why did he have to ruin it? She instantly frowned and

narrowed her gaze at him. "Why do I even bother with you? I said I was sorry!" she shot back.

"In the future try to be quicker and then you'd have less to be sorry about," he countered.

She stifled a scream behind tightly sealed lips and resumed her marching.

"Honestly, did you need to?" Bobo asked with a sigh.

"Of course, I did. If no one points out that she's being rude then she'll continue to behave like a spoiled brat," Leon informed, starting to walk behind the angry witch again. "Besides," he shifted the weight of his duffle bag before resuming his conversation, "It was weird having her apologize."

Bobo chuckled, and the remainder of the walk home was relatively quiet save for some minor chit chat between the men.

 *Chapter 11:*

"Oh, come on, Vanessa, it was funny!" Leon yelled after Vanessa as she practically ran down her apartment building's hall.

"Funny?" She stopped and twirled around to face him so quickly that her long, ebony braid flew like a deadly weapon behind her. "Funny? I could have died!"

"You're being dramatic, I had you. I was just teasing." Leon said with a smile. Bobo wasn't helping while he chuckled relentlessly into his closed fist behind Leon.

"Dramatic?" She shrieked.

"Okay, you can stop repeating whatever I say. I heard myself saying it the first time. And yes, dramatic," Leon confirmed.

"That is a flat," Vanessa screamed, pointing to the old school styled elevator as the man running the rope started to head back down to the main floor. "You hit me with a wind spell, and I almost fell off the edge!"

Leon looked back to the flat and giggled, remembering the little stunt he pulled. "Oh, knock it off. It was a tiny gust, and I grabbed your arm long before you ever reached the edge of it," he rebutted.

She threw her hands up in the air and turned back around as she raced for the door. "I hate you!" she yelled.

Leon jogged to catch up to her, only to be met with a door slamming in his face and hearing the deadbolt slid into place. He stared at the door with a deadpan glare, and his smile had faded from his mouth. He reached for the doorknob and jiggled it unsuccessfully before knocking on the door. "Open up the door, Vanessa, I live here too, now."

Bobo continued to giggle as he slowly walked down the hall and leaned on the wall next to the doorframe. After a moment, his laughter ebbed, and he started to reach for his pouch at his hip. "This might take a while," he said, retrieving his book and glasses from his side pouch and settling in to read a few chapters.

Throwing his head back and facing the ceiling, Leon groaned and knocked on the door again. "Vanessa, open the door."

"No," her voice snapped back through the door. He could tell she was still nearby, probably leaning against the door. So, Leon knocked a little louder.

"Seriously, this is childish. Unlock the door and let me in."

"Sleep in the hall!"

"This is going to take forever," Leon whispered.

"Tooold yooou," the singsong voice came from the ogre as he slowly turned a page.

Determination flared through Leon as he pounded on the door. "Open this door, Vanessa!"

"Not by the hairs on my chinny-chin-chin!"

"Why you little—" He balled up his fists and shook in anger for a moment. "I've got an ogre out here, and I'm not afraid to use him."

"You wouldn't dare."

"Oh, yes I would."

Bobo's voice was smooth, calm, and collected as he added to their bickering party, "Don't pull me into your squabble, please," and then turned another page.

"What is going on out here?" A woman across the hall had her arms crossed over her chest and hard glare set in place as she eyed over Leon. "Are you trying to hurt her? I'll call the Coven on you!"

Leon went to show his Coven insignia to prove he was a member but had a wicked thought slither into his brain. A wildly crazy smile coiled on his lips as he skillfully kept the silver emblem from sight. He thumbed back at the door. "You know how girls are. Make one joke about the size of their thighs, and it's out the door with you."

"Oh my!" The woman touched the side of her blushing face, and her mood went from cross to understanding all at once. "I did that to my husband once."

"I'm sure he deserved it just like I do now. Lover's quarrels are never easy, but she never likes to forgive me right away. Wants to make me simmer in guilt."

"That's a good woman right there," the neighbor replied with a giggle.

Suddenly, the door flung open, and Vanessa grabbed Leon by the back of his cloak and jerked him through the opening, leaving Bobo to waltz slowly to the front door while waving at the woman, "Have a good night, Mrs. Garrett."

"I'm glad you two made up!" she yelled to them before she shook her head and laughed and headed back inside her own home.

Slamming the door shut behind Bobo, Vanessa barked at Leon, "Are you crazy? Don't go telling my neighbors that you are my... my..."

"...Lover?" Leon finished while leaning into Vanessa.

Like a flare spell getting ready to explode, she turned so red she was practically purple and shoved him away from her. "Don't spread lies through my apartment building."

He chuckled and straightened up his cloak, "Very well. Then don't lock me out of *our* apartment."

"Fine," she muttered and brushed past him to get to the kitchen.

The apartment front door was right next to a coat closet, directly after that it opened into the rest of the living space. To the left was the kitchen. A stretch of gold-flecked, black countertops raced around the left-hand side of the room making a large breakfast bar. The opening for the kitchen was right next to the small dining area that neighbored a small hall that led back to one of the rooms. To the right was the living room, and another short hall gave way to the second bedroom and the main bathroom. The living room had a couple of bean bag chairs and a couch set that was oversized in Leon's opinion, and then he saw Bobo walk over and sit down on it. It clicked then, that the set was bought more for his comfort rather than having others in mind. Overall, the apartment was rather spacious in design, and it was a blessing considering Bobo's monstrous size.

Candles littered the coffee table and votive candles filled the sconces on the walls and dusted the counter spaces. The scent of cinnamon and vanilla wafted through the home and caressed his senses. It was a warm and inviting scent that gave the body a relaxed and energized feeling. He found himself smiling for no reason other than finding enjoyment in the scents floating about the apartment.

"It's a welcoming spell," Bobo spoke up from the couch as he flipped another page before he looked up from the edge of his book, letting the glasses slide down the bridge of his nose with the aid of his large index finger. "She figured that it would make people feel more welcome to come back when they visit."

"Does—"

"You're the first visitor," Bobo cut in before Leon could finish his question.

Leon looked through the home and then down the hall for Vanessa. It would have seemed that she had run away and locked herself away in her room. That was, until she yelled from behind her door, "I'm changing out of my dirty clothes."

"Sometimes I wonder if she can read minds," he said, turning and walking to sit down on the couch across from Bobo.

"She's a woman."

Blinking, Leon tilted his head and looked at Bobo, waiting for the beast to explain his comment to him.

Rolling his eyes and shaking his head, Bobo added, "A woman always knows. Even if you don't want them too. They are only dumb in one area if you ask me."

"What area would that be?" Leon asked with a laugh.

"They are clueless as to when someone is interested in them." With that said, Bobo pushed the glasses back up his nose and fell back into the words on the page.

From down the hall, the sound of Vanessa's door opening peeled Leon's attention from aimlessly wandering over every knickknack, scented candle, and the artwork lining her apartment. He scooted to the edge of the couch and looked at the plush carpet below. Noticing a spec of dirt on his boot, he reached down to brush it off and spoke to Vanessa as he toiled with the mundane task, "Where am I supposed to sleep?"

"Well, not in the room with me. That's for certain," she said with a snort of laughter nasally escaping her.

The comment caused Leon to snap his gaze to her and opened his mouth to say something but paused with his mouth open.

Vanessa stood behind the couch Bobo was seated in, her attention on the task of brushing out her hair that had been in its usual braid like it always was when she was at work. Deep ebony hair was gripped in one hand while a small toothed brush wrestled to comb through the many knots that had made a home in her long, silky locks that had become naturally crinkled by the braid. She wore a white tank top and a long, brown pleated skirt with a belt that cinched in the front through a gold emblem of the Coven symbol. It was a simple outfit, and for the life of Leon he couldn't figure out why she looked so appealing in it.

A flash of movement caught his eyes, and he turned ever so slightly to see Bobo waving to get Leon's attention, but trying to use his body to hide the motion from Vanessa. Bobo mimicked what Leon's mouth looked like in that moment before he put his hand under his jaw, and pushed up, closing his ogre mouth and then gave a mock grin to the man. Leon furrowed his brow and clamped his mouth shut with a heated look in his eyes. *As if,* with a look alone, he was telling the ogre it wasn't what the beast thought.

Bobo just rolled his eyes and mouthed, "Yeah. Okay." And moved on to read his story while saying, "I've heard the couch is comfortable."

"Why can't I sleep in your room?" Leon half-whined.

"Because I'm spoiled and like my privacy

Vanessa snorted with laughter and looked to the kitchen. "I'm hungry. We should order—," The thought was broken by a soft rapping on the door.

A brief moment passed as all three gave questioning glances to one another and then the door was suddenly thrown open.

Vanessa pulled out her wand, the only weapon she had now that her spell belt was off, and her staff was put away, just as Bobo jumped over the back of the couch and hooked Vanessa around the waist to drive her toward the floor just in case the intruder had a spell ready to toss out at the witch. The heavy thud of them hitting the floor resonated through every object in her home that had jolted about from the ogre's weight slamming with Vanessa in his grasp to the floor.

Instead of slinging spells and harmful magic being flung through the room as expected, there was a sultry voice that rolled through the apartment. "Honey, I'm home!" It sounded sexy and upbeat, not menacing and deadly.

Bobo's head shot up from the floor and he gave wild, fearful eyes to Vanessa, who felt squashed under the beast. "No," he whispered.

Vanessa whispered, "Force push," with her palm directed at the demon's shoulder and the ogre was hit with a small spell that caused him to roll off the witch. Crouching behind the furniture, she fussed with straightening her hair and clothes. Slowly, she peeked over the couch to see a succubus kicking the door shut behind her with her cloven hoof.

She had long, brilliant raven locks that fell in waves around her shoulders and flowed down the female's back in soft, tame half curls. Her near-perfect skin was pale and held a lavender hue to it and was covered (hardly) up in a short leather mini skirt and a gold and black leather corset, lavished with a line of gold buckles from navel to the swell of her ample mounds. Boots that mirrored the style of the corset rose up to the creature's slender legs but left open at the bottom for her cloven hooves to remain free. She had two black, long-sleeved gloves that seemed like a second skin they were so smooth and flawless as they ran up each of the demoness's arms. Two long, blade-like ears pointed out on the sides of her sharp angular featured face. Atop her head were two vibrant purple and black horns. On her back was a set of folded, red-violet wings, and dancing behind her, flicking from side to side in a seductive wave, was a tail with a spiked (and very venomous) tip. The succubus's brilliantly amber jeweled eyes seemed to burn with an otherworldly glow as she smiled to Vanessa when she saw the girl poke up from behind the couch.

"Lyx?" Vanessa questioned.

"Darling! Why are you behind the couch? Come, give me a hug." The succubus outstretched her arms and waited for the girl to come to her because there was absolutely no denying the demoness.

Reluctantly, Vanessa started for the succubus when she felt a sudden weight upon the fabric of her skirt. She looked down to see Bobo on all fours, or three's rather because one hand was clutching onto Vanessa's skirt like it would somehow save him. She awkwardly turned and gave a single finger, signaling for the succubus to wait a moment and quickly ducked back behind the couch.

"What?" she hissed.

"What is that … that … *woman* doing here?"

A wickedly sinister smile came over the witch's lips. "Oh? Aren't you happy that Leon's living with us?" She jabbed. He was so tickled earlier that she had to suffer through this arranged living situation with them that he had forgotten about Leon's pet.

Served him right…

As Vanessa stood, she patted the despairing ogre's head with one hand and snatched her skirt from his death grip with the other and then turned and skipped over to Lyx and flung her arms around the demoness's neck as she flew into the creatures embrace. "How've you been?"

"Oh, darling, I've been fabulous as ever. Leon is such a kind sir—"

"Stop calling me that."

She giggled and then pouted, all for show. "Why must you be so mean to me in front of company, Master?"

"Your charms don't work on me. Try to behave, I know it's a stretch for you," Leon huffed.

Lyx waved at Leon like he was a fly buzzing in her face. "What about you? Are you a Spellweaver yet?"

"Ha!"

Both Lyx and Vanessa shot Leon a look, and he sunk into the couch and covered the side of his face with a throw pillow as if it would act as a shield him from the eye daggers that were being shot at him. Melting back into their happy state once more, the girls continued with their conversation.

"No, not yet," Vanessa replied.

"It'll happen soon enough, darling. Don't beat yourself up." After saying that, the succubus started to stand on the tips of her cloven hooves to look around the apartment. Orangey gold orbs scanning the space that was visible for something. She stopped suddenly when her gaze locked onto Bobo's head that was peering sneakily (not really) from behind the couch.

Lyx practically tossed Vanessa out of the way before cupping the sides of her face with a wild smile and bent her knees dramatically as she spoke in a high-pitched voice, "BooBoo!"

"No," he gasped as he shot up to his full height suddenly and froze in place.

The succubus unfurled her wings and flapped them once to give her jump a bit more juice before instantly refolding them on her back as she landed a few feet away and started to run, almost skipping, toward Bobo.

"Stop."

"BooBoo!" she screamed excitedly again.

She outstretched her arms and went to hug him, but his mammoth-sized hand palmed the succubus's face, and he looked over the couch to Leon. "You!" he pointed a single digit at the man, and Leon dropped the pillow.

"What did I do now?"

"You are bunking in my room."

Leon grinned as he flung the pillow to the other side of the couch and crossed his arms over his chest. "Why the sudden change in heart, my good man?"

Bobo shook his index finger maliciously at the Spellweaver. "Don't test me. Besides, you're the only thing that can control this pet of yours."

Lyx reached up and jerked Bobo's hand off her face with a heated glare. "Why do you deny my love for you?"

"I…" Bobo seemed at a loss for words.

"Didn't you miss me, my love?" she pouted.

He then pointed the finger from Leon to Lyx. "Don't do that. We aren't together."

"You're fighting fate, my love. Isn't it better if you just," her voice dropped back down to its normal sultry tone, and she crashed into his side with a surprise half-hug and let a finger circle over the ogre's tattered button up, "…let go and let me have you?" Her hair turned into a bright magenta as she nuzzled into the demon's side.

Two hands clamped down on the succubus's shoulders and ripped her from his side as he glared down at her. "Harlot! I told you. I do not wish to have relations with you or court you."

Lyx shivered and moaned. "I do love it when you manhandle me," she cooed.

Instantly, like she had burned him, Bobo released the woman and cleared his throat while tugging on the bottom of his dirty jacket. "I shall retire for the evening. I'm in need of a shower and a good night's rest."

"What about dinner, won't you join us?" Vanessa questioned, but when the ogre turned his gaze to the girl he took note of the smile plastered to her face and narrowed his eyes at her.

"I'll have Lyx behave," Leon assured, understanding of Bobo's plight.

"Oh, imp poo," Lyx whispered under her breath.

With a sniff and a moment's thought, the creature nodded and said, "Very well. I shall return for dinner before I turn in for the night."

Leon clapped his hands together. "It's been forever since I've had a home-cooked meal. What are we having?" he asked eagerly.

Vanessa and Bobo cut him a look like he had lost his mind. "I'm not cooking tonight," Bobo said.

"I thought…"

"That I was cooking?" Vanessa asked.

Leon nodded and both she and Bobo burst into laughter that was so crippling that they held onto one another and hysterically hooted until they sounded like they were hyperventilating.

"I mean… If you want…. The house to…burn down…she could…" Bobo wheezed.

Vanessa could hardly catch her breath and tears were rolling down her cheeks that were split with her crazed smile. "He—he—he thought I could *cook!*" Vanessa cackled.

Leon looked at his pet. "I'm not cooking, I just had my nails done," she informed.

Bobo slowly regained his composure and patted his person for his handkerchief. Wiping his face and giving his nose a quick blow, he returned the cloth to his pocket and straightened himself up. "Oh. My good man. I so did need a good laugh." He cleared his throat again and fought the threatening wave of laughter before resuming with his idea. "I say we order out. We are all too exhausted from our days to try to cook. Let us eat and then retire."

"Do you have work tomorrow?" Leon asked.

Vanessa shook her head no. "Tomorrow is my day off."

"Plans?"

"To sit at home and read, if you are asking me," Bobo admitted.

Leon turned his attention back to Vanessa who was already trying to distract herself with anything but answering his question. "Oh, my goddess, Lyx. Your hair smells fantastic!"

The succubus perked up instantly. "I know, right? They washed it with this jasmine and white tea shampoo, and I was in heaven the whole time. The smell is to die for!"

"Vanessa," her name came across like Leon was an upset parent. The tone alone insinuated that a scolding was in order, but the child may not be so sure as to why.

"Hmm?" she hummed.

"What were you thinking of doing tomorrow?"

"Nothing."

He narrowed his eyes at her. "I don't believe you."

"I'm sorry that you don't."

"Tell me."

"Tell you what?"

"What are you planning in that harebrained mind of yours."

"I don't know what you are talking about, Leon. Clearly, you are tired from your day and need rest."

"Vanessa, by the goddess I swear I'll bind you for a day!"

She growled. "I was going to go to the academy and see if I could find any traces of where those hellhounds had scampered off to."

"Vanessa!" Bobo and Leon yelled in unison, and she cringed like they had both slapped her.

"What?"

"Whoa. Whoa. Hold the crystal ball for a moment," Lyx said turned toward Leon. "What in the name of magic is she talking about, Leo?"

He looked guilty for a moment. "You didn't tell her?" It was Vanessa and Bobo's turn to speak in unison to Leon.

"I've been a little busy," he shot back.

Lyx put two hands up at her sides, closed her eyes, and took a deep breath. But as she did, her hair turned flaming red before dimming down until it was the usual glossy ebony shade. "Leo, darling. I need you to tell me what, in the name of magic, is going on."

Leon rubbed the back of his neck and groaned as he massaged some of the tension that was growing there out. "We are in a bit of a… pickle… Lyx."

"I'd say! Hellhounds? Do you have any idea how long it's been since one was last sighted?"

"I'm aware."

"Do you have any idea of how difficult those atrocious beasts are?" Lyx asked.

"I am now."

She blinked with her mouth open. Whatever she was going to say was stolen by the fact that Leon had admitted that he had encountered one personally. "You *saw* one?" she screeched.

"Well, it was more than one…"

For a moment she stared at Leon like he had turned into a unicorn, and then gasped and turned around to face Vanessa and Bobo. Instantly, she started to let her hands race all over Bobo, even forcefully turning the massive creature around as she inspected him for more than the soot and scraps that covered him. "That's what happened to you?"

"Of course, woman. What did you think had happened to me?"

"I… well…" she blushed and looked to Vanessa, "Sorry, darling. But I thought you might have messed up another spell."

Leon started to chuckle, and Vanessa raised the wand and pointed it at him. He raised one leg off the ground and put out both hands in front of him to ward off a possible oncoming spell. "Don't point that at me," he ordered.

The succubus forced Vanessa's wand hand down and whispered to her, "At least not in the house. You'd never be able to get the stains out of the carpet." Vanessa sighed and dropped her hand completely to her side.

"I think we need to order food and talk about what's happened today," Bobo advised.

 *Chapter 12:*

The four of them fought over what to order and settled on Merlin's restaurant. It was a bit pricier than the usual takeout but well worth the extra coin. Besides, they were all splitting the tab evenly.

They sat around the living room explaining the events that lead to Leon having to live with Vanessa for the next two weeks and peddled back to what they had seen down in the boiler room of the academy, right down to the tunnels. Lyx listened, hardly saying a word the whole time. She just looked like she was trying to evaluate a long math problem with no pen or paper.

When the group fell silent, all eyes were on Lyx as she stared down at her lap. Glowing amber eyes rose to meet with those that were spread out around her. "You realize that this is bad."

"I do," Bobo replied.

"Really bad," she said while looking between the Spellweaver and Hunter.

"I know that it's bad. It's for that reason that I'm so upset with the Council giving up on the search like that," Vanessa started.

"They are going to be sending Summoners out. People far better suited for the job than inexperienced Hunters and newly made Spellweavers. It's a death sentence."

"He's right. You need to keep your mitts out of this case, Vanessa. It's too much for you to handle alone, much less at all," Bobo said softly.

"Your pet is trying to keep you safe. Heed his warning, please. I don't want you to get into a predicament that even I can't save you from," Leon spoke in a half-hushed voice.

The comment caught Vanessa a bit off guard, but before she could question anything any further, there was a knock at the door. This time, everyone wasn't tripping over themselves expecting an attack, they expected food.

Vanessa opened the door to find an oversized floating white

bag filled with takeout boxes. The aroma of the contents caused Vanessa's mouth to water with anticipation of devouring the food. Grilled meats, roasted red potatoes, steamed veggies, soft and fluffy freshly baked loaves of bread topped with salt and butter. It was enough to drive her starving belly into a grumbling beast. Her stomach wasted no time in letting a growl breakthrough the silence.

"Whoa, don't eat the messenger," a small voice teased. That was when Vanessa heard the soft flapping of tiny, leathery wings. She peered out into the hall and around the bag that appeared to be floating. On the other side was a bat, and she could see the mist magic that he was using to keep the bag afloat. "One hundred and eleven Poppy Lane, apartment three?"

She nodded. "That's me."

"That'll be fifty-seven gold and three silver," the bat said as a puff of smoke seemed to burst out of the bat and shadows enveloped the misty clouds until it formed a tall, lanky male vampire.

"Just a second," she said, fishing through her pocket for the funds that she had gathered from the group earlier. "There ya go. Keep the extra coin."

The vampire quickly counted the gold and nodded with a smile to Vanessa and handed her the bag. "Enjoy your meal!" With that, he poofed back into a bat and squeaked before furiously flapping his wings and bolted out of sight.

"Thanks!" she called to him before closing the door and heading to the living room with the food.

Each of them got their meals as Bobo handed out the silverware from the kitchen. "Those plastic forks never hold enough," he said.

"That's because you are enormous and have a mouth to match it," Leon said with a short laugh.

"They always break too," Vanessa added in the ogre's defense.

"That's because you are careless," Leon stated after quickly letting his laughter end to make the joke at her expense.

Vanessa squeezed her metal fork and imagined it was Leon's neck as she glowered at the man. Regardless of how cute or smart or funny the guy may or may not be … he was a jerk. One day, she'd be a Spellweaver too, and he could just stuff all his snarky comments into a complaint box at work!

The meal was enjoyed in silence after that. Bobo retired to bathe as he had promised to do before they had ordered food, and Leon used Vanessa's private bathroom, even though she didn't want him anywhere near it. But, the sooner he bathed, the sooner he'd go to bed, and the sooner he'd be out of her hair. Sacrifices for the greater good must be made.

While the men showered, Lyx and Vanessa cleaned up the living room and put the dishes away. It dawned upon Vanessa in that mundane moment that she had never really spoken to Lyx alone with no one else around. She did a few double-takes before she quitted her voice and spoke to the succubus like she was asking for a taboo secret potion.

"Hey, Lyx?"

"What is it, darling?"

"Can I ask you something?"

"Well, you are now. I thought that it would be obvious, but sure. Fire away."

"Why are you so infatuated with Bobo?"

The succubus stopped in her slow exit of the kitchen and turned to face the young Hunter. She tilted her head to the side and watched as the young witch poured two glasses of lemonade. Vanessa looked up and smiled nervously before she shut the icebox and turned around to face the succubus head-on. Lyx searched around the corner to make sure the coast was clear and gave Vanessa a come-hither finger as she walked into the living room to gain both distance from possible eavesdroppers and give them some privacy if one of the men entered the room unexpectedly.

Not that the succubus was shy by any means, but she could tell that the girl wished for less to hear the conversation that was sure to ensue thereafter. Lyx situated herself on the couch and fussed with her mini skirt and fluffed her curls with her fingers as those amber eyes fixed on the witch that chose to sit next to her. Vanessa handed her the lemonade and sipped from her own glass.

"Darling, do you know what it's like in Hell?" Vanessa shook her head no and Lyx continued. "Flames, rivers of blood, endless screams, and there is not a sin or pleasure that could be offered that you can't find down there. If there is a dark itch that needs scratching, you'll find the means to relieve yourself down there." She spaced out while staring down at her glass. "There are a million voices matched with a million screams and yet, so many of us feel completely alone. Most of us don't even realize it. We aren't aware that we are lacking what you Coven members give us. You give us something that we've craved for so long, and we just didn't realize that it was something that we desired, or it was something that could be obtained. The intelligence and morals that come with the spell that you all throw at us when summoned is a most powerful thing." She sighed. "Having said that, to answer your question. There is muscle down there. Dime a dozen, really." Lyx gave Vanessa a look that said it all. "But brains aren't exactly overflowing in the underworld."

Vanessa blinked and rubbed her arm with her free hand. "So … you have a thing for Bobo because he's smart?"

Lyx shook her head and locked amber eyes with the witch. "He's smart, sophisticated, wears a suit … girl, you know we die for a man in uniform. And he has a job? Darling, I'm hooked. Toss in his love for the arts and that he's witty as can be and I'm instant putty," she said while theatrically throwing herself back into the pile of throw pillows and pretending to 'melt' into the couch.

"I suppose I can understand," Vanessa admitted.

"But, that's not the main reason," Lyx said, slowly rising and straightening herself out.

Raising a brow over one eye, Vanessa stared at Lyx and waited for the explanation that she was hoping would come without prompting. Lyx giggled faintly into a lightly closed fist. "Darling, a muscled man is nice. A demon of your current make and model has its perks. But sometimes, a woman wants a guy that has charm, brains, *and* the muscle. Beyond all of that? He isn't on a one-track mind. For some reason, him not giving in to me," she looked off in space and smiled like no one was watching her, "…makes me want him even more." Her smile softened, no longer holding hints of madness but warmer, gentler thoughts. Her eyes sparkled with it. She laughed to herself quietly and added after emerging from her small quiet moment, "That's a demon you wanna take home to momma…" She snapped out of her happy daze at the realization of what she had said. "Well, not *my* mother, she'll try to steal him away, but you get the picture."

Vanessa laughed lightly. "Sounds like you know what you want."

"Of course, I do. I'm a woman, and a woman knows what she wants, a girl can be persuaded, and a lady needs to be won. No matter the species, we are all pretty much the same. We have standards for it, but we all want love."

It was Vanessa's turn to laugh again. "I'm glad you have it all figured out." She took a sip of her drink.

"What about you, any male suitors catching your eye? Or females. There is no judging here, darling. Spill it."

Vanessa choked on her sip and coughed furiously into her elbow until she was sure she could breathe without tasting lemons. "Do what?"

Lyx gave Vanessa a look that said she was not amused with the girl's lack of understanding. "Come now. Spill who you have a crush on." She got a devious sparkle in her tawny eyes. "Is it Leon? Tell me. Promise I won't say a thing," she whispered excitedly.

Looking as though she'd been told that there was a pop quiz on demonology, Vanessa bulged her eyes as she swiftly put down her drink and then Xed her arms out in front of her. "No. No way. I have no crushes and even if I did, it would *not* be on that stuck up Spellweaver."

The succubus rolled her eyes hard. "Okay, darling. I'm only the manifestation of lust incarnate. I ooze desire and want on an hourly basis, but … whatever you say. No crushes. It's fine." She turned her head and looked at the witch from the corner of her eyes and attempted to hide a wild-growing grin on her face. "I mean, I understand a strong woman like yourself not being fond of the idea of marriage and family and all that. Hex it all. If you ask me, it's overrated."

78

The thought of settling down wiggled into Vanessa's thoughts. She'd have a child, maybe two, a home… a family. Things that she never grew up having. Allowing herself the briefest of moments to think of a being to fill in the blank face of the male that she envisioned standing next to her, overlooking her shoulder down at a bundle of joy resting in her arms, she began to have small details color in the blank space of the daydream. She saw sandy hair and piercing blue eyes. Instantly blushing, she shook her head and tried to deny what she thought of just then while she spoke to Lyx.

"I-I didn't say that. I wouldn't mind settling down with someone…" Vanessa lost some of the aggression in her voice, and Lyx pounced on the opportunity as she turned around, bouncing as she did, to grab the witch's hands and shake them in an energetic fashion.

"Who? Hmmm? Are they cute? Charming? Intelligent?"

"I don't know if you'd call it a crush… I mean…" the blush was becoming violently apparent and was quickly taking over every inch of her features.

"Who's the unlucky guy?" Leon practically yelled as he crossed his arms over the back of the couch and leaned in on the appendages.

Not expecting the man to be there, and given the delicate topic that was being discussed, Vanessa half-screamed and jolted so fiercely that she fell off the couch and crashed to the floor, which didn't aid the red cheeks that she was already sporting. She slammed her hands down on the couch cushion. "Do you have to sneak up on us?"

Leon blinked, not understanding why she was so upset. "I thought you heard me…"

"Yeah… well… I didn't."

"What's the big deal?"

"Nothing, dear, you just interrupted girl talk," Lyx said with a sigh.

"It wasn't girl talk. I just was asking Lyx something…" Vanessa corrected.

"Oh. I just thought you two were talking about crushes. Thought I'd warn the guy that you fancied."

"You don't have to. I don't like anyone!" Vanessa barked

before dusting off and storming into her room and slamming the door shut.

"What's her problem?" he asked while thumbing in the direction of the brooding witch behind the closed door.

"You wouldn't understand it if I explained it, dear." Lyx patted Leon's shoulder and walked past him. She opened the door to Bobo's room and waltzed inside.

Instantly, she was met with a harsh tone and being ushered out of his space, "Do you have no shame, woman? Shoo. You'll find your quarters elsewhere!" The door was closed and Lyx huffed while staring at the barrier that was now before her.

"Can't blame a girl for trying," she whispered and then flipped her hair over her shoulder before she headed for Vanessa's room and closed the door behind her. Leon was left leaning on the couch looking absolutely perplexed more so than usual.

"… Seriously. What just happened?" he asked no one in particular before he sighed and headed for bed.

 *Chapter 13:*

"You aren't the boss of me," Vanessa snapped.

"Of course not, but I am here because I'm supposed to babysit you and make sure you don't do anything stupid," Leon reminded as he followed Vanessa into the kitchen.

"You're stupid!" she fumed.

He stared at her, unimpressed. "Really? That's the best you've got?"

"I haven't even had coffee yet. You're lucky that I'm not resorting to pure violence as a witty comeback, Leon."

At that moment, Bobo exited his room, his nose stuck in a new book. His large paw patted the counter and after a moment of thumping about barren counter space, he looked away from the worn pages to search the breakfast bar more thoroughly. He pouted and dropped the hand holding the book to his side, the action causing a loud smack that gained the attention of both Leon and Vanessa. Palm up, the ogre motioned to the empty space upon the peninsula. "Where is my cappuccino?" he asked in a monotone voice.

Vanessa cut her heated gaze to Bobo. "I'll tell you where it is." She pointed to the machine that looked as though it were cut off in mid-use. "Leon decided that I was interrupting his beauty sleep and came in and unplugged the machine!"

Leon gaped and looked between her and Bobo and then he started to try and gain sympathy as if it were a competition all of a sudden. "I asked her to cut it off and wait a while. That blasted thing makes more noise than your snoring," he whined while gesturing to the ogre, and the gentleman-beast instantly flushed in embarrassment.

"I-I realize that this isn't the most favorable of situations, but I was trying to be a gracious host. I'm sorry that the manner in which I sleep forced you to the couch. I hope it wasn't too terrible to sleep on."

Leon looked as if he instantly regretted what he said and was about to comfort him when Vanessa chimed in. "So that, Bobo, is the reason why there is no cappuccino for you this morning."

Bobo sighed heavily and removed his spectacles and motioned with them to the – now unplugged – cappuccino machine. "Honestly, Leon…" he started while shaking his head slightly in disappointment, "… it's the one thing the woman can do right in the kitchen. Must you take that one pleasure from me?"

Defeated, Leon groaned and scratched the back of his head aggressively. "Fine." He mumbled something and went to find his shoes, "I'll buy you something from the Grim Bean, but all I ask is for a few hours, your bed, and everyone leaving me alone, so I can get some sleep."

"Done," Bobo barked and then took note of Vanessa staring at him in awe.

"Are you that easily bribed? The man robbed you of a daily ritual and you dismiss it as if it never happened?"

"He also offered to pay for what I'm now lacking, and I'm a sucker for the Grim Bean. Don't look so surprised."

"Mark me, this is the start of him trampling all over our home life."

"I'll buy you something, too," Leon added coolly.

She darted her eyes to the corners and looked Leon over for a moment. "Anything?"

He rolled his eyes. "Yes, yes. Anything."

"I suppose I'll go get my cloak then…" Vanessa said, throwing her black mane over one shoulder and marching confidently down the hall to her room.

"I can't blame her," Bobo whispered. "That stuff is like black magic."

Less than twenty minutes later they were walking out into the hall as Leon and Vanessa's bickering continued all the way to the flat opening. They whisper-argued as they performed the usual daily task of walking, stopping to greet the neighbors as they departed for their day, and stopping to pull the rope to ring the flat bell that hung on the wall next to the shaft opening.

While the two of them continued with their back and forth banter, Lyx slowly tried to inch her way over toward Bobo while she smoothed out the side of her plaid skirt and pushed and squeezed her breasts until they threatened to spill out of the top of her half-buttoned button-up shirt. Looking down to inspect the respectful amount of cleavage, Lyx pursed her lips to the side and was still a second before she popped an extra button out of the slit and fussed with her hair before sidestepping until she was bumping – quite literally and purposefully – into Bobo.

The ogre looked down with a blank expression and was met with Lyx batting her luscious lashes while smiling up at him. The second look to the cleavage made the poor demon snap to a stiff stance and lock his eyes into the blackness of the flat hole and pray to the goddess that the flat driver would hurry the hex up.

Giggling, Lyx went to walk her fingers up one of the pinstripes of Bobo's suit jacket arm when the flat driver finally arrived. The man peered out from a blue-gray, worn cadet cap, hints of deep chestnut hair peeking out from the edges of the hat's border that snuggly hugged the man's head. His pale face paled even further as his hazel eyes grew three times larger than their original half-tired appearance, and the man let out a semi-girlish scream before releasing the ropes that helped pull the flat up to the level that he was at.

The ropes slacked and then went tight again as a second voice from the roof level of the apartment building yelled down through the hole. "John, what in the name of hellfire is going on down there?!"

"It was a bloody ogre! First a succubus and then that lady with all the imps this morning. You think you could warn a guy?"

There was giddy laughter from the roof level. "Yeah, you'll see some things in this place."

"Really, Raymond?"

"What?"

"I quit. I quit yesterday. I'm so done that you can go ahead and count me as not here today."

"Oh. Suck it up, John. I was just having a bit of fun. I'll tell you about the residence here at lunch. Come on."

"Took this job because you said it was easy coin. You just wanted to scare me. I should have known better…" the man said more to himself than the one he referred to as Raymond as he pulled himself back up to Vanessa and the other's floor. "Pull yourself together, John. You can do this. Those imps threw far worse at you this morning. It's just an ogre and a succubus. You're not going to die today. Come on, ol' boy."

"Lad, you realize we can hear you, right?" Bobo asked with a bored expression.

The man forced a smile and said to himself, although not really controlling his volume, "You're not going to die. It's okay, John. Pull yourself together." The smile grew painfully wide and appeared to almost hurt the man as he tried to speak to the group and only squeaks were produced. Clearing his throat, John attempted to speak again. "Good day. Where to?"

Leon was laughing into his fist and trying to hide it while Bobo looked insulted and Lyx was trying too hard to cling to the ogre to care about anything else while Vanessa rolled her eyes and stepped onto the flat saying, "To ground level, please."

"Of course, you're going to the ground level…" the man sounded defeated and lost the edge to his smile. He attempted to pull himself together before asking the next dreaded question. "All of you?"

"That's right," Leon said before stifling another chuckle.

"If I wasn't going to the Grim Bean, I would have just gone back to the apartment by now. Rude," Bobo whispered the last word.

"I'll buy you a little something extra, big guy. Come on. John didn't mean it."

"That's right, sir. Not every day that you meet a sophisticated ogre like yourself," John quickly added.

"Well, I suppose it is pretty rare. I am an oddity," Bobo seemed to loosen up as he straightened out his jacket, the compliment had done well at feeding the creature's ego, and he happily stepped onto the flat. The wood creaked under his massive weight.

John had to hold the rope a little tighter, and the leather gloves he was wearing groaned under the stress of holding the ropes in place as they all piled on. The other person that was waiting motioned for John to go on, "I'll take the next one," he assured, and John mouthed *thank you* over and over until out of sight.

After they reached the bottom, the man bowed and smiled telling them all to have a nice day and waited a minute before yelling up the shoot, "I'll kill ya, Raymond!"

 *Chapter 14:*

As they were walking through the city, the icy winds blasted through the piles of white powder and sent the glittering flakes spiraling down the semi-quiet streets. These winds were the start of the usual winter blizzard that would find its way passing through the heart of Aeristria each year, and already the northern winds had brought in a thick overcast of gray clouds that draped over the sun, causing the channels to seem duller than usual. The lack of life added to the dreary feeling that seemed to take over the usually busy city roads. The traditional street shops were all put away for the season. It was too dangerous for the shopkeepers. They typically had agreements with the local stores and set up small stands there during the winter season. During the spring, they'd resume their normal posts outside.

The Grim Bean rested on the corner of a crossing where quaint met questionable. Most of the shops and stores that lined this part of town were old and historical. But this particular corner is where the city started to become less casual and the average person needed to be on their guard when passing through the alleys and thinner streets that were nestled between buildings. However, the Grim Bean was not the only reason that this corner was well known.

Turn down the silent, dirty alley that was between the Grim Bean's side and a local tailoring shop and you would stumble upon two old, bent townhomes sandwiched together like two lovers lost in the large city. And in one of those crooked townhomes lived the disreputable Leslie Templeton. An imp that knew more about getting into trouble than out of it. Everyone, *yes everyone*, knew Leslie at the Coven.

Lose something? He was either the one that tried to steal it or managed to get his sticky fingers on it by other means and is selling it to an unsuspecting customer. Need something? He probably has a knockoff of it for a fraction of the price – *maybe*. Looking for information? He more than likely has the connections, but the amount of street jargon and bargains that you'll have to wade through to get it may not be worth it in the end. It's a coin toss, really. Leslie Templeton was, without a doubt, the most annoying imp and butterfingered pickpocket Aeristria had to offer.

There was hardly a day that went by that the imp wasn't getting into some sort of trouble. With that thought in mind, Vanessa took a few steps backward, away from the front doors of the Grim Bean and stepped toward the corner of the establishment to peek around the wall and see if the mischievous little imp was up to no good, per usual.

Vanessa sneakily inched her face close to the stone corner of the building and looked down the long, dismal alleyway. She wasn't at all surprised when she found that Leslie was, in fact, trying to fool some passerby into buying some of his busted goods. She sighed and rolled her eyes, getting ready to rush off to save the day when the attire the woman that Mr. Templeton was trying to con made the Hunter give pause.

Upon closer inspection, Vanessa realized that the female had curly light brown hair that glistened with a golden hue in the gloomy sunlight that the early day had to offer. She had a black face mask hiding most of her feminine features and blocking most of the winter chill, but it was the silver Coven insignia that caught Vanessa's attention and made her lips twitch in a devious smile.

Turning on heel, she resumed her post with the others as Leon tried to gain a peek at what was going on around the corner. "Is that imp up to no good?" he asked.

"Yeah, but he won't be for long. Seems he picked a Coven member to try and sell to this time."

Leon snorted and shook his head. "That little devil can't stay out of trouble to save his life."

Bobo poked his head out the door sniffing the air and fluttered his eyes at the delicious scent that he was taking in.

"Does the coffee smell that good, Bobo?" Vanessa asked in a half-tease.

"Not half as good as that crispy batwing spaghetti that I smell cooking." He looked down at Vanessa as she tried to squeeze by him. "Was Leslie there? Oh, I do so adore his mother. Perhaps we could pop in for a moment. She's always fond of feeding anyone that comes her way."

"He won't be there for long," Vanessa informed and then instantly her mind went back to the time that Ma made bumpy toad lasagna and had offered her and Bobo a plate. Bobo was in heaven, while she was trying her best to find the courage to swallow the first, and only, bite that she had taken of her meal.

She felt her face pale, and her hand wrapped around Bobo's wine-red tie and tugged hard enough that the ogre followed the tiny hand that had caught him off guard. Their eyes locked, and Vanessa's voice dropped into a dark whisper, "Never mention eating there again." She released the tie and had a chipper tone as she motioned for everyone else to hurry up. "Come on," she announced like the incident had never taken place.

Bobo cleared his throat and smoothed out the wrinkles in his tie. "That was a touch unnecessary."

"Awww... let momma help," Lyx commented as she started to fuss with the tie.

For a moment, Bobo was so baffled by his owner's actions that he let the demoness carry on for a moment or two before slapping her hands in rapid succession as he whisper-yelled, "We are in public woman. Restrain yourself!" and then huffed as he stormed toward the counter inside the Grim Bean. Lyx giggled and skipped happily along to catch up with everyone.

Inside the Grim Bean, there was the usual long lines and idle chatter. People sat all around drinking coffee, lattes, cappuccinos, and iced drinks or indulging in the delightful muffins and scones that the shop had to offer while browsing things on their crystal balls or chatting with friends. A few read the newspaper or books while some scribbled in art pads or wrote vigorously inside of notebooks between longing gazes out the large windows that lined the front of the barista.

Up at the front, Leon and Vanessa bickered back and forth over how much Vanessa could and could not order. She seemed fully prepared to eat and drink her weight in what the Grim Bean had to offer, and Leon would not have it – and neither would his coin satchel. Bobo scanned his options while playing with the rims of his glasses, and Lyx was too focused on the ogre to take note of anything on the menu.

Two, floppy, olive ears with black, jagged stripes, bounced behind the counter as the sound of bare feet slapped the tiles underfoot. When the bumpy skinned ears stopped at the register, a gremlin climbed up a step ladder and stood on top of the counter, locking its dingy gold eyes with the next person in line and waved them forward with a series of nonsensical guttural sounds that made up the gremlin's speech. Knotted fingers with sharp, shiny black claws tapped away at the register with each person that stepped up. Meanwhile, at the side of the gremlin, there was another writing down names on cups with a permanent black marker.   The problem with gremlins is that they understand you … and that is about it. Gremlic is incredibly hard to learn as well, and rarely will you find the most gifted learner trying to get a grasp on it past a few words before they give up. Imps typically run gremlin owned establishments. A sort of language barrier manager. They make sure that everyone understands one another. Why imps? Because imps can speak all languages. Having the gift of tongues came in handy with these money hoarders. Yet, people have become very aware of the body language of the creatures, and the managers aren't needed all the time.

Before they knew it, the gremlin running the cash register was dinging the bell resting on the counter with its large floppy foot relentlessly and motioning with urgency for the group to come forward while the gremlin with the marker threw various-sized cups all over the counter and climbed up to stack them all while uncapping the trusty writing utensil.

"Radda ratar a?" The gremlin questioned in its complex language and tilted its head while waiting for them to reply.

"Excuse me," a male said while scooting between Vanessa and the counter.

"Ratta. Radda. Rad rad radda ra," the gremlin snipped and pointed to the back of the line.

"No, I will not go to the back of the line. You messed up my order. This is cow milk. Gross. I ordered unicorn milk. And this is Leprechaun Brew when I specifically asked for Banshee Blend. Also, I asked for two shots, not one, not one and a half, but two shots of espresso. Honestly, how hard can that be?"

"Radda." The gremlin's response was short, and the look in the creature's eyes seemed dulled over with boredom and lacked a sense of care toward the man's plight.

"I am a paying customer. I demand my order be remade."
"Baka."
"What did you call me?"
"Rara."

The gremlin added a forced the-customer-is-always-right smile that was accompanied by far too many pointed teeth to be genuine. It snatched the cup from the man and flopped over to the trash bin behind the counter. After stepping on the peddle to lift the lid of the wastebasket, flames two feet high and no wider than the width of the can spewed out, and the gremlin tossed the cup into the fire breathing receptacle as hellish screams and tormented cries rose and faded. The peddle was released and the fire disappeared after the lid shut tightly closed. All the workers around the front had put on black sunglasses after they heard the commotion and removed them once the messed-up order was thrown out.

The large, oversized feet of the gremlin slapped rhythmically on the coffee shop floors as it made way for a door marked in multiple signs and all of them screaming in one language or another to not enter unless an employee. It stopped just shy of the branded door and looked back to the man and then sighed before reaching for the knob. It didn't seem pleased at all about whatever lay behind that door.

A series of sounds poured out of the room as the gremlin yelled at the workers and a series of gibberish sounding barks were returned along with assorted coffee beans flying out from the crack of the door and insane giggling followed by the head gremlin yelling at them in a sterner voice and slamming the door shut and making his way back to his post at the front.

"Radda ra ra." The gremlin pointed to the side and the man said his thank you's as he slipped over to the side to wait for his order to be remade.

Vanessa waited a moment or two before she ordered, making sure that there was going to be no more interruptions from anyone. After a short while, she and Leon made their orders and stepped off to the side. The gremlin with the marker was poised over the side of the cup while the one at the register was ready to smash buttons to his heart's content with Bobo's order.

Flattening his tie and smoothing it out over the front of his button-up shirt, Bobo cleared his throat and approached the cashier and made his order. "Good day, my good fellow."

"Radda."

"Yes, I would like a large vanilla cappuccino with a shot of espresso, one Monstrous Muffin, bran please, and two blueberry scones." The ogre thought about his order for a second and then added, "Cow milk is fine."

All the gremlin's seemed to lose tension as they openly sighed with relief. Just as the gremlin holding the marker went to gain Bobo's attention a loud crash made all those within the walls of the coffee shop turn their gaze to see what was causing the commotion. Countless beings turned just in time to see a gremlin flying with a large streamline of puffy rainbow-colored clouds seeming to force the creature to be propelled across the barista and slam into the exposed brick wall on the opposing side of the 'Do Not Enter' door. A wet sounding slap enveloped the coffee shop as the gremlin made impact with the barrier. Its voice was groggy and strained as it spoke Gremlic, "Ra-daaaa-raaaaa—" and then fell face-first to the floor, hand twitching as it held firmly a lidded jar of sparkling milk.

Bobo and the two gremlins at the front counter stared at the face-planted creature, waiting to see it slowly lift up from the floor, and – noting that the gremlin worker was fine – resumed their exchange as though the occurrence never took place. It wasn't strange, after all. The gentlemen before them did order unicorn milk…

The gremlin holding the marker locked eyes with Bobo and waited for a name. The large, floppy ears of the creature tweaked from one side to the next as it waited for the massive ogre to speak.

"Ah, yes. My name," Bobo stood straight and cleared his throat before saying his full name proudly to the gremlin. "Botobolbilian."

The gremlin nodded and then paused after squiggling a B onto the cup. Its ears twitched, and it slowly looked back up to the ogre, eyes glittering with confusion.

He bent down a bit and repeated, "Botobolbilian."

Again, the gremlin gurgled Gremlic and started to write the O and paused. Instantly, the creature's ears drooped, and the second gremlin snipped at the first and took the marker and cup away from its co-worker and pointed to the register where the other slowly walked over, looking utterly dejected.

"Rada ta?"

"It's quite all right. The name is Botobolbilian."

"Ra-da-ra...." This one too paused and looked to the ogre with a face of pure confusion.

This is when the poor ogre began to blush with embarrassment before he whispered, very slowly, "Bo-to-bol-bil-ian."

Rusty yellow irises stared back at him before it muttered quickly in Gremlic and scribbled *Bobo* onto the cup.

"No!"

The gremlin motioned for Bobo to move to the side and let the next customer in line step up. Defeated and hanging his head in shame, Bobo sulked over to Vanessa who was giggling into her hands out of sheer joy from what had transpired.

"No respect even amongst my own kind..." he muttered pathetically.

"There, there, Botobolbilian. Your name isn't hard to say," Lyx assured, but the ogre was too lost in self-pity to take note of the succubus trying to make him feel better.

Leon jabbed Vanessa with his elbow, and she hissed in pain while giving the Spellweaver the dirtiest look. In return, she was faced with a glare and a pointed look to her pet, and she eyed over the ogre before sighing heavily and rolling her eyes. "Hey, Botobolbilian, want to pick out a booth for us and I'll bring everything over to the table?"

The ogre lifted his head just a smidgen and stared at his master in, what could only be described as, a look of amazement mixed with pride slowly being regained. "I ...I do enjoy a good window seat." With that, he strolled off more confidently with Lyx following close behind, her tail swishing from side to side happily.

Vanessa turned to Leon grumbling, "I'm not doing that ever again."

Chapter 15:

Vanessa sat across from Bobo at a table near the window, while Lyx scooted her chair as close to Bobo as she could get before the ogre gave the succubus a glare filled with warning. As Lyx toyed with one of her horns and bit her index finger while eyeing over the demon that had just asserted himself, Vanessa tried to not laugh at the spectacle and stared out the window to the snow-filled roads lining the edges of the river that ran through the center city.

Winds lapped at the hills of freshly fallen powder, and the skies were a deeper gray than usual. The yearly snowstorm would soon descend upon the heart of Aeristria. It seemed to be coming in faster than usual this year. The harsh elements would surely make the search for the hellhounds more difficult for the Coven, even if they were Summoner status. This single thought unnerved Vanessa, and it showed on her face as her brow bent in deep thought, and her eyes mindlessly followed the spiraling snow that zipped through the wintry blanketed city.

"Here's your coffee…" Leon spoke, breaking Vanessa's train of thought as he put her order in front of her and motioned at her breakfast. "Don't say I didn't do anything for you." With that, he turned on heel and headed for the exit while cupping his own cup close to his chest as if it were a precious treasure.

Doing a double-take from the spread of her sausage, egg, and cheese biscuit to Leon rushing for the exit, Vanessa looked confused and called out to him, "Hey, where are you going?"

He waved at her without looking and called back, "I was promised a bed and silence." Then he stepped out into the snow.

The first gust of wind caught the Spellweaver off guard after opening the door, and he almost fell over but clung to the cup as though it were his lifeline, not spilling a drop of it as he muscled through the icy gales and marched on in the direction of the apartment. Vanessa hummed to herself for a moment as she watched Leon fade from sight.

Bobo stirred his coffee and then pointed at Vanessa aggressively, "Stop that."

"What?" she snipped defensively.

"You know precisely what I'm talking about."

Lyx blinked, "What is she doing?"

"Don't encourage her," Bobo pleaded under his breath.

"Is she thinking about something?"

"I was just thinking that the whole hellhound matter won't be solved if the Coven just sits on their butts waiting, and the blizzard is going to hit us any day now. Someone should take a deeper look into the academy." Vanessa took a victorious sip from her cup after motor-mouthing her thoughts to Lyx.

"I told you not to encourage her," he sighed.

"I ... I'm so confused," Lyx drooped her shoulders and sunk down in her seat a bit.

"And you," Bobo started while turning a heated stare at Vanessa, "you'll not step a single, troublemaking foot into the academy or, so help me, I'll buzz Leon on a crystal ball so fast that you'll wish that you were being punished by the blue cloaks themselves."

Vanessa looked like she had been physically slapped and went stiff for a moment, blinking rapidly as her mind tried to catch up to what had just transpired. Quickly, the young girl regained her composure and retorted with, "I wasn't going to do anything of the sort."

"Mhmmm..." Bobo sounded unbelieving.

"I was going to suggest that we dig up some information on just what exactly is going on in the academy's basement."

"Who would have information like that?" Lyx asked.

"Oh, I know a place that's just full of gossip."

Everyone thought of it, without a word, the one place that was full of more gossip and dirty secrets that no one should even know about was Clipped by Magic, the local beauty shop. Bobo groaned displeased. "By the goddess. Must we endure that place today?"

"Oh, come on, it's just a little intel gathering," Vanessa tried to convince him with an innocent smile and batting her lashes.

"You are the furthest thing from innocence, Vanessa, so you can stop with the little charade."

"I thought it was rather adorable. Besides, it'll keep her away from the academy," Lyx stated plainly.

Rolling his eyes, Bobo sighed deeply once again and lifted one of his scones. "Fine. But let me at least enjoy fifteen minutes of coffee filled peace while I pretend that I'm not tortured daily with being your pet…"

"That was harsh," Vanessa grumbled and turned her face to hide the slight pout.

"Booboo, that was pretty mean," Lyx whispered.

"I refuse to feel bad for my comment. She gets into trouble on a daily basis, and I'd enjoy a single day where it isn't filled with her crazy antics."

"She's at least trying to follow the rules," Lyx whispered in a peppery tone.

Bobo peeked over to Lyx, looked to Vanessa, and then to his scone, "I wouldn't have it any other way, though." He stuffed the treat into his mouth before he said anything else he'd regret and before anyone could question him. Vanessa heard him but acted like she hadn't, and Lyx was happy that Bobo wasn't being a complete grouch anymore.

The world, for fifteen minutes, was blissfully bland, and Bobo couldn't have been happier.

Chapter 16:

Bobo was rubbing his chin and cheeks as he silently gauged whether he should have a nice, relaxing shave while they were in the shop. After all, he had endured this week, he thought that he was in line for a good bit of pampering. A day where he had a quiet breakfast at the Grim Bean and a shave at Clipped by Magic was as close to heaven as a demon of his stature could get. Besides, Vanessa was going to be gathering information. She was having her fun, why shouldn't he have his?

The beauty shop was the one-stop-shop for any demon, human, or mythical creature, and was rated the number one salon in Aeristria one hundred and fifty years in a row. Need your fangs sharpened, tail waxed, horns polished, hair styled, or claws clipped? Clipped by Magic was the best place to go and well worth the coin spent to get it all done. What was better than talking mirrors that would tell you how fabulous you looked with your new appearance? It was run by pixies.

Why was that so grand? You might ask… well, for starters, they were wizzes with scissors and spot on with detail. But the main factor in why pixie ran hair shops were some of the best in the land was because pixies can read your thoughts. Dirty secrets and gossip don't have to leave your lips. These crafty, flying, hell-with-wings will pluck it from your mind without you knowing and do it all without batting a perfectly mascara battered eyelash. But, aside from that small detail, the fact that they could read your mind made explaining the look you were going for a breeze.

The shop itself was two stories tall and had endless rooms and amenities, including a spa, private nail salon room, and a fitness center. Bobo double-checked his attire in the faded reflection displayed in the window and opened the main door. The bronze bell overhead chimed delightfully as the trio entered the shop.

Mint green and pearl white tiled floors gleamed in the high-lighting of the beauty shop. A cluster of pixies stood at the register giggling while two other fluttering busybodies tended to clients. There were a few customers sitting in the chairs lining the wide windows facing the streets, browsing through magazines as they waited. Two rows of pink, tall backed salon chairs lined the sides of the room, and in front of each of them were magic mirrors waiting to drip with compliments at those that peered into it.

One chair spun relentlessly near the front desk, a woman gleefully clapping her hands therein as she said, "Cressi! Come, sit on my lap and spin with me!"

A woman wearing a wide-brimmed, black dress hat and a rather large pair of matching sunglasses sighed heavily and brought the glasses down to the center of the bridge of her nose and flickered a green-eyed glare to the hyper-active woman. The chair slowed in its spinning. Slower and slower until it came to a complete stop, and the brightly dressed woman in the seat pouted to the glare. "Fine," she said, almost sounding defeated. After a short moment of silence, the woman kicked her foot off the counter and sent the chair spinning once again, making the poor pixie that was trying to style the outlandish hairdo on the young lady extremely difficult.

"How can I help you?" asked a pleasantly plump pixie with a curvy body – thick thighs, wide hips, large breasts, and happy round cheeks – and an outrageous, lilac-colored beehive hairstyle sporting a solid white band of hair that spiraled up the bumps of the hairdo. She wore a pale, dandelion-yellow dress with a large white flower slap dap in the center of her chest. Her deep mulberry eyes scanned the group awaiting their reply.

Her face was shoved to the point that her squished cheek made her lips form an awkward kiss pose to the side, the hand causing the face squishing belonged to another pixie who had short, electric blue hair and deep brown eyes. She wore black and white striped knee-high stockings and a black skirt with a blue tank top that matched the color of her hair. Freckles adorned her cheeks and gave her usual harsh stare a softer appearance. "You are so right, sir, you *are* in desperate need of a shave." The hand, voice, and face belonged to the pixie co-owner, Nym.

Bobo looked relieved and happy at the same time. "I thought I looked like I did."

"Oh, you do, and you are so right! You *do* deserve a clean shave." She gasped, bringing the tips of her fingers to her lips. "I just thought of something. A warm towel on the face, open those pores up and then a nice, tasteful smelling sugar scrub to bring out that baby soft skin."

"That sounds like a dream. Take me away. I'm all yours!" Bobo held out his massive hands in front of him, and the pixie took them into her own tiny grasp and tugged him with fluttering wings to the far end of the salon.

"Imp poo… I wanted to do that…" the lilac-beehive haired pixie said with her lower lip poking out. She sighed, shook it off, and faced Vanessa and Lyx. "Well, what can I do for you girls today?"

"Drop the formalities, Bidelia. You know I don't come here for anything other than information," Vanessa said with a bored expression. Lyx kicked an imaginary rock behind Vanessa as she pouted, with her arms crossed over her chest, and she looked absolutely pitiful now that Bobo was gone. The succubus was now engaged in her super sulk mode, and Vanessa couldn't try to bring her out of it because she was hard-set on finding out any information that she could about the academy.

The pixie looked surprised, and she darted her gaze around the salon while looking for anyone that might be interested in her and the new customer's exchange. Finding no one looking at them, she returned to Vanessa with a harsh whisper and narrowed eyes. "I don't need my clients knowing that I freely exchange information with the Coven." A single, small digit extended and pointed repeatedly into the top the register that Bidelia was practically laying on top of as she heatedly spoke in the softest voice possible. "I am swore-bound to keep the secrets of my clients and to not use the information that I have in order to sell it to others or use it as blackmail."

Vanessa motioned her hands up and down to visually tell the pixie to calm down. "Bidelia, can we talk somewhere more private?"

The owner looked around and took note of a few people looking at them strangely. She straightened herself up with a bright smile and giggled. "Girl, I'm gonna manicure you so hard that you'll swear I chopped off your own and sewed on a pair of hands that belong to the goddess herself!"

Vanessa mouthed *I hate you* before she forced a smile – one that held a promise of pain – and giggled loudly (annoyingly loud) and jumped up and down in a dramatic half-angry way as she bellowed, "Oh my goddess, yaaaasss!"

"Girl, follow me before you hurt somebody… Or I wind up hurting someone," Bidelia said through gritted teeth, and Vanessa instantly dropped her smile and gulped.

Why is a one-foot tall and eight-pound heavy pixie frightening? Because pixies can lift fifty times their own weight and Vanessa was only weighed a hundred and forty-five pounds. She'd fly like a sack of potatoes being hurdled by a veteran discus thrower.

"Looks like you were lucky today," Lyx whispered in Vanessa's ear, and the poor girl practically hit the ceiling.

Bidelia turned and fluttered her wings in place before heading for one of the back exits that would take them into the manicure and pedicure room. As Vanessa and Lyx followed close behind, there was a soft toot from the pixie leading the way and she swiftly turned around with a deep flush red all over her round face. "Oh, my goodness." She waved at the bright pink puff cloud that clung to her backside. "I had poisoned apples at Merlin's today. That poison is no joke," she tried to make idle conversation as she frantically fanned at the fart cloud.

"You did it on purpose," Vanessa claimed while trying to help wave the smell away from her face and the succubus at her side.

Lyx smacked loudly with her tongue hanging out and a look of disgust and confusion on her face. "Does anyone else taste cotton candy?"

"I'm so sorry…" The pixie, now glowing crimson in shame, turned and hurriedly escorted the two into the next room and shut the curtain behind her.

 *Chapter 17:*

As soon as the curtain dropped, a privacy spell cloaked the doorway. Typical with most places ran by mythical creatures. Occasionally, wards and spells would have to be replaced by a contracted enchantment smith. Otherwise, you had to pay extra for privacy spells if you desired the secrecy.

"Well, are we actually going to do anything with those man hands of yours or is it all business and no pleasure?" Bidelia asked while throwing a hand upon her hip.

Lyx stifled a giggle that was sure to have been a bursting cackle and stared off in a random direction – any direction was better than the one facing the fiery glare of the short-fused Hunter. Taking in a long, thoughtful breath, Vanessa calmed herself before she sassed herself right out of any information she came here to possibly get. "Bidelia, what do you know about the academy?"

The pixie looked confused for a moment before speaking in a drone tone. "The academy was created in the heart of Aeristria, in the very center of Tolvade, to teach young magic users and aid in the growth of properly trained—" she started to recite the information on the academy like she was giving Vanessa and Lyx a history lesson from the back of a pamphlet.

"No, Bidelia, listen. I need to know if you know anything about...." she looked around the room, wary of saying anything too loud, and wondering if this was a whole new can of worms she was about to open. "... what was going on in the basement level of the academy?"

The pixie gasped and nodded, seeming to know precisely what Vanessa was asking. "That... is something that I don't know anything about. Not in detail, anyhow."

Vanessa looked disappointed and slumped her shoulders disheartened. "Double dip a candlestick," she cursed under her breath.

"Hold your Pegasus. I didn't say I didn't know where you could get the information from. Just that I don't have it." She fluttered over to another door and motioned for them to follow. This door led straight into Bidelia's office and, once there, the pixie started to dig through her desk drawers until she found her orb. "This is my personal crystal ball. I have a contact that I chatter with from time to time, and she's the one you'd want to talk about when it comes to gossiping about the dark dabbling's of the Coven and academy." She withdrew the crystal ball completely from the dusty reaches of her desk drawers and blew some of the clinging cobwebs from its surface. With a smile, the pixie turned her attention fully to the orb and concentrated on the person she was about to contact. After a moment, the ball buzzed with life and levitated ever so slightly in her tiny hands. A one-sided conversation was overheard by Lyx and Vanessa as they waited.

"Hey there, sugar, it's me. ... Well, yes, I know you can see it's me, but I thought it would be polite to let ya know. ... Stop your sassin' and listen to what I've got to say. ... Yes, it's important this time!" Bidelia looked over her shoulder with a quick grin and then back to the crystal ball. Now she was whispering, and the two of them could only wait until the call was ended.

It didn't take very long for Bidelia to end the call and turn her attention back to them. "Good news, my friend said that they can fill you in on anything they know, and trust me, they'll know something. You can find them at Tasgall's Tavern."

"Hold the crystal ball," Vanessa said with a huff. "You mean *the* Tasgall's Tavern?"

"Uhm... I only know of the one, sug."

Vanessa pinched the bridge of her nose and tried to not yell out in frustration. "I could have just gone to the tavern from the start of this nightmare and gotten everything that I wanted. What a waste..."

"I wouldn't say it's a complete waste. Bobo got a little pampering in, and you found out that the information that you're looking for is indefinitely there. And," she turned her attention to Lyx. "Now, how about we do something with that hair—" her thought was cut short by the swift crack of Lyx's tail slapping against the floor like a bullwhip. Two angry, golden eyes glowered at Bidelia daring her to suggest *anything* to her.

The pixie cleared her throat and clasped her hands in front of her and pouted playfully. "Guess that's a no." Instantly, that pout shifted into a devious grin that faded so no one would be able to tell that the flying creature was concocting a delightful plan in her head. "I thought that that ogre friend of yours would have liked what I had in mind for you … but, alas, you're not interested." She sighed heavily for theatrical purposes.

Lyx's ear perked up at the news, and she looked out the corner of her eye to the pixie. One step was taken and then another before, slowly, the succubus had inched and scooted herself right up to Bidelia's side. "What did you have in mind?" Lyx asked in a curious tone.

The pixie spun around and instantly grabbed one of Lyx's hands. "Oh honey, that hair needs a touch-up, and those horns need polishing," she leaned over to fluff the succubus's hair and then looked at Vanessa mouthing that the horns were in desperate need of a heavy filing. She pulled back and smooshed Lyx's cheeks in her hands. "Girl, he won't be able to look away!"

Sold! The poor succubus's eyes were twinkling with hope and joy, and she was smiling crazily to the pixie's promise. "Come with me, honey. You are going to look fabulous!"

With that, Vanessa was forced to follow the two that were in their own little world. Lyx was flushed at the cheeks and lost in a dreamy daze, while Bidelia was happy that she'd be able to do more than tend to the cash register.

It was about forty-five minutes later when Bobo and Lyx were both done. Bobo confidently walked out from one of the back rooms. Strutting over to one of the magic mirrors on the sidewall with no chairs in front of it. Side to side, he inspected his close shave in the mirror.

"Your skin is absolutely radiant today, sir. And that shave was just what you needed," the well-mannered mirror gushed compliments to the ogre.

The sound of manicured cloven hooves clicked over the polished tile underfoot and slowly the owner of them stopped at a mirror next to Bobo's. He was standing hero-posed while admiring his reflection, and his elbow grazed the being standing next to him. He turned and bowed halfway to them. "Extremely sorry for—" He forgot what he was going to say.

Lyx turned from fluffing her hair in the mirror and faced the flabbergasted ogre. Her hair had more pronounced layers and had been lightly styled, her horns had been filed smooth and polished to a perfect gleam, her smile radiated as she flipped her hair behind her shoulders and winked at him. "Like what you see, big boy?"

"I know I do," the mirror in front of Lyx oozed with its praises. "You are absolutely stunning, girl!"

Shaking off physically, Bobo cleared his throat and looked back to the mirror to straighten his tie and fuss with his cuffs. "Stop flirting in public," he muttered lowly before walking toward Vanessa.

The succubus looked deflated even with the mirror trying to lift her spirits, and she appeared to be on the brinks of tears. Soft flapping wings carried Bidelia over to Lyx, and she laid a hand gently on the succubus's shoulder. "What's wrong, sugar?"

"He didn't like it…" the demoness sniffled.

Bidelia looked back to the ogre who had made it, almost, to Vanessa – who had passed out in one of the waiting chairs. He looked back to the mirrors and craned his neck, trying to get a better look. The pixie grinned wildly and patted Lyx's shoulders. "I wouldn't say that, sug. I wouldn't say that at all."

 *Chapter 18:*

Vanessa woke up and wiped the drool that had collected at the corner of her mouth. While Vanessa attempted to wake up, Bidelia brushed through the young lady's hair while the witch tried to tell Bobo what she and Lyx had found out. All the while, she swatted and shooed the persistent pixie away. In the end, Bidelia got her way and managed to make Vanessa's hair look semi-presentable. It lasted only a brief moment before the witch put it up in a sloppy pony-tail.

"One of these days I'm going to make you look like a girl," the pixie swore.

Vanessa retorted with, "Yeah, yeah. Thanks for the heads up," and the trio headed out the door and on their way to their next destination.

Tasgall's Tavern was run by a fiery ginger that had a love for money and information. She was the only one in the city that had more information than a nosey pixie. What's worse? She had two pixies aiding her in running the bar. Talk about bad luck. To sweeten the deal – at least on Tasgall's side – she offered drinks half off to Coven members.

Got a mind like a steel trap and enough will power to keep pesky pixies and other dirty information diggers out of your secretive mind? Doesn't matter when you have a set of loose lips after consuming one too many ales in this establishment. And be warned, you'll definitely have one too many at this tavern. Between the trio that ran the joint, and your potentially wandering gaze, you're going to be slipped a few tankards of booze you didn't order and be charged for it to boot.

It was a harmless sham that no one felt the need to turn the girl in for because, hey, half-off drinks, great food, and – for a few coins more – you can order a privacy spell and whisper whatever you want without fear of who's listening.

Well, almost no fear...

Besides all that, she was the daughter of a blue cloak. What harm could someone associated with that kind of authority really do with random dirty laundry aired accidentally in a bar? Didn't like being slipped drinks and having a harmless eavesdropper looming about your barstool? Go to a different tavern. Rarely did anyone venture to a different establishment. At least, not those from the Coven.

Years ago, before the days of the academy and Coven, Vanessa would frequent this place with the few coins she'd made from odd jobs and pestering. Vanessa, even then, had a knack for getting into trouble and knowing things she shouldn't. So, naturally, she and Tasgall hit it off tremendously. The short ginger would ramble about Coven secrets she got her hands on at the tavern, and the lazy witch would gossip about the dirty tidbits she heard on the streets. Together, they'd piece together some dark stories and gasp and giggle at their findings.

Today, Vanessa didn't think she'd do too much giggling. The front door to the Tavern felt heavier than usual, and there was an unsettling feeling growing in the pit of her stomach as she braved the bard's usual bellowing songs and loud chatter that was hidden behind the door.

As expected, the song was upbeat and worldly as the tune of the bard rolled through the afternoon crowd. Even if they weren't there for a cup of ale, it was well past noon, which meant most were on their breaks and just grabbing a bit of cheap grub with good company. A few imps laughed as they played a card game in the corner, tossing in coin instead of chips to bargain with. An incubus whispered into the ear of a blushing woman while a few couples spiraled and laughed on the dancefloor to the music. A group of centaurs and a couple of trolls sat in the corners exchanging tall tales of valiant battles, that never took place, with red dragons in the north. It was a usual day in here.

Boisterous laughter roared from the tables where the trolls

and centaurs sat as Vanessa took a lonely seat at the bar. Tasgall walked by with two enormous, frothing mugs in each hand and shot a comment her way without really taking a look at who was in the seat. "Be with you in a minute." She paused in mid-stride and shifted her gaze over to Vanessa. "Mark the stars, it's you! Dang girl, where have you been?" She turned her attention back to the mugs and twitched her lips. "Hold that thought, let me serve them, and I'll be right back."

Vanessa laughed and motioned for Tasgall to go ahead. "I'll be here."

Tally score: Laughing – 1, expected non-laughter – 0.

A few moments passed while Tasgall made customers happy, so she could gab with Vanessa uninterrupted, or as much as one could be while running such a busy place. However, Me'Glach and O'Glach could manage for a short while without the bartending rogue.

With no warning, the short in stature, ginger headed Tasgall leaped in front of Vanessa and rested her chin in her hands. "Okay, let's have it."

She smiled and stifled a light-hearted laugh. Double dip a candlestick. ... *Tally score: Laughing – 2, expected non-laughter – 0.*

A deep sigh escaped Vanessa, and that was when she realized that this whole thing was weighing a lot heavier on her than she knew. "I've been dealing with one hell of a case, Tasgall."

"I could tell. You sighed like a centaur galloped over your puppy."

"Sort of feels like it." She looked around and then back to her. "I need the special."

Tasgall's eyes widened greatly and then nodded. "I got just what you need." She turned to gather a pinch of dust to make the spell while Vanessa followed the line of the bar over to Lyx, who was practically trying to sit in Bobo's lap. Bobo, who was being served by Me'Glach as he attempted to keep the temptress at bay, floundered about with where to put his hands on the demoness in order to remove her from his person.

A set of wings that looked like they had been touched by the fingers of fall fluttered as the pixie they belonged to put a large drink on the bar top in front of the ogre. Wild brown curls covered her naked upper body, and her leaf skirt brushed the bottom of her ankles as she hovered over the cup and pushed it over to him. Bobo reached out to grab the large tankard with some foaming drink inside. Vanessa hoped that it wasn't alcohol...

Just then her thought process was broken when Tasgall returned with the dust and threw up a quick privacy spell. "Privacy I seek; privacy I demand, keep my words secret from the rest of the land." Her hand hovered in the air for a moment before falling quickly to the top of the counter, a ripple of magic growing in girth before falling with the hand in an unseen sphere barrier around her and Vanessa. "Okay, you're all set. Spill those magic beans, Vanessa."

She needed no further spurring, Vanessa unleashed upon Tasgall the past few days that she had endured all while Tasgall crept in closer and closer like the witch was telling a good suspense story. Finally, she explained what happened in the catacombs below the academy having forgotten that detail in her excitement. "We barely went in them, Tassie. There were tunnels for days, and the blue cloaks called us out of there, swearing that they'd put Summoners on standby to have come search them later..." She shook her head.

Tasgall made a nasally hum before she leaned in the whispered, "I have heard from all the Coven members here, even some of the Summoners that are on 'standby,' that not a single one has been instructed to go down there yet."

"What?"

"Right? I thought it was nothing at first, but my dad's been acting weird all week, too. Something isn't right."

"Hmmm... that's not good at all. Plus, any day now we'll have the blizzard hit. I'm sure the blue cloaks won't let anyone search the rubble or the catacombs with the snowstorm whirling about the city. It would be too dangerous even if we went in prepared for it."

"What are you thinking?"

"I'm thinking that if they won't do it, maybe I need to see what they are trying to hide from the rest of us."

"I smell trouble. Better not let Leon find out or he'll make a shackle spell for you and make sure that you never leave the apartment again."

Vanessa sighed. "I need to get Bobo and Lyx back home and

find a way to—" she grunted as Bobo landed on her without warning and hiccupped loudly.

Swaying, even while leaning against the poor girl, Bobo started to slur his outrage to her, "Get tha' grabby handed female away from me." He pointed a large digit back to Lyx who sat in a barstool inspecting her nails like she had no idea what was going on.

The smell of honey mead rolled off Bobo like he was the one that brewed it all day. "That reminds me, looks like you're gonna have your hands full in a minute, so I took the liberty of paying your tab!" Tasgall grinned and threw Vanessa's significantly lighter coin purse back to her. Probably was swiped by a pixie during the time that she was debriefing Tasgall on her week's happenings.

"Ugh, Me'Glach," Vanessa whined while searching what remained in her coin satchel.

"It's not that she's not pretty. It's just so unbearably unsophisticated to rub her hands all over me like a common floozie," Bobo went on to explain. "If she'd just conduct herself in a more," he hiccupped again, "proper manner, I wouldn't mind her company so much."

"Okay, big guy, you've had enough to drink…" Vanessa said, grabbing the tankard from Bobo's grasp as he poised his lips for another swig, only to turn up empty and blink at his hand where the cup had vanished from.

"Hey, that's not very nice…"

Reaching into her satchel at her hip, she found her crystal ball and pulled it out. The moment she saw the clear glass waiting for her to make the call she hated the object. "I really don't want to call him," she admitted out loud with a sigh and then closed her eyes to think about Leon. Mid thought, Bobo used Vanessa's shoulder to try and stand up straight, and she groaned in pain. The crystal ball hummed with power and then jolted with electric blue crackles before resuming its usual normal buzz.

"Banish a banshee…" Leon answered the call groggily and one finger was digging into his ear.

"Sorry to wake you."

"It wouldn't have been so bad if you concentrated better. The darn thing screeched so loud I thought your apartment was haunted again." He blinked in the dark room, the illumination of the crystal ball lighting up his features, and he brought the orb close to his face to inspect what was going on in her surroundings. "Is that... Bobo?"

"Yeah. They slipped him a few when I wasn't looking. Think you can help me?"

"Nope, you're on your own," Leon quipped.

"Come on!"

"I refuse to aid you in this."

"Why not?" she snapped.

"Because you should have known better than to take your light-weight pet to the booze slipping triplets."

"Fair enough." For whatever reason, Vanessa went from full of pepper and sass to ... accepting that she had made a dumb choice. Maybe it was all the stress, or maybe she was just too tired from all the excitement in the past twenty-four hours to fight him on the unfairness of the situation. But she threw in the towel on the argument, and it sent Leon's head spinning.

"Whoa. Are you okay?"

"I'm fine," her tone didn't sound fine, hex, if she could see the worn-down expression he saw in his crystal ball, she would have understood why Leon stood up so quickly from the bed. She wished she wasn't looking at the ball when he stood up because she saw bare, well-toned muscles staring right back at her. Instantly, Vanessa went stiff and held her breath.

Leon snagged a shirt off the footboard of the bed and slipped it on while speaking into the crystal ball. "I'll be there in a few. Stay inside. I don't care if they try to run up the bill, I'll pay it."

She couldn't protest if she wanted to because as soon as he said it, he cut the connection. The orb was dropped back into her satchel with a drawn-out sigh. Turning around in her barstool, Vanessa came to find Bobo singing an upbeat demonic song at the top of his lungs, and he practically had the whole tavern singing along.

She felt her jaw unhinge as she eyed over where he had his feet planted. On top of one of the tavern tables! His weight had the poor wooden structure bowed heavily in the center and with each joyful bounce of the ogre – who was singing painfully off-key – it threatened to give way any moment with a profound cracking sound.

As the wood whined with its promise that it would snap in two, Vanessa heeded the warnings of the furniture and scrambled out of her stool to rush over to the now-turned-pop-star ogre. "Bobo, get down," she ordered.

It was at this precise moment that her eyes noticed the first set of Coven members that had taken a seat at the bar. By the silver and golden insignia perfectly pinned upon their person, they were higher rank than her. The male with long black hair and striking eyes more so than the honey blonde haired partner that was grinning triumphantly at his side. There was a rusalka playing with her drink rather than downing it as she eyed over the two members with a knowing gaze, and the two Coven members seemed to be coming to a mutual agreement after a short argument. How long had they been there?

Double-dip a candlestick.

It dawned on her that the tavern would soon have the regular crowd of Coven members that frequented the bar after work. She bit her lower lip and tapped Bobo on his leg. "Bobo, get down now," she begged as she began to tug at his arm aggressively. Bobo didn't expect the tug, and even if he had he was not the graceful creature he had been before consuming his drink. He wobbled atop the table and started to stumble back, knocking into Vanessa and causing her to lose her footing and flop backward.

Vanessa hit the ground first. Her vision saw bright bursts of white and then a darkness overshadowing her. She opened her eyes just in time to see Bobo lose his balance on the edge of the table before falling backward and heading her way. There was a choice to be made, become Coven jelly on Tasgall's floors or roll out of the way and live to tell the tale.

Choosing life over the death by ogre squishing, Vanessa rolled to the side a fraction of a second before Bobo slammed against the floor. The whole Tavern jumped, even the furniture and beings, before slamming back down in its proper place. Crawling over to make sure he wasn't hurt, her heart racing from all the excitement, Vanessa was met with the goofy laughter of her pet as he lay there on his back. Instantly, she rolled her eyes at having been silly enough to worry about the blasted beast.

"I think you should just stay right there, Bobo," Vanessa griped while tucking her legs under herself.

"If he breaks anything, I'm charging you," Tasgall warned in song form behind the bar.

It took everything in Vanessa to not say something sassy in reply. Her mouth had gotten her in enough trouble today, after all. She sighed and tried to help the giggling ogre up off the floor. "Come on, Bobo, stand up."

"What was that delightful drink? I think I'd rather enjoy another."

"Oh no. No. No. No. You aren't having anything else," warned Vanessa.

"Booboo, look at you. I don't think I've ever seen you like this," Lyx practically skipped over to them.

"You mean drunk?"

"He only had two honey meads," she said with a pout.

"Two?" Vanessa exclaimed. "I only saw him with the one cup!"

"I might have snuck in another one without him noticing." Lyx bit the tip of her thumb as she took notice of the heated glare that Vanessa tossed the succubus's way. Vanessa didn't know if she wanted to laugh or cry or scream.

There was a good chance with those nimble little buggers fluttering around, that Bobo had three drinks in total. As she did the possible math in her head, Lyx asked, "Is two bad?"

"He has the alcohol tolerance of a colo colo." A colo colo was a feathery rat that slowly drains a person of energy and lifeforce. They, like Bobo, had no stomach for alcohol.

"Oh, dear. That *is* a problem." Lyx made a loose fist and brought it to her mouth as she bit her lower lip. "I... I didn't mean to. I was just trying to loosen him up. I thought..."

Even though she wanted to be upset, she could understand where the succubus was coming from. She didn't approve of her methods, but she did understand, at least. "I hope I never see you try that again. It's not right, Lyx, and you should know better..." she sighed and looked at her pet on the floor. "Come on. Don't worry about it. He'll blame the pixies even if you do confess. Just help me get him to a chair near the exit where I can keep him out of trouble."

Nodding compliantly, Lyx stood up and reached down to pick up Bobo with Vanessa. "Don't you start getting handssy again. I'll have nun of tha' in public, you hear me? Nun of it!" Bobo barked and then giggled to himself and closed his eyes before stifling a hiccup.

"Stay awake, Bobo. We'll go home soon."

"Oh, I do say. I'd very much enjoy that."

"Gotta... help ... stand...up...Booboo," Lyx groaned as she tried to pick up Bobo. It was no use; the ogre was a bag of muscle and lead. They huffed and puffed and failed in every attempt until a set of deep voices caught the girls off guard.

"Need a hand?" A large, muscular, male centaur with deep chestnut hair in curly waves that masked a strong squared jaw asked them. The centaur's back leg tapped at the wooden tavern floors as he watched the succubus and witch eye him over. His deep black fur of his horse body glistened in the oil lamp lighting of the tavern, and his silky night shaded tail slapped at his hip. A quiet moment passed as Vanessa tried to collect herself and catch her breath before she looked at the male centaur in his hazel eyes, only to find them gleaming back at her with the hope that she and Lyx would ask him for help.

A more feminine – but equally as deep-toned – voice spoke up. "Clearly, she does, friend," a female troll said with a light laugh. Turning her attention to Vanessa and Lyx, the troll said, "I can help you out." Her deep forest green dreadlocks hung well past her shoulders. Her long face and sharp-pointed wide nose almost devoured her beady yellow eyes. Long, clawed fingers unfurled at the two ladies as the troll extended a hand coated in her lime-colored skin and deep olive-toned bumps. She wore a simple brown leather skirt that appeared to be more of a loincloth and a matching shirt that left little to the imagination. Her feet were large and bare, and they brought her closer to the passed-out ogre. When the female troll smiled at the girls, her fangs made it look more vicious than friendly.

It was clear that the centaur and troll saw an opportunity to test their might and offered to help them out. Lyx nodded while Vanessa replied for them both, "Yes. Please. We need all the help we can get."

Without delay, the two strangers dipped down and picked up Bobo like it was nothing and followed Vanessa as she guided them to the bench located near the exit where they plopped him down. The ogre giggled and hiccupped in a drunken slumber as he was dumped onto the seat.

"Need anything else?" The centaur asked, but his eyes were transfixed on Lyx who was so concerned with Bobo that she didn't take note of the male's lustful gaze.

"Give it up, Hurro," the troll groaned and pat the centaur on the shoulder.

"Thank you for your help," Vanessa said to them as the troll nodded and jabbed an elbow into her drinking buddy to spur him into returning to their respective table.

"I ... I suppose you're right, Felic'ma," the centaur groaned and then forced a smile to Vanessa before sighing and trotting back with his friend.

Sitting down on the bench on the vacant side of Bobo, Vanessa settled in to wait for Leon, so they could all go home and get some much-needed rest. Lyx constantly pouted and mumbled something to Bobo that Vanessa couldn't make out over the tavern's usual commotion that was mounting as the sun relinquished its throne in the sky.

Each time the cowbell over the tavern door chimed, Vanessa would toss a hopeful glance over to the entrance and stand swiftly before slinking back down into her seat after realizing it was just another customer joining the growing crowd. Finally, Leon came rushing in through the front doors and scanned the bar until he spotted them off to the side.

"This looks like a big ol' mess," he looked at the half-awake and very much still drunk Bobo and shook his head. "Did we learn anything today?"

Lyx and Vanessa both nodded their head frantically, and he gave Lyx a glare and she shrank a bit. "Please don't tell me you had a hand in his current state."

The pet pinched her fingers together to show the proper measurement of her meddling and tried to give a small, believable smile. Her owner was not at all trusting the minor fib of his pet. His narrowed gaze and crossed arms solidified the lack of pleasure he was taking in the whole ordeal, and that she had aided the horrible situation. "I'm disappointed in you, Lyx." The succubus opened her mouth to speak. "Don't even try to apologize to me. You really need to be thinking about how to apologize to Vanessa and Bobo." She held her breath, looked down to the ground, and nodded while playing with the tassel of her whip hanging from her belt.

Putting his hands upon his hips, he turned his somber gaze to Bobo and sighed heavily. "Got any gold dust on you? I might need a small feather spell."

Vanessa nodded and fished around her many bags around her casting belt. "Yeah, I just bought more the other day." After some quick thinking and slight digging, she managed to make an easy feather spell. One that wouldn't eat up a lot of her materials on hand and would aid Leon in carrying Bobo back to the apartment without breaking his back.

She sprinkled the dust all over Bobo while concentrating on the spell and then stepped back. "He should be a great deal lighter now," she said. "Helps when they are thinking happy thoughts, too."

Leon cracked a smile then. "He should be just as light as a feather then, he has a grin a mile wide!"

Double-checking what was mentioned, Vanessa noted the perfectly grand and goofy smile that graced Bobo's mouth, and she burst into laughter. It was that deep laughter that rolled up from the belly and sent zips of energy coursing through her chest. Tears welled up in her eyes, and she noticed that she hadn't chuckled like that in so long. So long, in fact, that it hurt her throat to be laughing so heartily. But it felt good to just let go and laugh.

… *Tally score: Laughing – 3, expected non-laughter – 0.*

 *Chapter 19:*

It took every shred of concentration and strength to get Bobo back home. Thanks to the blistering cold, he started to regain some of his senses, although not much, but enough to enable him to walk on his own two feet the rest of the way. Once out of the bitter chill of the streets, they headed upstairs to their apartment, and all of them practically fell in through the front door.

Bobo bee-lined a wobbly path straight to his room and caressed the wood under his enormous paws and kissed the door curtly as he turned the knob. "I wish to retire," he mentioned before hiccupping, stepping back – whilst attempting to take off his loafers – stumbled on his footing and fell into his room.

"He's home, I've done my job as roommate and owner."

"One might even claim your job as a friend," Leon teased.

She gasped playfully. "Never." She fell back onto the couch, her legs randomly placed upon the cushions and her arms outstretched to the sides. She stared at the familiar ceiling of her home and sighed. "Thanks for your help tonight, Leon."

Leon approached her side and stood perfectly still as he looked down at Vanessa's sprawled out form. A long moment passed, and she was starting to feel unnerved under his unwavering stare and silence. Just when she thought he would say nothing, he said, "You're welcome. I normally would have let you handle it yourself, but you seemed to ... not be yourself tonight. So, I figured I would come rescue you." He crossed the room and sat on the sofa on the opposite side of the living room.

"Gee, thanks, oh great and wonderful Leon. My knight in shining armor! I didn't realize I needed *saving*."

"I don't think you're understanding what I'm saying, Vanessa." His tone wasn't mocking or correcting her, it was different. It was a tone she hadn't heard from him before. That caught her attention, and she turned her head to the side to look Leon in the eyes. Sometimes people say things, and you don't really need to look at them to get what they are saying. But there are those rare occasions where, when a person speaks, you *need* to look them in the eyes to really hear them because the tone, the sincerity, the raw emotion is staring back at you from their gaze. "I'm saying, I have always thought of you as a pretty tough girl. You never really relied on anyone. From the first time you set foot into the Coven, you walked with such confidence and you seemed so sure of yourself. You never slumped your shoulders. You never looked down. You walked into the Coven like you owned it," he laughed lightly and shook his head. "I never looked at you and thought of you as weak."

All she could do was blink rapidly as she stared at him. Was he playing with her? Where was the punchline? He was going to laugh …

… Any minute now.

But he never did. The more she let it sink in, the more difficult it was to find the words to respond. She could only look at him dumbfounded as she lay there on the couch trying to process that he was being honest with her. She and Leon had always held this ongoing battle. Always arguing. Always bickering. She never really understood when or why it started, but she didn't hate the man, just his love for following the rules and the enjoyment chastising her brought him.

For some reason, Leon's confession made Vanessa tear up once she soaked it all in. She quickly looked away, praying to the goddess that he didn't notice. If he did, he didn't make fun of her for it, and he didn't mention it. "It was all fake," she finally said. "I was so scared the first time I stepped foot in that place. But I never really had anyone. Growing up in an orphanage was one of the most crowded and lonely experiences of my life. The Coven? It was crowded, sure. But I was finally seen as a somebody. Not just another parentless kid stuffed away in an orphanage." She felt the first tear betray her, the hot, burning trail it left behind on her skin made her realize just how much she kept to herself, what really ate away at her every day, for years on end. "Even if no one else believed in me, I had made it into the Coven. I had actually achieved my dream. No one, not a single soul, was going to take that away from me." She smiled then. It contrasted against the slow-rolling tears that cascaded down her cheeks as she still tried, to no avail, to hold them back. "That's probably why I looked so confident. I was going to defend myself with my dying breath. I had earned my right to be there and, in turn, to be proud of myself."

"Well... I was always impressed with you. Not just because you had come from an orphanage but because you were so different than a lot of the people that wind up joining the Coven. Orphanage or not," Leon admitted.

She turned to face him and whipped her face with her cloak. "Thanks," she whispered.

Just then there was a sharp, male scream, and slurred speech that erupted from Bobo's room. "Away foul beast! I shan't have you trying to woo me with your vixen tongue and wildling ways," Bobo's command thundered out from the confines of his living space and soon after Lyx was seen spiraling out into the hall with the door swiftly slamming in her face. In a huff, the succubus frantically removed the hair that had fallen like a veil in front of her eyes. Once freed of the coal-colored curtain of hair, her amber gaze fixed on the door and then they all heard the lock as it turned over. She sucked at her teeth and flicked her tail while staring at the door like the crude barrier it was.

"I was so close," she seethed.

Leon chuckled and held his stomach, "You're going to give that poor ogre a heart attack one of these days, Lyx."

"Or an aneurism," Vanessa added under her breath.

"I'm just trying to make him see that I'm the best thing for him," she said, flipping her hair behind her shoulder and sashaying down the hall to Vanessa's room. "I need a nap," she said with a yawn.

Leon cozied into the couch across from Vanessa. "For a guy that had a nap already, I'm still pretty tired." He yawned as well and crossed his arms over his chest and started to close his eyes.

"It's been a rather long day," Vanessa agreed feeling sleep tug at her lids without relent. She too yawned and turned over onto her side as she drifted into a light slumber. Home safe and sound and warm, it was hard not to sink into the cushions and give in to the sleep she so desperately needed.

When Vanessa woke up, she noticed that everything in the home seemed a touch darker. It had been quite late in the afternoon when they all passed out. Now the sun was starting to set, casting shadows of the neighboring buildings through her windows. The inked replicas of the surrounding city stretched out through her apartment and inched across the carpet with every moment that ticked by. Spreading out on the couch, she wiggled her fingers and toes and cracked her back before she slowly sat up. The home was quiet. Everyone must still be asleep. She looked over to Leon who was passed out and hugging a throw pillow. Her eyes followed the sunset hues that splashed against her apartment walls and fixed on the window across the room as her mind mischievously wandered.

Now would be the perfect time to slip out. No one would stop her, and no one would be any wiser. But leaving the home without her staff and a few extra powders would be silly, if not downright stupid. Sneaking around the apartment, Vanessa gathered a few things and double-checked her satchels and person and headed out the door before anyone could bring a halt to her plans.

She took the stairs down instead of waiting for the flat. Less chance of being caught that way. Racing down the stairwell, she hurried for the exit and then trekked through the less-traveled areas – at least the ones with the minimal amounts of snow – and headed right for the academy.

Whatever they were trying to hide, the academy, the blue cloaks, whoever, she was going to find it even if she died trying.

… And she reserved herself to the fact that that just might be what would be written upon her headstone if things went south tonight.

Chapter 20:

The storm clouds circled around the clocktower of the academy. Yellow rope and caution signs littered the busted portion of the building. They had marked off the area and were already starting to form the framework for them to start rebuilding the academy's walls. Most of the rubble and debris had been cleared away after Vanessa and the other Coven members had left the sight a couple of days ago. The school made sure to keep all students safe while making sure that the incident, and the wreckage it had left behind, didn't disrupt classes any further than it had already.

A gust of snow-filled air made Vanessa's cape billow in the wind and sent strands of hair that weren't confined by her hood fluttering about her face. There was no way in hellfire that she was turning back now. Something wasn't right about this whole thing, and she'd never forgive herself if someone got hurt because she didn't at least try to find some shred of evidence that the hellhounds had moved on or found out what secrets were being hidden away in the depths of the tunnels.

As she stood there on the sidewalk staring at the building that seemed to now hold an ominous aura to it, she noted the full moon attempting to shine through the swirling deep charcoal snow clouds and the yellow glowing clock tower that was now strumming eerily that the hour was seven o'clock. The final chimes were accompanied by heavy footfalls crunching through the snow-covered sidewalk behind her.

"I thought I'd find you here," Bobo's voice was calm and low. She figured that there might have been a thread of heat to it, but there wasn't.

"Did you come to take me back?" she asked him while staring at the academy.

"Nope," he replied simply.

Astonished, Vanessa turned gradually to face him. "Really?"

Bobo, in turn, faced her and replied, "Really." They held each other's gaze for a long while. "You might get into trouble a lot, and I will forever complain about it. But, Vanessa, your heart has never been in a bad place. Everything you try to do is to either better yourself or save others from possible torment. If you feel that strongly about it, I'm going to be right there at your side when you walk into that building."

A warm smile slowly built over the hard line of Vanessa's lips. "You are honestly the best pet any witch or wizard could ask for."

He straightened up and squared his shoulders. "Of course, I am." She laughed through her nose at him. "Now, let's get on with this."

"Right."

Clutching her staff a little tighter and fidgeting with the amulet around her neck, she mentally prepared herself to take the first step forward. Each soft sinking step into the mounds of collected snowflakes sounded so loud with how quiet the world had become. The plastic that was stapled to the wooden beams where they were rebuilding the walls flapped in the growing wind. To say she wasn't scared would have been a lie. She was terrified. Over and over she remembered the horror that had transpired down in the basement, and she couldn't help but physically shake. She could blame the cold if Bobo asked, but she knew the truth. Bobo probably did too. But appearances must be kept.

The front doors were locked with giant iron chains and multiple locks, some of them spelled. That was the first sign that something on campus wasn't quite right as if the other hints leading up to Vanessa feeling the need to come back here weren't enough. She and Bobo slipped behind the sheet of plastic on the side of the building and retraced the steps to the boiler room door that they had taken only days ago. There was yellow rope and caution signs, but no real way to keep anyone out. Vanessa looked over her shoulder to Bobo who shared her furrowed brow at the sight before them.

"Shouldn't they have locked this?" she whispered.

"Oh, yeah. And spelled it and warded it. Not just a few signs and some rope," he replied.

She looked back to the boiler room door. "And the easy entrance from the lack of walls … It's like they didn't want it to be locked."

"Like they wanted to be able to get in and out without fuss or detection," he added.

Their eyes met, and they knew that whoever was causing all of this was still making trips down there. Meaning many things. 1.) Someone has visited since the incident. 2.) The culprit doesn't have any intentions of stopping. 3.) And – the one that Vanessa feared most of all – the person or persons could be down there right now.

Both nodded at one another and Bobo withdrew his battle-ax while Vanessa readied her staff. She concentrated enough to make the tip of her weapon have a soft yellow glow, just a low enough spell that she could maintain it for a long period of time, yet, if they were attacked, she would have the harder part of the counterattack spell ready on her staff.

There was a moment in time where they just stood there, preparing to go into darkness or battle. She pursed her lips to the side and seemed to be in deep thought. "Hold on," she whispered and dug around her pockets. Eventually, she stopped and nodded to Bobo. Stepping forward, the ogre watched as Vanessa poured a small vial over the seam of the door. "This way, if anyone tries to come in after us, we won't be caught by surprise."

"Marvelous, I really don't want to be caught by whoever is conjuring feral demons," he admitted and then opened the door slowly.

Creak… The high-pitched whine of the door sent Vanessa's heartbeat to a frantic pace, and she swallowed hard as her eyes cast down into the black abyss of the basement level. Was it that dark the last time? She nervously checked the front doors to the academy just a few feet away and noted the now even darker skies. Last time it wasn't at night in the middle of an oncoming snowstorm.

Taking a deep breath, she pulled out a bit of gold dust and whispered to it. Tinker Bell's spirit jingled and rose above her head and then floated a few feet ahead of her and Bobo.

"Going to turn on the lights?" Bobo whispered.

"No. Going to have to go in with just a little illumination. If someone is down here, I don't want to give them any more of a warning that we are heading their way."

He nodded, approving of her methods. "Wise choice."

A quick smile and then a soft exhale before Vanessa finally gained the courage to descend into the nightmare below. On one hand, she hoped to find adventure and answers, on the other she hoped that all her gut feelings that were keeping her up at night were wrong, so terribly wrong because it wouldn't just mean that the academy was comprised with corrupted board members, it would mean that the blue cloaks and Coven were somehow tied in on all of this as well.

She wasn't sure that she could handle that if it came to pass. The Coven was, in her eyes, the epitome of truth and justice. Corruption couldn't touch it. It was immune … wasn't it? A naive thought, but everyone has one. The Coven being pure and untouchable to dishonesty and black magics was hers.

As she went down, she tried to rid the negative thoughts from her mind. It didn't help much, for every bend of the wood sounded like shrieks of a banshee and every soft tiptoe thundered in her ears like a giant's footsteps. Her poor heart couldn't handle much more of this.

Once at the foot of the stairs, she turned her staff to each side, using the illumination of the premade attack spell in combination with Tinker Bell's spirit to light the surrounding area. All seemed clear, and she gave Bobo a signal indicating that there didn't appear to be any foes around.

After a quick nod, Bobo was behind her, and a step to the side with his battle-ax gripped in both of his hands he turned his gaze to Vanessa and motioned with his head for her to go ahead and he'd follow. If anything came out to attack her, he'd step in front of her and deliver a powerful blow with his blade.

They checked the main area around the steps and then proceeded toward the hall that led to the summoning room. Slowly, they made their way to the white hall. She could smell the lavender through the musty scent of the basement. It wasn't an unpleasant smell, but the memories that it stirred up left her stomach feeling a touch sour. Vanessa steadied her hand and focused on breathing for a moment. The light spell dimmed from her rattled concentration and then resumed the brighter glow that it had previously.

The candles lining the walls seemed to be almost untouched. Outside of the black wicks showing that they had been used at some point, there was no dried wax drippings or pools of wax around the collected candles. Just almost pristine white candles, unlit and lining up and down both sides of the narrow passage toward the room with the summoning circle.

Her heartbeat was thundering like the hooves of wild unicorns within her chest. The silence that filled the air around her made it all the more eerie to her. One step further into the closed hall. She felt her hands start to shake again. *Steady your breathing.* Another step further in, the dirt under her boots crunching into the cement floors. Her heart picked up in tempo, and she thought that she couldn't swallow, her throat felt so tight. Again, she had to focus on the spell or she'd lose the light. One moment the hall was silent, the next it was filled with soft whispers. Words from voices not of this realm echoed around her.

> *May the light be with you.*
> *Be brave, daughter of Saellah.*
> *The power is in you.*
> *Defeat the darkness.*
> *Daughter of Saellah, push back the evil!*

Vanessa froze in place just as the last whisper was called out, louder than the rest, and the white candles all erupted to life with flames. Bobo stopped a few steps behind her and blinked at his master. She slowly turned to face him and tried to not shiver in fear. "Bobo... please tell me that you heard that."

"I cannot deny it. I most certainly did," he admitted.

"Please tell me the candles all didn't light on their own," she begged in a whiny voice.

"Well... I mean..." he motioned around them by circling his hand palm down in front of his body like he was washing a small, imaginary table. "At least it was the white candles."

Her expression looked less than amused by his statement. However, he had a point. Had all the darker candles in the room ahead burst into flame she would have turned on heel and abandoned any further investigations.

She slowly turned to eye over the spread of candles and nodded so much that her head felt dizzy with the action. "Yeah. Yeah, I suppose you're right." The confidence that she once had in her steps were now drained from her footwork. As they inched closer to the next room, she walked slower than before and was ever constantly craning her neck to see in areas up ahead or looking back over her shoulder to the endless void of the black abyss behind them that lead to their only escape.

"I'm right here, Vanessa," Bobo whispered, and she snapped her vision from the ink-black behind them to his sincere gaze. Who would have guessed that an ogre's eyes could calm the swelling fear she was faced with?

Letting go of a breath she hadn't realized she had been holding, Vanessa nodded to him and turned to face the mouth of the hall, dumping them into the summoning room dead ahead. A few steps pulled her further and further from the comforting glow of the white candles and the soft scents of lavender. She stood just past the entrance. Nothing happened.

The deafening heartbeat that suffocated her thoughts ebbed, the tension in her shoulders lightened, and the illumination spell grew in brightness. Scanning the summoning circle, she took note of all the deep-colored candles and the mounds of wax puddles that they had been reduced to. Some candles were lodged into the mound of another – long since dead – candle. Others were submerged in wide-spread dark pools of wax from countless previous candles. Unlike the hall, these candles had been used and replaced numerous times. Soon her eyes were fixed on the dreaded corner where the hellhounds had last appeared from. Nothing came. Not a sound. Not a light. Nothing. It was blissfully … silent.

As soon as Bobo left the white candle hall and came into the room, the candles in the corridor went out. Snuffed by winds not felt by the duo. Bobo jerked and turned on heel to stare back into the hall and gulped before turning back to Vanessa to whisper, "Well, that wasn't ominous in the slightest." The event had rattled them both, but his joke managed to somewhat lighten the mood and enabled Vanessa to find the courage to march on toward the catacombs.

When Bobo and Vanessa reached the entrance for the tunnels, there was a light breeze coming from deep within the winding shafts. It smelled of dewy and rich, dark soil that had never seen the sun. They feared that they would smell sulfur, or some other tell-tell that there were hellish things within, but it never graced their noses. There was a minor spell over the tunnel. Nothing that would be terribly hard to remove, but it was enough to stop them from heading further in without thinking.

"It's like a tripwire spell. It'll leave someone dazed if they try to go in or out," Bobo said while looking at the entrance with a furrowed brow.

Vanessa was crouched on the other side of the tunnel and eyeing over the magical essence. "It's not concealed very well, but if we hadn't been looking for a spell, we would have activated it." She glared at the entrance and at the forcefield that couldn't be seen.

"What are you thinking?"

"It's just a hunch, but I think … it might be mixed with an alarming spell. A spell that will notify the caster that something's passed through. Regardless of if it's in or out."

"Should we go back then?"

"No!"

"No need to snip, Mrs. I-Seek-Danger. It was just a question."

She stood dusting off her hands on her robes. "We'll just make a rip in the spell. We'll pick a spot that you and I will remember, and we can slip in and out unnoticed."

"Banish a banshee, you're going to use your sneak spell, aren't you?"

"Why yes. Yes, I am, Bobo. It's the perfect spell for this!" She started to dig through her pouches.

A sneak spell was a one of a kind spell that was of Vanessa's own making. She learned it from a collection of magic users at the orphanage and mixed it with the knowledge she had gained from the academy. It would make a tear in the spell that the user made and after two passing's the spell would mend the tear and return the original spell back to its normal state. It would allow her and Bobo to go in, search the tunnels, and then come back out without triggering the spell and without leaving a trace that they had ever been there.

"If I didn't know you any better, I'd swear that spell was dark magic."

"Hush, I need to concentrate."

"Well, this is going to take all night," he grumbled.

"Shhh…" she hissed.

Vanessa slowly wrote with a charcoal stick onto a small piece of paper a few runes and then sprinkled gold dust onto it. As she rolled it up, she recited a few words to fuse the two spells together and then spoke the spell out loud as she held the mini-scroll a hairs distance from the spell guarding the entrance. "Rip in the spell, only a tear just for me and my friend, I'll slip right on through and be back soon, mend upon return so no one can tell, we were here or made this spell." She slammed the paper forward and it was like her hand hit a brick wall. The paper made contact with the previous spell, and the middle of the scroll started to burn yellow and then burn in an orange shimmer until it was slowly consumed into the barrier of tripwire/alarm spell.

"Really, that was the incantation?"

"I was ten when I made it, cut me some slack."

Very slowly, a rip started to grow and made a hole large enough for her to pass through. Bobo cleared his throat and eyed over the hole. "There is no way."

"I thought you were on a diet," she teased. He flushed and growled. "Calm down, big guy. The spell will enlarge for you and me to pass through and then will become small again until we return."

"Very well then," he said, flattening his tie against his chest and making sure it was clipped properly to the front of his button-up shirt. "However, Vanessa…"

"Hmm?"

"Crack a joke at my weight again and only one of us will be passing back through here." He grinned wildly and motioned for her to go first. "After you, my dear."

"Could you say that without the battle-ax in your hand and a creepy grin on your face? Sheesh…"

She stepped through and then waited for Bobo. As promised,

the spell grew to match Bobo's size and then shrunk to a pinhole size when he was completely on the other side.

"The easy part is done," Bobo said in a hushed tone.   "Yeah, now we have to locate what they are hiding down here."

They both turned to face the long tunnel ahead and sighed heavily. This was going to take them a little while. It was going to be harder than prying an ale from a clurichaun. But, with hope and careful steps, Bobo and Vanessa traveled through the tunnels searching for possible clues. They felt like they were making no headway in their travels as all the tunnels looked the same. Some were narrower, others shorter, and then some were a mix of width, but, somehow, they all seemed the same to them.

A little over an hour passed inside of the passageways before Bobo and Vanessa started to feel the frustration eating at them.

"We're lost."

"No. We aren't. We can find our way out easily," Vanessa stated in a heated whisper.

"There isn't anything down here," Bobo almost sounded upset about it.

"There has to be. I know it."

"Admit it. This has been a wild goose chase, and now we are lost. Fish out a useful spell from one of your pouches and let's be done with this already."

"I refuse to give up just because the answer isn't falling into my lap."

"Well, pardon me, my dear, for bursting your bubble but we aren't exactly finding anything rummaging through these cold, and musty I might add, caves."

"Oh, ye have little faith—" her comment was cut short by a humming sound coming from one of her satchels.

"Please tell me you did not bring your crystal ball down here…"

"Of course, I did!" she spat back hoarsely.

"If there is anything down here, you'll get us killed with a crystal ball call."

"Good thing for us, like you said, there isn't anything down here. So, we should be golden," she said and swiftly stuck her tongue out at him.

"A whole lot of nothing is going to kill us, mark me, Vanessa."

"Besides," she started, fishing the crystal ball out of her pouch, "I'd rather have it on me in case of an emergency." As soon as the crystal ball was pulled out, she concentrated on linking her power to the ball and a picture came to life. Leon's face was so close to the ball that Vanessa held it at arm's length away and gave a nervous smile. "Oh. Leon. It's you…"

"Don't you act like you are all innocent. Where are you?"

"Oh, I'm just—"

"Before your lips even think about producing a lie, I've been to Tasgall's, the salon, Merlin's, and I even made a pitstop by the Coven. You don't have friends, so don't try to use that as an excuse…"

"Ouch," she mumbled.

Bobo whispered into her ear, "The truth hurts, my dear. Embrace the ugly truth."

"Spill it, Vanessa!" he barked.

"Shhhh!" She looked around nervously as his voice echoed through the tunnel.

He pulled back and then she saw his eyes darting around. Instantly, she pulled the crystal ball in toward her chest, clutching it closely and letting her hair drape around the orb as she looked at it from above. "I'm just walking around before the blizzard hits," she lied.

It was too late, though. Leon had seen where she was. "You idiot. Tell me you aren't where I think you are."

"Don't tempt her," Bobo mumbled.

"I don't know what you are talking about," she whispered and giggled.

Leon's gaze darkened. "Vanessa, how long have you been down there?"

She said nothing. Her heartbeat was slamming against her chest like a war hammer, and her mouth felt as desperate as Aeristria's grasslands after weeks of being deprived of rain. He knew where she was, and she couldn't lie her way out of it. She cursed in her own head. Well, she was already this deep, right?

"Oh..." she waved the orb from side to side as she attempted to shake the man up and make it appear more convincing that she was losing the crystal ball call. "Wha...t...wa...s...tha...t?" She shook it even harder.

"Stop that," Leon's unamused voice commanded.

"You...re... brea....king...—"

"No, I'm not."

"—up. I'm.... los...ing.... conne...ction..." She waved it even more.

"I can see you just fine," he remarked in the same deadpan tone he had the whole time she tried this little connection charade.

In a panic, Vanessa tossed her crystal ball over her shoulder and stared at Bobo like it was the best option that she had and that he should agree with her course of action. Only, Bobo's eyes weren't on Vanessa. They were steadily watching the crystal ball as it bounced off the shallow ceiling of the tunnel, clanked against the wall, and hopped further behind Vanessa until it rolled to a half-stop and then began to roll back toward her.

They were on a decline...

Before long the crystal ball rolled back and through Vanessa's stance until it came to even ground. Which was, you guessed it, directly in front of Vanessa. His expression was zapped of anything that could be remarked as his usual approachable self. "You are in the basement of the academy, aren't you?" Leon's disappointment seeped from his gaze and dripped from every word spoken.

The witch's eyes were everywhere but upon that cursed orb. She dodged his question with silence and avoided making any eye contact with the crystal ball and the very angry face of Leon peering through it. "Vanessaaa?"

She looked to Bobo and fake gasped. "Do you hear something, Bobo?"

"I can still see you..."

Vanessa bit her lower lip and cringed before looking through one eye at the crystal ball on the ground. Instantly, as soon as her eye was on it, a handkerchief was tossed over the glass ball. "Don't say that I don't do anything for you, darling. I'll be offended and remind you of this moment," Bobo warned with a sigh.

She smiled, only to have that smile snatched by the snarling voice under the cloth by her feet. "I can still hear you!"

Again, Vanessa panicked, and she reared her leg back and kicked the orb full force. *Roll back now, you cheeky piece of junk!*

The orb flew like she was a professional runeball player. From down the hall, there was a sound that was most unnerving to both Vanessa and Bobo. The crystal ball flew a short distance before clattering on every wall and bouncing with high-pitched tings off the rocky ground below and then bounced on something hard, only this didn't make a sound like rock. The sound was more like a grunt from a person … or creature … being slammed with a heavy crystal ball unexpectedly. In fact, the duo was almost sure that is exactly what that sound was.

Two yellow eyes peered from the furthest reaches of the tunnel. A rumbling growl reverberated off the stretch of space and rolled over the witch's skin like thunder sweeping its warning over the plains. Vanessa took a single step backward and froze before the icy touch of chills walked up her spine. The eyes belonged to a creature with a voice that lacked a higher level of intelligence, which told the pair that the owner couldn't be reasoned with.

"Pretty lady," the deep voice said as the creature removed the handkerchief from its snout.

A set of cloven hooves pranced and dug excitedly at the ground beneath the furry legs and man-like torso. Bulges of muscle stacked on top of each other made up the broad-shouldered, barrel-chested creature before them. A set of horns jutted out from the top of its large, hairy head and the face mirrored that of a bull, and it shook its head from side to side. Spurts of hot air protruded from its nostrils as it snorted in the cold confines of the tunnel. "Pretty lady, stay with me."

"Oh, dear. Look at that, Vanessa. You have an admirer."

"Pretty lady," the minotaur grunted.

"I do believe he's speaking to you, Bobo," Vanessa urged.

"Pretty lady, stay. *You die.*"

"No. No. I think we are seeing your future husband, and you know me, I won't stand between two young lovers. Go. Greet your lover with a warm embrace. I give my blessing to you."

The minotaur roared and then barreled through the tunnels, and Bobo and Vanessa tripped over their feet as they spun around and scrambled through the halls. "You really shouldn't leave your man waiting," Bobo said, pulling Vanessa back behind him, so he could take the lead as he started to run as fast as he could.

Vanessa squeaked as she was dragged behind Bobo. She spared a look over her shoulder only to regret the action. "You no trespass," the minotaur snarled, and she fumbled with her pace before she found herself spurred by the image of the monster racing his way through the tunnel in hot pursuit of them. Nostrils flaring, eyes wild, and a deep guttural howl echoing off the rocky walls.

"Move your butt, Bobo!" Vanessa pushed Bobo and saw a tunnel up ahead, she switched from pushing to tugged at him and forced the ogre to follow her lead. They tumbled into the tunnel toppling over each other just as the minotaur raced by and slammed his horns into the wall. The sound of his horns scraping across the solid stone screamed out like nails on a chalkboard, but worse. A lot worse.

They wasted no time. The two of them rapidly got on their feet and ran further into the tunnel. "He doesn't turn very fast!" Vanessa yelled to Bobo.

"A lot about the creature is slow, dear," he said. "Let's use that to our advantage."

"Right." She strained her eyes. In the near pitch-black of the tunnels, it was hard to tell a dip in the wall from a possible opening to another tunnel. Grabbing and fumbling over dusts wouldn't help either, she wouldn't be able to concentrate long enough to make a worthwhile spell. There was always her staff, but she'd have to find somewhere to hide and meditate. There was no time for that now. Even if the minotaur was sluggish in turns and speech, it was still fast and full of brute strength. Vanessa couldn't last two minutes without Bobo to back her up. Still, the light spell wouldn't be worth the injuries they would, without a doubt, be inflicted with.

"What in the bloody hellfire is a minotaur doing down here anyway?" Snapped Bobo between attempts to catch his breath.

That was a good question…

Why was a minotaur down in a series of tunnels that seemed to have absolutely nothing contained in them? Minotaurs were a type of scroll-summoned guardian that were task-based. They guard a specific item or place and upon completion of their duty, the spirit disappears. Minotaurs, sphinxes, gorgons, and nagas were all types of scroll-summoned guardians and were a spirit form of their free-roaming relatives. The only reason one would be summoned down here would be to guard it, and right now the creature was doing that in aces.

With that in mind, it would mean that this one was summoned, and recently, to guard either the tunnels themselves or the secrets they contained. A living one wouldn't have roamed down here and claimed the tunnels as their own. Vanessa had a hunch that it was keeping guard of the secrets the tunnels had tucked away. Her attention was snapped back as she and Bobo skidded and slid on the smooth surface of the ground and clambered over themselves to dodge another blow from their pursuer and dive down another opening.

"This way!" Bobo barked, and they were at full speed again.

The roaring moo of the minotaur rang through the tight space and rumbled in her ears, rattling Vanessa's brain as she tried to focus on searching for the next tunnel. "It's too dark," she sputtered between heaving breaths.

"I can see just fine, follow me," Bobo advised.

The ground rumbled beneath their thundering feet as they felt the galloping monster swiftly gaining ground on them. "Bobo!" Vanessa screamed with her eyes barred shut.

"Here! Go here!"

When Vanessa opened her eyes, Bobo was already turning to the left and dead ahead was nothing but a stone wall. She screamed as she felt the pounding footwork of the minotaur close behind. She'd be a wall ornament if she didn't think fast. Seeing a black hole in the wall, Vanessa beamed and turned abruptly to dive into the tunnel only to have her vision blur in a sea of starbursts and then be consumed by darkness.

She felt something hot and wet run down the bridge of her nose and drip from the tip of it and land on the top of her mouth.

Instinctively, Vanessa licked her lips and tasted the sweet metallic perfume of blood upon her tongue. She could barely hear what was going on around her. It was like she was submerged in water. Her vision swam in and out.

"Vanessa! Vanessa!" It was Bobo's voice. She turned and felt the dip in the wall that she had so gracefully assumed was another tunnel and had gifted her with a rather large wound from the mistake. Luckily, the dip in the wall was enough to escape near-death by bullhorns.

Scraping her shoulder and back as she turned to face the direction of Bobo's voice, she felt the world spin, and she let her hands grasp at the grooves of the wall behind her to help steady herself. The howling call of the minotaur mixed with the sounds of bits of rubble that fell to the floor. Blinking, she turned her gaze to the beast and saw it struggle with its horns stuck fast to the dead-end that she had so desperately attempted to avoid mere seconds ago. Its horns were only embedded a few inches into the rock, but, with a bit of a struggle, it would be free any moment.

Her ears were ringing, and her dizzy spells were as nauseating as they were distracting. Bobo had braced himself in the tunnel's entryway and had one hand extended out toward her. "VANESSA!"

The rubble resounded as it fell all over the floor below the feet of the minotaur as it freed its horns from their prison. Instantly, it turned and locked her in its sights before scraping the ground with a cloven hoof and making a mad start for Vanessa. She felt her heartbeat leap, and it was enough to force her to her feet. She ran the short distance between them and as she lunged at Bobo, he pulled her into his chest before rolling his back against the wall, and the monster continued to plow through the tunnel again. It didn't turn down the passageway that Bobo and Vanessa were in, but that didn't mean it hadn't caused any damage as it ripped through the tunnel in a blinding rage.

Bobo roared, and the caves shook with his piercing cry. One of the horns had clipped Bobo as it barreled by the opening, and the ogre had a long gash from shoulder to elbow that was spewing blood profusely.

"Bobo. You're hurt. I need to mend it."

"There's no time."

"But, you're hurt—"

"And so are you. But if you want the mending to matter, we need to get the hex out of here and find somewhere safe."

She nodded. She hated that it was true. He was hurt. She was hurt. No spells could help them until they were no longer pursued by the minotaur. Just then, the beast came back and slammed into the entrance as it tried to slide and shift direction. "Pep talk over," she announced with wide eyes.

"Yup. Time to go, my dear."

They turned and ran just as rocks from overhead bounced off the floor around the minotaur, and its breath fogged around its angry face as it settled in on its target.

"We've got to figure something out. We can't just outrun it forever."

"I don't know. I was rather enjoying the workout."

"This isn't the time to joke."

"I don't have any ideas, Vanessa!" Bobo snapped, and she bit her tongue.

She felt so worthless. All the years at the academy, at the Coven, training and learning. For what? So, when she was faced with hardships, real ones, in the real world, she could just see if she could outrun them? No! She was on the streets and alone, surviving by herself before the Coven. All the academy did was help her reach her dreams and broaden her magical capabilities and knowledge. She wasn't some half-baked spellcaster.

As they ran her mind raced. The floor thundered. Their footwork pounded. And then, as she stared at pebbles vibrating from the impact on the floor, she realized something. Looking up, she saw bits of dust and rock falling from the ceiling.

That's it!

"Bobo. I need you to yell!"

"I'm not that kind of ogre, Vanessa."

"*No.*" The minotaur was gaining ground again. They saw another opening and dove into it and kept their pace. Blood was flowing over Vanessa's face and Bobo ignored the throbbing pain in his arm as he clutched his battle-ax.

"I need you to cause a cave-in," she explained.

Bobo looked over his shoulder at her and studied her expression for a moment. He seemed to ponder over the idea before nodding to himself and saying, "All right," in a low tone. A moment passed, and nothing happened.

"Bobo!"

"What?"

"Well?"

"Well, there is a lot of pressure on me."

The minotaur raced up faster than expected, and Vanessa swore she could feel its hot breath on the exposed skin of the back of her neck. She squeaked in surprise and ran a bit faster, spurred by the thought that that thing wanted her to keep it company down here … that is if it didn't kill her first. The bull-man roared and stomped loudly as it rushed forward and at the last second slammed into the wall near Vanessa, narrowly missing her. She screamed as she saw the beast shake it off like it was nothing and then regained lost ground to attempt to slam her into the wall again. The next slam caused the minotaur to crash onto the floor, and it scrambled on all fours before standing back up to catch up to them.

"Yeah. I have nooo idea what that's like…"

"It's not that easy to tap into that primal side, Vanessa."

"Try."

"I am."

"Not hard enough."

"How about *you* do it?"

"Oh sure. Let me turn into a fat ogre and yell like an idiot!"

Bobo stopped dead in his tracks – she slammed into his backside, not expecting the sudden halt – and he turned to face Vanessa and roared so loud that her hair fluttered in the breeze of his bellowing shout.

She inhaled sharply and went stiff for a moment. "Nice one!" Vanessa said with a satisfied grin.

The minotaur was still racing toward them, and Vanessa quickly turned around and braced her staff out in front of her, holding it on each end to attempt to block the blow. She was thrown out of the way at the last second, and she watched as the flat end of Bobo's ax blade made contact with the rushing ram of the monster. Again, Bobo roared, and the caves rumbled like a growing storm was swirling within them. Pebbles fell, and dust drifted in the air as a split in the ceiling grew.

"Time to go, Bobo!"

The ogre blinked out of his primal spell and looked around him to see the catastrophe that was sure to ensue. He kneed the creature in the chest and slammed it in the face with the flat side of the blade again, this time sending the minotaur flying into the side of the wall, and that was when the ear-shattering crack pealed overhead.

Running like his life depended on it – not like it hadn't since the start of this whole minotaur marathon – he snagged Vanessa by the arm and dragged her to her feet as they made way for the only open tunnel. Hopefully, it too wouldn't cave-in on top of them. Just in case, Vanessa reached up and grabbed for her amulet around her neck and peered back to the creature that was still trying to regain its lost senses from Bobo's monumentally powerful blow.

They ran into the side shaft just as the minotaur straightened up and bellowed out an impressive rage-filled scream. Right after, the tunnel caved-in with heavy boulders slamming all around in a deafening maelstrom of rocks and rubble.

 *Chapter 21:*

Bobo's cough was unrelenting as he and Vanessa sat in the middle of the tunnel catching their breath within the safety of her amulet's fading barrier. The last-ditch spell for any Coven member was their amulet, and hopefully, they wouldn't need it again anytime soon. It would take almost an entire day to recharge the power for that spell again.

The entrance was sealed so tight with fallen rocks that it looked like just another dead-end, and the other side was buried in a ton of boulders and rubble as well. Nothing could have survived that. Nothing.

"And your blossoming love affair has come to an end. How tragic," Bobo said between gasps for air.

Vanessa coughed and sucked in air sharply as she touched a few fingers to the gash on her forehead. "Yeah, well... he was abusive."

Bobo couldn't help but roll his eyes and laugh to the point of another coughing fit that brought him to tears. Some pain-filled ones, others joyful. "Come then, on with the healing spells." Bobo motioned while rolling his wrist to have her hurry and mix up something to tide them over until they could get proper treatment outside of the caves. He did a double-take then, seeing the blood-caked to her skin around the wound made him sigh and walk on his knees over to her. "Confound it all, Vanessa. You really walloped yourself good there." Bobo moved a few tangled strands of hair that were plaster to Vanessa's forehead with drying blood and sweat. She made small sounds of pain and cringed, but once her face was free of the knotted, gory mess, Bobo withdrew a handkerchief from his breast pocket.

Vanessa looked confused at Bobo. "I thought you lost your handkerchief right before we were chased by the minotaur."

He laughed and shook his head. "Vanessa, when will you

learn? I'm a sophisticated gentleman. I ooze intellect, charm, and handkerchiefs."

She laughed lightly to his joke as he dabbed at the wound. "Sorry for calling you fat…"

He stopped and sighed as he looked her in the eyes for a split second and then resumed cleaning the wound. "Oh, please. I'm a highly intelligent beast, Vanessa. I knew you were trying to rile me up. Even so, thank you." He puffed out his chest. "Besides, I'm fit as a fiddle. No way that I'm fat. I'm just trying to tone up, that's all."

Again, she laughed. For a few moments, they tended to their injuries. Bobo's arm took a little longer due to how deep the gash was. After that, they gathered themselves and stood facing a fork in the road that now lay before them. Just beyond the passageway that they had found solace in, the tunnels branched off into three different directions. Bobo stood inspecting each one of them as Vanessa did some spell prepping. She didn't want to be stuck in another situation like she had been with the minotaur.

First, she prepped her staff for a light spell so they could see better. Bobo had night vision, but that didn't help Vanessa in the slightest if they got separated again somehow. Second, she prepped a few barrier scrolls. And finally, third, she premixed a few battle spells into a couple of spare pouches and came to Bobo's side.

"I've made a few spells to aid us if we have something like that come up again. I even made two barrier spells just in case we come across any hellhounds or other demons. I prepped my staff as well, so we'll have light too." She rubbed her arm. "I should have done this from the start…" she admitted.

Bobo patted her shoulder. "You're a hasty creature, Vanessa. I walked in just as blind as you. So, stop blaming yourself and do what you have been. Learn from your mistakes, not live in them."

She smiled and then motioned toward the spread of dark burrows. "Which one is it going to be?"

Bobo scratched the back of his head and sighed heavily as he looked at the choices one last time. The hand holding the battle-ax rose and pointed to each destination ahead of them. "Those two have strange smells and sounds coming from them. They are faint, but I can still sense them. Something is definitely there." He then pointed to the one on the far right. "That one has airflow. I can smell the lavender too. This tunnel probably winds back to where we came in and connects with the main passageway." The information wasn't as comforting as she thought it would be. *Something* meant it wasn't human, but at least she knew which tunnel to take if anything started to chase after them.

"So, we search one of these and then make our way back to the surface."

He nodded. "Staying down here with minimal supplies and poor lighting won't give us anything but trouble. If there is something down here, we'll find something down just one of those tunnels, that and the minotaur should be enough to spur the blue cloaks to resume the search down here with the Summoners that have been on standby."

"Good. We have a plan and are prepared for an attack. I say we move forward so we can get the hex out of here."

"I agree."

She pointed to the middle tunnel. "Let's take the middle."

"The middle it shall be."

The two of them started through the chosen tunnel. Lighting her staff, Vanessa once again led the way and inspecting every crevice as they slowly went deeper into the shaft. Not wanting to be caught off guard for a second time that night, they made sure to be a little more careful than before. Each possible corner was checked, each step was quiet and well-placed, and their concentration was set dead ahead.

It didn't take them too long to reach a point where even Vanessa could hear the sounds and smell the scents that Bobo had picked up on back at the entrance. The sounds were like moans and grunts, sniffles and hacking like they had entered the recovery ward in Coven headquarters. Their footwork would teeter somewhere between speeding up and slowing to a crawl. Part of them wanted to see what was producing those sounds and the other part of them feared it.

They never stopped, though. They pressed on until the stench made Vanessa gag, and she paused to tie a bit of cloth around her nose and mouth to repel some of the revolting odor. But the smell wasn't even the worst of it.

It wasn't until the staff glowed off something other than rock and stone that Bobo and Vanessa realized what was making the sounds and why.

Rows upon rows of bars lined the stretch of tunnel. Each side providing a tiny carved out space. A cell. A prison. A private cage. And in each cage?

Bobo's face twisted in horror.

This was monstrous! Who would do such a thing? He dropped his battle-ax and rushed over to one of the cages. Both his hands gripping the bars that held the captive inside and the disturbed Bobo and Vanessa out. His mouth moved in a way that told Vanessa he was holding back a series of curses, screams, rants, and possibly even tears. She couldn't blame him.

"What … what have they done to you?" He asked one of the prisoners.

He received no reply. Just a tired expression from a worn-down ogre. Its eyes were sunken in and seemed half-starved. In some places, it was charred as if it had been burned and never properly treated. One of its fangs that jutted up from the bottom gum line was broken off and a portion of its chin missing. A bright pink scar was on the side of its head, and it seemed to be partially blind in one eye. Its neck was clamped in cold iron and a chain connected the creature from the cruel collar to the wall. It moved, and the skin of the demon would sound as if it were being burned. It would wince in pain, but not make a sound. The ogre's hands outstretched as if to receive something from Bobo, and it opened its mouth. But no words came. Just pleading eyes and begging hands.

"This is wrong." Bobo turned, and, to his undying horror, he saw hands sticking out from all the bars that lined the channel. All large. All like his. All burned, or stitched, or missing fingers, limbs, appendages. As he walked, almost too quickly, and turned to face each prison cell, he was greeted by a new nightmare therein. Ogres that looked like they had been tormented and then collared in iron were sitting in each one of the small barred rooms.

Vanessa took her time, even though it made her sick to her stomach, to look into each cage and inspect the prisoner. She didn't like it. Some looked like they were dead, rotting in corners hugging themselves, and the skin looked strained as it stretched over the large creature's bones in a way that let you see every dip in the structure and ripple of the ribcage. Others looked like they were in a daze or deep trance, their eyes glazed over with a fog of sadness, drooling while staring off into space. Some looked like they were infected, bits of their bodies missing in various spots. The more she looked, the more she was sure she was going to lose whatever contents were in her stomach.

Only a handful of the poor creatures spoke. But the hope that their voice produced was quickly stamped out by the words that they spoke. They weren't any better than the others. Their speech was broken, mixed with equations, poems, and half-remembered spell incantations and murmured with a scratchy voice that was hardly audible. It was like … she looked at Bobo and then to the bars and the sad eyes of one of the ogres that lay beyond them.

It was like an intelligence spell had gone wrong. All of them appeared to have been summoned, blasted with an intelligence spell but … but something went wrong. Either the caster wasn't paying attention, or the ingredients weren't right, or they weren't skilled enough to perform the spell. Or they had been blasted with *two* intelligence spells at a fast rate. No matter the case, the demon was injured and then left to rot in this place? This was what the minotaur was hiding. Failed summoned pets.

Frowning so hard she thought she'd never smile again, she touched one of the bars and stared into one of the cages again. The ogre inside stared at the ceiling unblinking. "Bobo, get your ax, we're leaving." She looked over to Bobo, he was on his knees and staring into a cage further ahead. "Bobo," she called softly to him again, and he didn't move. "Bobo!"

He jolted and looked around him. Sniffling and wiping his nose on his sleeve, Bobo rose to his feet and walked to his forgotten weapon like he was drunk. His back was to Vanessa, and he was facing the floor and the tunnel that would lead the way out. "Vanessa," his voice was hoarse and hardly audible with all the pitiful sounds that surrounded them.

"Yes?" she answered, but she feared his next words. He was

going to ask to save them. She didn't have the heart to list protocol. They weren't tethered. They weren't spelled with a proper intelligence spell. Hex, most of them were hardly classified as living. There was no way that they could get all of them out and not have the Coven find out or cause city-wide panic.

She inhaled, ready to speak the bad news in the softest tone she could muster, but his question made her lose her breath and it came out of her in a half-croak. "We need to put them to rest," he said.

That was not what she was expecting. It was nowhere near the anticipated question. She stammered for a moment and then finally found her tongue to be able to speak again. "I wouldn't even know what spell—"

"A Rip Van Winkle curse," he said in a tone that lacked his usual spunk and life. He sounded monotone. Plain. It didn't suit him at all.

"I suppose I could try if I could find something to ground me—"

Again, he interjected with an answer, "Use me."

"What?" she gasped.

He turned to face her and raised his gaze from his reflection in the blade to meet her eyes. "Use me to draw your power from. I'm a demon. I've got enough power in me to supply you with what you need to perform the spell."

She was lost. He was determined, that was to say the least. But a spell like that and on such a grand scale. It would take a team to perform it. She was just one witch. There was no way she had that kind of ability, even with Bobo using himself to ground her. "I ... I don't know if I'm—"

Once again, he shot in a reply before she could finish a sentence. "You are strong enough." He stepped forward. His voice wasn't playful. It was serious. "I've never doubted your power. Never. You have always doubted yourself. I give you hell for it. Leon does too. You are a good witch, Vanessa. You are a powerful witch." He slowly approached her and knelt down in front of her and bowed his head. "Please. I'm begging you to tap into that power. Believe in yourself like I believe in you and put my brethren to rest. This…" he looked around the cells again and a tear fell from his eye before he locked gazes with her. "… This is worse than hell." The weight of that statement rested upon her heart as she heard it and played it over and over in her mind.

Vanessa stared at him in half-awe. The proud and intelligent Botobolbilian was on his knees and begging her for her help. "Get up."

"Tell me you'll do it."

"All right! I'll do it. Just … by the goddess, stand up," she urged him as she dipped down and started to aid him to his feet.

Bobo's hands clamped down on her arms. His tear-filled eyes burrowed deep into her own, and it felt like it reached a bit further. "Vanessa. I need you to believe that you can do this."

"I …" she hesitated to tell him the truth and just nodded a bunch, hoping it would be enough for him to let the matter go.

"You can do it," he whispered and tightened his grip on her.

"I'm not sure that I can," she admitted.

"I know you can," he was half smiling and half crying.

"I can try, but I'm not sure if I have that kind of power, Bobo."

"You. Summoned. Me!" he yelled, and his bellowing voice snatched her body into a stiff, unbelieving mass. She started to blink as she tried to remain still. Bobo had *never* used this tone with her. It scared her a bit, but, more so, it hurt her to hear him use it with her. He indignantly shook her in his grasp with eyes of frustration and pain. "You summoned me." His voice was strained, and his eyes frantically searched hers. "Not even trying or paying attention, this little witch with a whole lot of sass, horrible table manners, and one nasty temper, summoned me… you are what most envy, Vanessa. You have what others crave. Power." He stared at her for a long moment and another tear dripped. "Use it. Save them from their suffering."

She nodded. She didn't know what else to say. She had never seen him like this. If he believed in her, then she had to try. He looked to the side, realizing he'd been crying, the shame settled in. Retrieving his handkerchief, he wiped his face and nose before resuming some of his normal stature.

As Bobo collected himself, she prepared a salt circle, a

nightingale feather, and a mini-scroll with charcoal runes written on it. She stood outside the circle staring at the white salt lines that surrounded Bobo. He was holding out his massive paws while waiting for her. Vanessa stared down at them as she bit her lower lip. She wasn't killing these poor creatures… she wasn't. She was setting them free from a fate worse than death. She was giving them the freedom they deserved. Free from pain. Free from a slow death. Free of prison walls and dark tunnels and cold nights.

She wasn't unsure anymore. She took one of his hands in her own and stepped into the circle. With her free hand, she laid the feather in Bobo's palm and released a slow calming breath. Within the circle, a soft wind picked up and moved their clothing and danced with strands of Vanessa's hair. Closing her eyes shut, she focused on the words and dug deep to have the strength to say them and not breakdown. The inhale of air was tainted with the must and putrid scents of the tunnel, but her voice was sweeter than honey as she slowly prayed out loud, "A nightingale to show a melody to the shade of night, the feather a gift for one last song, may their sleep be sweet, and their final moments not prolonged. The scroll a final moment, a memory, a dream, goddess give them a quiet passing, a release from anguish and pain. May their death be like the last breath of winter. Gentle, relenting, and giving way to new life, a spirit's spring."

The feather shimmered and rose, floating away from Bobo's hand. The scroll drifted from Vanessa's, and they danced between Bobo and Vanessa's palms. They watched it ascend above them. A silver light emitted from the two and then, the feather burnt slowly with the scroll and turned into sand, which drifted on an unseen and unfelt wind to each cell. It lazily wafted through the bars, glided through the cell, and landed softly into the eyes of the ogres. One by one, their eyes closed. Their breathing slowed. Rest took over. A final deep sleep. And a final dream before they would pass from this world onto the next.

Bobo watched as the sand drifted from cell to cell. Bringing the peace that he had wished for each of them. Soon, the whimpers and sniffles and moans all stopped. Bobo didn't know if he should smile or weep.

The Rip Van Winkle curse was gray magic, meaning it was

neutral magic. All neutral magic worked the same. If there is ill intent, the magic picks up on it and will turn the spell into black magic. If there are good intentions, the magic remains gray with an aura of white. It would still ping on the orb back at headquarters. Normally, gray magic wouldn't do that, but a spell this big most certainly would. They couldn't stay much longer. If anyone in the Coven was part of this horrendous act, they'd notice the activity here and be on their way before dispatch could send out investigators for the gray magic spell.

"We can't afford to stay; we have to leave," she reminded Bobo, and he just nodded as he looked from cell to cell. A strange calm washed over him as he watched his brethren slumber.

"Of course," he whispered. The way that he looked, the tone of his voice, and how slow he seemed to be moving almost broke Vanessa's heart. But they couldn't spare any more time down here. They needed to get out of there and tell Leon what they had found.

Gathering up her belongings, she took the time to double-check everything on her person. When they left, she didn't want anything to tie her and Bobo to the spell or give hints that they had been down there since they were ordered to stay out. She was making sure all her pouches were secure before kneeling to pick up her staff when she heard it.

That dreaded sound.

A growl that rattled with the sounds of hell as if the mouth that produced the horrific melody was the doorway to the fiery pits of torment itself. Vanessa froze, and her heart broke free from her ribcage and clawed up her throat, each beat snuffing out the ability to draw in a full breath of air.

Slowly, her eyes walked the narrow corridor between the cells and rested on the end of the tunnel where, not one, not two, but three hellhounds stood. Lava-like saliva dripping from their boney charred mouths and singed the stone ground below. Their throats rumbled with their menacing guttural warning. Any moment they would rush at them. One of them gnashed its teeth in the air, and one of the others barked and snipped in their direction. It wasn't until the third one craned its head back to howl – the sound a cross between a large dog and a woman screaming – that Vanessa snatched her staff up quickly and pointed it at the trio of hellhounds.

The tip glowed like white fire. "Force push," she yelled, and a ball of power spat out from the staff and grew into a massive disc shape that took up the width of the channel as it sped faster than she could blink toward the hounds. The spell hit them, and the dogs yelped as they flipped back and hit the bars of the cells and the stone walls. She knew they wouldn't stay down. They healed like nothing she had ever seen before.

"Bobo!"

"Already one step ahead of you," he said as he grabbed her by the arm and forced her to run down the other end of the tunnel.

"If we can get to the original tunnels, I can post a barrier spell. It won't last long, but maybe long enough to get away from them."

"Wait…" Bobo stopped and looked around, then ran down the other tunnel, the one that only led to more prison cells and possibly a dead-end.

"What are you doing?"

"I've got a plan," Bobo said as he searched each of the cells and stopped when he got to an empty one. In an unexpected display of brute strength, that she always knew he had but hardly saw him demonstrate, he ripped off the door to the cell and chucked it behind him carelessly.

It clanged as it slammed against the opposing wall and dropped to the floor with a reverberating thick, dull toll. "I hope you weren't trying to be quiet."

The howls echoed in the other tunnel, and they both turned to face the direction the sound had come from. There wasn't much time. "Look, Vanessa. I need you to trust me. Those things, we can't kill them. But we can trap them."

"With what?"

"A talisman spell." As soon as he said it, she had her mind relive the moments that Leon had come down and saved them. A barrier spell had repelled the hounds.

She snapped out of it and looked at Bobo shaking her head. "But those are temporary."

"Not if you etch the runes into the wall. It could last a day, maybe even two or three if you do it right. Enough time for the Coven to get prepared and come down here to retrieve them to take them to a better holding dwelling."

"I … I dunno…" The snarling was now at the mouth of the tunnel. There was no more time to argue. She growled and nodded. "Fine. I'll do it. Only because those things roaming free down here is bad news. If they get out. A lot of innocent people could get hurt."

She fished a piece of chalk from her pocket and crashed into the wall. "Keep them away from me," she commanded as she started to scribble a rune onto the rough stone.

"With pleasure," Bobo wrung the handle of his battle-ax and then ran down to greet the hellhounds as Vanessa frantically etched runes around the stones of the cell. Each time she heard a yelp, or cry, or heard something slamming into a wall she resisted the urge to look. She had to concentrate.

She was shaking, her breathing was hitched and shallow, and her mind was racing through every spell and incantation that she knew. Another piercing bark tore through the tunnels, and a roar of pain ripped from Bobo's throat. The sounds filled her with urgency and caused Vanessa to drop to her knees and dig out a piece of parchment. Her fingers fumbled over the crinkled paper as she smoothed it out. She scrambled to gather the chalk after it slipped from her grasp and rolled across the ground.

Crazily, she made a talisman and hastily slapped her hands together to pray. Closing her eyes, she started the most dangerous part of the spell. She couldn't open her eyes. She couldn't stop chanting or the spell would fizz and die.

"Burn it into stone!" The talisman lifted from the ground as the coal markings sparked, like a flame catching to a line of gunpowder, and etched the runes magically into the stones. Then, the parchment rose to the top of the cell and hovered there as she kept her hands in prayer form. She mentally tugged at their connection. Tethered together since summoning day, there was always an invisible line, a cord, that connected pet and owner. A spiritual link that can become so strong between the two that some could even speak telepathically. Bobo and she were not that lucky. But she could tug on that string, she could get his attention and that would be enough.

"Just…a …second… dear!" she could hear Bobo struggle with the dogs, but her eyes were shut as she focused on the spell. She heard, no … felt the ogre's thundering feet as he raced over to her. As he skidded to a stop, she heard his labored breathing and then his words graced her ears. "No matter what you do, Vanessa. Trust in me," his hand gripped her shoulder tightly, "and believe in yourself."

The hellish sounds of the hounds pierced the air around her and made her flesh ripple in goosebumps, the hairs standing on end instantaneously as she kept her eyes shut and her mind reciting the spell continuously. She could feel the air as Bobo twisted his torso and, with all his might, smashed one of the dogs into the cell so hard that she heard multiple snaps resounding all at once. The next dog tried to bite at his feet while the other went for his arm.

Crunch! *Thud*! The neck of the hellhound that went for the ogre's legs was stepped on full force, and he proceeded to swiftly kick it into the cell. She could hear the heavy body landing on top of the first, and she felt her lip tremble. Still, she managed to keep up with the spell. Her wrists were shaking to the point that it was hard to keep her hands in prayer form.

Bobo gave a sharp, loud roar of pain and she heard him hit the floor. What happened? Was he okay? Was he conscious? She almost opened her eyes to check, but she didn't dare. She only jerked her head in the direction of the cry and then went perfectly still. There wasn't a sound. Silence descended upon the tunnel. She couldn't stop mentally reciting the incantation. Her hands trembled no matter how hard she tried to control it. She wanted to see if Bobo was okay. She wanted to see if the other two were still knocked out in the cell. But, most of all, she wanted to see where that last hellhound was.

The sound of lava-like spit hissing as it burrowed through rock sizzled mere inches from her. Vanessa moved her foot to escape the saliva but didn't know exactly how close the hellhound was until it growled, displeased with her movement.

She frowned. Her lips twisting into such deep grief that she was sure to wail and cry out loud, but she restrained and only sniffled. Her lower lip quivered. She shook and sniffled a bit more. Hot tears burned her eyes as she squeezed them shut even harder. No matter what, she never stopped reciting the incantation. Her body was wracked with quivers, but she never stopped reciting. Bobo told her to trust him. It couldn't end like this.

...she had tried so hard...

It lunged with hate and hunger and Vanessa felt the warmth of the hellhound's breath as it washed over her face causing her lashes to curl from the intense heat, and she felt a fang scrape over her neck. She jerked back but kept her hands in prayer form, her mind fixed on the spell, her heart sunk with despair. The beast yipped in pain and gargled like its windpipe was being crushed. "You won't touch her, you mangy beast," Bobo snarled into the hellhound's face and then thrust it into the opening of the cell. "Now, Vanessa!"

She opened her eyes and bellowed, "Let it be sealed on Raen as it was below!" The conscious hellhound leaped for the opening only to be greeted with the spill of golden light falling like a curtain over the front of the cell. It hit the barrier and whimpered as it was zapped with a jolt of power that threw it to the ground. It whimpered again before limping away from the doorway. Glaring at the two that had trapped the beast within, it circled the spelled cage with a menacing snarl.

"Nice job!" Bobo commended her victoriously only to be greeted with a flurry of Vanessa's tiny hands flying at him in a series of uncalculated slaps.

"Don't you *ever* do that to me again!"

Even though the slaps hurt, Bobo couldn't stop laughing as he covered his face to avoid the blows.

 *Chapter 22:*

They didn't exactly rush to leave, but they didn't take their time either. There wasn't anything chasing them anymore, but they still needed to get out of there before they were caught by the Coven or bumped into whoever was responsible for all the atrocities the caverns had stored away if they came to check on their experiments.

A little reluctant to leave the hellhounds caged with such a slap-dash spell, Vanessa continuously looked behind them as they made their way for the main tunnel. Each time she saw the golden splash of light illuminating the passageway it brought her some comfort, even as the sight faded from her vision. Once out of sight, worry gnawed at her relentlessly as they walked.

Bobo bumped her with his elbow and she jerked with surprise. "It'll be fine, Vanessa. You did good. Stop worrying about it."

She nodded. He was right. They did what they could. For now, they needed to get out of here and head back home to tell Leon about what they found. Hopefully, he would know what to do. She didn't trust her judgment anymore. The Coven could be infested with corrupted members. Right now, she only trusted Bobo, Leon, and Lyx. Everything else was blurred lines in the sand.

She sighed while in deep thought. If anyone would know what to do in a crisis, it would be Leon. His ability to be able to come up with a plan, and multiple backup plans, always amazed her. Not to mention his skill in reading people. She'd probably never tell him that, but that didn't mean it amazed her any less.

"What are you thinking about?"

"What I'm going to eat when I get out of this musty underbelly," she said with a snicker. "I'm starving!" She heard a grumble that made her turn to face Bobo and chortle, "If you were hungry too you could just say something, big guy. No need to be shy.

I was only teasing you about your weight, earlier." Bobo froze where he stood, and she was forced to stop and look back at him. "Bobo?"

Shaking his head, he spoke in a low tone to her. "That... wasn't my stomach..."

She looked confused for a moment and then the severity of his words sunk in. Her eyes grew bulbous and she leaned back on her heels to look behind them, down to the vast stretch of tunnel. At first, there was nothing. However, that didn't last long. Slowly, four obsidian black, leathery skinned legs crept from behind the corner of the passageway. A cat-like flame-tipped tail was swinging back and forth behind the bulk of a massive, dark body and a wild, greasy, matted mane of hair like a poised scorpion tail. A bright ember, like a lump of burning coal was lodged within the creature's throat, glowed profusely. When the beast growled, the throat vibrated and shook, and the ember flared to life like a wildfire. Smoke circled in fading rivulets around the broad-shoulders of the hound's body.

"Bobo, how many were in the cage?"

"Three. We checked and double-checked. I'm sure of it."

"They travel in large packs. Why didn't I stop to think of that?"

"What should we do?"

"Run." It wasn't a suggestion, it was an order, and she didn't wait to see if he'd comply. She turned and darted through the long corridor and let her mind race with plans. They needed to get out of there. Going back and trying to re-do what they had just done would only tack on time they didn't have and would put them in further danger. The hellhound couldn't be killed by any means that they had available, not that they knew how to kill one, to begin with.

Banish a banshee! She was getting nowhere in her plotting. She just needed a moment to stop and think....

That's it! She started to scan the tunnels and quickly came up with a plan. It wouldn't be much, but they didn't need much. "Bobo. We need to lose it and find somewhere to hide."

"What?"

"Look, we won't be able to outrun it, but we can lose it for a short time in the tunnels. I can cloak us with a spell. I already prepped one, I just need enough time to cast it."

"Then what?"

"We'll discuss that after we succeed with part one."

The ogre's tone dropped in pitch, "Understood." There was no sense in explaining an escape plan while huffing and puffing and trying to ditch a speeding hellhound.

Up ahead was a passage. "There. Turn up there!" She skidded and hit the wall and picked up the speed again. "Take every turn we can!" And so, they did. Each time, the sound of the hellhound's paws thundering behind them became more distant.

Vanessa searched for the cloaking spell in her satchel as she ran. She pulled open one of them and saw the nightingale feather buried in gold dust. "I found it," she practically laughed, half-crazed, and they turned down another tunnel. She started to slow her pace. The caves were crudely carved, and there were many dips and holes where they looked like they started to dig but changed their mind at the last moment.

Bobo slowed and looked behind him, his chest heaving as he sporadically looked from her to the end of the tunnel to make sure the hellhound wasn't there. "Vanessa, what are you doing?"

"I need a…" She stopped speaking and walking at the same time. Instantly, she beamed and motioned him over. "Quick!" She said, and he rushed over not questioning further.

Shoving him into the carved-out space in the rocky wall, Vanessa quickly squeezed in next to him and started to cast the spell. Just as she started to mumble the incantation, they heard the hellhound's claws scraping over the stone flooring and start to trot and then slow to a walk as it growled, sniffing the air. It knew they were close by.

"Vanessa," Bobo urged her to hurry with a frantic whisper that she almost couldn't hear. She focused on the spell. She hadn't concentrated so hard in her life.

Just as she opened her eyes, the hellhound's face was on the other end of the opening.

The molten saliva dripping from its sharp fangs and its feral burning eyes peering into the crevice they had tucked themselves away in. It snarled, its black, leathery lips quivered angrily. Her hands, that were outstretched near its snout from performing the spell, shook profusely in place, and she dare not move or speak or scream.

The hellhound sniffed around the edges of the hole, howled its scream-like howl, and Vanessa bit her lips to try not to shriek. Her heart was scratching at her chest like a caged hellcat. Just as soon as she thought that the beast would lunge and devour them both, it turned, sniffed the ground, and bayed into the darkness before running off further into the tunnel.

Her body relaxed so much that she was sure she had melted into a puddle on the floor. "That was close," she breathed.

"Too close," Bobo said what she was thinking.

After taking a quick moment to collect herself, Vanessa turned to Bobo. "Hand me your crystal ball."

He snapped his gaze to her. "My what?" he whispered.

Her hand was open, ready to receive the orb, and she bobbed it up and down impatiently. "Ha, ha. Hand me your crystal ball," she urged.

"I... Vanessa. I don't have it."

"You what?" she snapped hoarsely.

"I. Don't. Have. It."

"Why not?"

"Well, dear, I wasn't expecting to need it. I left it at home in my haste to chase after the young and restless troublemaker." He leaned in and cupped his mouth for theatrical purposes, as if to shield his words from an unseen crowd, "That would be you, by the way."

Her face twisted in anger. "Why in the name of magic would you leave the house without your crystal ball?"

"I didn't think I'd need it, for starters. Nor did I expect you, oh fearless master, to go kicking yours into the ugly face *of a minotaur*," Bobo sounded exasperated and strained the last few words in a breathless whisper scream.

"This is just perfect," she muttered.

Bobo gasped, and she braced herself on the small enclosed walls, half expecting the hellhound to have returned. The ogre fished around his satchel on his hip. Removing a pair of glasses, a book, and finally a compact mirror. "Ah-ha!" he exclaimed right before she snatched the compact mirror from him. "Rude," he whispered.

"This will do just fine," she said with a gleeful lilt in her voice and hope glistening in her eyes. Soon that look turned into confusion as she turned her attention to her demon pet again. "Wait… why do you have a compact mirror?"

He looked a bit bashful and pinched his fingers together and brought them to the space between his brow line. "Sometimes I get these few stray hairs betwee—" He shook his head and came out of the daze of explanation. "You know, it's none of your business! Just make your confounded call, woman."

She shook her head and opened the mirror. "Fine. No reason to be short. Sheesh."

Mirrors could be used as communication devices just like crystal balls, but she preferred to use a crystal ball. They could do more than a compact mirror as well. Because of their ability to do more than make calls, the crystal balls were all the rage in Aeristria. It didn't mean that mirrors, lakes, and anything that was reflective wasn't able to hold a call, it was that the calls were distorted and glitchy. Too much outside interference jumbled up the connection between the callers. Crystal balls and compact mirrors were more common than anything else to hold a call. This was primarily due to how they were made. Crystal balls were imbued with more magic and from start to finish were infused with spells and magical items to aid them in being the best item to have for calling other witches or wizards.

Right now, it didn't matter what she was holding as long as it could make a call. She thought of Leon, his pinched brow and angry eyes, his long sandy-colored hair and frowning mouth, the last face he made before Bobo draped his handkerchief over the object. She waited. Barely two buzzes went off before a frantic Leon picked up. His mouth was in a hard frown, his eyes searched the orb wildly, and he combed the area before he spoke in a whisper. Was he… worried?

"Vanessa, where are you? Are you all right? Where is Bobo? Is he with you? Are you in the tunnels? The front door is closed and locked from the inside, I can't get down into the basement. I've been pacing for hours." Everything came out in rapid succession, and Vanessa couldn't answer one question fast enough before he shot out another. She waited until he was done before she replied.

"Bobo's with me. We're fine. I have a plan to get out, but I needed to let you know that we are all right. We need to talk, but after I get out."

"What's wrong?"

"There is a hellhound down here..."

He yelled, and she heard the distinct sound of something soft hitting something hard. His face disappeared from the sight of the mirror for a moment. Quickly he came back into view with his features twisted in pain that he was poorly trying to mask. "Can you get away from it?" he whispered crossly.

"I think so. The tunnel has a daze spell. I made a rip in it that Bobo and I can slip through, after that anything that attempts to come through will be stunned. But that thing is fast."

"I can smell us out of here, but it's a bit of a ways. There's no telling if we can beat it," Bobo added.

Leon stared at the orb. "Vanessa..."

She cut him off, "I was calling to tell you ... If I don't come out in the next fifteen minutes ... I need you to do something for me."

"No." She blinked, baffled at the compact mirror. "You get out of there and tell me what you need to."

"Leon."

"I'm not saying goodbye. You are going to get out of there." He looked sternly into his crystal ball. "I'm giving you ten minutes, not fifteen. Don't make me wait." The connection cut off.

"Well, can't blame the man for being upset," Bobo said with a sniff.

She sighed and closed the compact and handed it back to Bobo. Leon was mad, and he had every right to be. She was stupid coming down here on her own, without preparations, without consent from the Coven, and without letting him know. She looked without poking her head out from the cloaking spell and saw nothing. "I think we are just going to have to make a run for it and pray to the Goddess it's enough." She turned and looked at her pet. "You lead the way. Get us out of here so we can go home."

Bobo nodded to her, and she took one final look before inhaling deeply, holding her breath, and stepping out into the tunnel. The silence that surrounded them was horrible. Every little sound made her heart skip, and every breeze made her skin shiver with fresh goosebumps.

They carefully and quietly made their way back to the main tunnel where they could see the opening to the system of passageways. Nothing ever looked as sweet as that sight did. She was tired of the scent of mildew, must, and soil. She was tired of being chased by monsters. She was tired of thinking of all those ogres she had … she frowned hard and looked at the floor passing under her feet.

"Come on, Vanessa, we're almost there," Bobo whispered.

"I'm coming."

The sound of claws dancing on stone made her heartbeat climb to a painful patter. She turned just to see a few feet behind them, the hellhound emerged from a tunnel dumping out into the main passage. She slapped Bobo's back repeatedly right as it started to snarl. "RUN, Bobo!"

He only looked to confirm that the beast was there before breaking out in a sprinting start. How could such a massive creature be that fast? She followed close behind as best she could. The hound scrambled, feet slipping a bit as it tried to catch traction and then hauled off after them in a raging rampage.

Sweat beaded over their faces and dripped from their chins. Vanessa's lungs felt like they were on fire, her legs felt so sore she was sure they'd give up on her, and she'd fall to the ground any moment. Every breath in was like needles scraping at her dry throat, and her lips and tongue felt as though they were cracking like she was stuck out in desert heat. She whimpered as she started to fall behind Bobo.

"Pick up the pace!" Bobo growled.

"I'm *trying*," she whined.

That sound wasn't something she produced often in the face of danger. The whine made the ogre turn on a coin, kick off the wall, and remove his battle-ax from his hip as he hit the ground and bravely went to face the hellhound head-on. As though the weapon was a golf club, the ogre brandished it like a sports tool, scraping it over the ground as he ran at the nightmarish dog. Sweeping up from the floor, Bobo swung, connecting the metal with the meat of the hellhound's chin and slinging it several feet behind them with a bellowing roar.

The creature yelped and then bounced and slid to a stop a good distance away. But it didn't stay down. It slowly rose, shook off the blow, and erupted in flames as it gave a shrieking howl right before it picked up speed and resumed racing back to them.

Bobo spun around and caught up with Vanessa. "I did what I could, dear."

"It was more than enough," she admitted. The end of the tunnel was there. So close she could taste it. She never ran so fast and hard in her life. As soon as she reached the opening Vanessa dove through. Bobo close behind and the hellhound inches behind him. The spell crackled as it widened its birth and Bobo lunged with all his speed and might through the opening.

A short bark echoed in the main room before the spell exploded in a deep-blue light and slammed a ghost-like image of a hammer down on the hellhound's body. It was dazed.

Vanessa crab-walked backward as her eyes dared not remove themselves from the hellhound knocked out on the floor a few feet away from her. Bobo rose and didn't bother with dusting off as he picked her up and raced for the summoning room. "It's dazed," she reminded him between panting breaths.

"It's a hellhound, Vanessa. They regenerate faster than most demons," he explained. She looked back and saw the dim fire start to grow in illumination.

"Double-dip a candlestick," she hissed and patted at him. "Best pick up the pace or let me down to run," she told him.

He put her down once they reached the white candle hall and they bolted for the stairs and the main door. They heard the shrilling howl of the hellhound just as Vanessa whispered the unlocking word to her spell. They tugged on the door hurriedly, squeezed through the opening, and frantically slammed the boiler room door shut. Right after, Vanessa whispered the locking spell.

With that spell, she felt spent and slid down the door huffing and puffing. The pain was starting to sink in as the adrenaline ebbed from them.

"Come on. I want to get as far away from here as possible," Bobo said while catching his breath. She nodded in reply and they hobbled, holding onto one another, to the exit through the plastic curtain down the halls. They practically fell out of the opening on the side of the building.

Once out in the snow, they saw Leon racing through the almost knee-high mounds of white and sending flurries of snowflakes dancing in a kicked-up mess behind him. Slamming into Vanessa, he hugged her hard and strong. The feeling of his embrace made her go stiff, and she felt confused. But the longer he remained there hugging her, the more she let go of trying to pick apart what was happening and just lived in the moment. Her body ate up the warmth that he provided, despite him standing out in the cold for hours, and she felt that he cared for her for a moment. There was comfort in knowing someone had waited for her. After all that she had been through, there was someone waiting on the other side of that curses door that caged so many nightmares.

She let her guard down at the same moment that Leon pulled away and started to shake her as violently as he dared to shake a woman. "Are you a blasted fool! What were you doing down there?"

"Be gentle with her, Leon. She's been through enough," Bobo spoke softly, but Leon was furious and didn't listen to the wise words of the calm ogre.

He shook his head. "You had no business being down there. You can't handle taking down a hellhound!" he snapped at her.

One moment she was feeling things she only had glimpses of in her dreams and the next they were ripped away and followed by Leon yelling. She felt a swirl of emotions and said the first thing that came to her mind. "You said you didn't think I was weak!" She screamed it in his face. How dare he lie to her, try to make her feel better just because he thought she was having a bad day. What a typical male. Saying something to make her feel better but not meaning a lick of it. She wasn't his charity case.

Her yelling in his face didn't bother him in the slightest. He just stared at her and furrowed his brow in anger. "I wasn't afraid of you not being strong enough, I was afraid I was going to *lose you*!" He yelled back in her face, and it caused her to pull back as much as his tight grasp on her would allow. Her eyes widened, and he continued to yell at her, "You could have *died*, Vanessa. You would have died, and I would have blamed myself for the *rest* of my *life* for not being able to stop or *save you*."

She didn't know what to say to that. He was right, but when her mouth opened to speak, nothing came out. That was the moment when she realized that she was crying. Hot tears blazing down the sides of her frozen cheeks as she stared up at Leon, bewildered by his worn and worried expression. He sighed and pulled her into his chest and just silently hugged her as Bobo tried to shield them both from the blistering cold winds that whipped around them.

The three of them stood there in the start of the blizzard, holding onto one another like they were life rafts amidst a stormy sea.

 *Chapter 23:*

The teleportation spell dropped them in the middle of Vanessa's living room. Clumps of snow that were clinging to their clothing fell from their attire and landed on the carpet, making the fibers soggy as it quickly melted from the warmth of the apartment.

"What in the name of magic?" Lyx said as she put down a teacup onto a small saucer and rushed over to the living room. She stared down at the melting mounds of white and then to them. "That is going to make a mess," she added in a hushed voice.

Taking a moment to look them over, she saw the drying blood on Vanessa's forehead and her eyes widened. "Vanessa," she gasped and reached for the girl's face to draw her in close and inspected the rather clean wound. The small healing spell sealed the gash and managed to clear up the more problematic bits of the injury. But, once at the witch's side, Lyx's eyes wandered over to Bobo's tattered clothing and inhaled with a startled expression. "Booboo!" she turned on a coin and snatched Bobo's arm and tugged it to her. There was no finesse or gentleness to her touch. The ogre hissed in pain and pressed his lips tightly together as he turned his head away and stifled – as best as an ogre could – a growl of pain. "What is this?" A sharp nail pointed at the half-closed, blood crusted wound on his upper arm.

Vanessa and Bobo cast their gazes to the floor and avoided the heated glare that Lyx was mentally melting them with at all cost. The succubus whipped her attention to Leon and snarled in a whisper, "And you! Leaving the house in a rush. You didn't even wake me up. You went out in the start of a blizzard, Leon. A blizzard!" Her harsh tone made him look away as well. He had put himself in harm's way to come after her and greatened his chances of being hurt by not bringing his pet with him. This made Vanessa turn her head just enough that she could see him and looked the

Spellweaver over. He was that worried about her? She felt bad now. Not only was Bobo put in harm's way, and she had made Lyx worried, but she had caused Leon so much trouble and had him driven up the wall with his concerns over her wellbeing.

She frowned and looked down at the living room floor covered in puddles of melted snow. As her gaze floated down, she caught sight of skin slightly frayed and a burst of red on Leon's knuckles. That was when she remembered the crystal ball call with him in the cave. Vanessa frowned deepened as she realized that the sound she had heard before Leon went off the glass was him hitting a wall. Just as Leon looked over to her, she averted her gaze and fidgeted with the spell bags dangling from her hip.

Lyx eyed them all over quietly and huffed in a rage before fluffing up her hair. As if the simple action had washed all the aggression out of the succubus, her voice returned to its usual sultry tone. "Well, fussing won't fix anything. Come on then. Let's get you guys cleaned up and out of those wet clothes before you wind up finding your death from a cold." That would be the hellfire of it all, wouldn't it? Escape death countless times within the tunnels only to find their foot in a grave from being soaked to the bone and chilled by the elements.

They were ushered out of the room to wash up, Leon to one bathroom and Vanessa to her own. Meanwhile, Lyx made Bobo sit on a large stool at the breakfast bar as she tended to his wound while he waited for a washroom to open.

He squirmed in the chair, and it whined under his weight, but he complied with the woman nonetheless. "I'm fine," Bobo tried to reason with the fussing demoness.

"Hush," she snipped sternly. She would have none of his excuses. She wanted a reason to play nurse to him but more so, she wanted to make sure that his wounds were properly tended to. Lyx fetched the first aid kit, and Bobo stared at the breakfast counter. There was a cobalt and pearl tea set with a thin gold line separating the two striking colors. It was a set for two, and one cup was on either side of the wooden serving tray.

Lyx came back with the kit and watched Bobo as he looked at the set. "I bought it for you," she said and then turned to the open bag, inspecting each item withdrawn until she had everything she needed to tend to his wound. "I got it a few days ago. I just haven't found the right time to give it to you."

Slowly, Bobo turned from her, a bit awestruck, to the tea set before him. "That's for me?"

She nodded. "There is a cinnamon and clove blend in the pot. It's been steeping for a few minutes. I thought a spicy tea would help warm you up and relax you after your unexpected adventure," she spoke calmly. Moments like this didn't happen between the two. She was always battling for his affections while he spent every ounce of his energy trying to escape them.

He looked at her like he was seeing Lyx for what she really was for the first time. Not just an affection starved woman that pawed at him relentlessly like a begging kitten, but like a kind and friendly she-demon. His mouth was parted like he had gone drop-jawed and caught it at the last minute. She took out a wipe and started to clean the wound on his arm causing him to slowly screw his mouth shut. Her amber orbs were fixed on the task at hand and didn't take notice. Bobo slumped his shoulders a bit before he spoke in a soft manner to her. "Thank you, Lyx. I very much appreciate the gesture."

The succubus stopped mid-motion on her handy work and flashed an astonished look to the ogre, but he was focused on using his free hand to pour a helping of tea from the pot into the delicate cup. He drew the steaming cup close to him and sipped from it. Holding the sip in his mouth to enjoy the taste upon his pallet a bit more, he looked down at the cup and nodded with a slow-growing smile inching over his lips. "Very nice," he whispered.

Lyx beamed, elated with the compliment and went back to fixing up his arm until they all could get to a medic who could perform a better healing spell on the gash.

The three of them bathed, changed into a set of fresh, warm clothes, and healed up with minor mending spells once again. Despite Lyx's nagging, the trio explained that leaving the house to visit a healer wouldn't be the best option. Though she didn't understand, she relented in her begging just as Leon motioned to the living room. "I think we need to discuss a few things," Leon announced and ushered everyone into the seating area.

Bobo and Lyx drank tea while Vanessa and Leon had hot chocolate. All the while, Bobo and Vanessa explained everything that they had endured and seen down in the twisting tunnels beneath the academy. The look on Leon and Lyx's face was one of deep-seated concern. Vanessa's fears were confirmed with Leon's first comment since she and Bobo had weaved their tale to them.

"This means that there is a group of people at the Coven that has been covering this up." He paused and thought for a moment. "And they'd have to be pretty high up to hide something of this caliber."

"I was afraid you'd say something like that," Vanessa grumbled.

"The fact remains that we have to let someone know about all of this," Bobo said.

"Yeah, but if we tell the wrong person we might wind up M.I.A." Leon sighed and threw himself back on the couch. "Why couldn't you just stay home, Vanessa?" he half-whined.

She rolled her eyes. "Not much can be done about that now," she grumbled. "If they've been covering all of this up then I can promise you, they know that we were down there tonight, and they will assume that I've already told you."

"That's a pretty hard-lined assumption, Vanessa," Leon warned.

"But an accurate one," Lyx defended.

"True," Leon exhaled like he had just returned from a long day of work. "This whole thing is just a mess. Let's just ... let's all just try to get some rest for now. Let me think of a plan and get back to you."

Vanessa rubbed the back of her neck before saying, "Yeah, you're right. Even though that healing prayer spell helped out a bunch, I'm still pretty worn down from all the magic I had to perform tonight."

"And all the running," Bobo added with a slight laugh.

"I haven't run like that since the training period my first year in the Coven," Vanessa groaned.

Everyone laughed. The mood had been lightened, but it was the tug of sleep on their eyelids and the pleas from sore limbs for soft feathery beds that sent them swiftly to sleep that night. For their minds were troubled with the worries of who at the Coven was betraying them all and whether they'd be coming for them when they least expected it.

No matter the foe or dangers, lack of sleep and tired bodies wouldn't get them very far in a fight. So, with mumbled "goodnights" uttered between long stretched out yawns, they each departed to their rooms with their bunking partners and settled in for a good night's rest.

 Chapter 24:

The sudden thundering knock on Vanessa's door a few hours later made her lunge upright and leap out of bed. Miscalculating the distance of the edge of her bed and her body, coupled with the fact that she was twisted in her sheets, caused Vanessa to fall flat on her face. A sharp cry was short-lived before it was quickly stifled by her plush carpeted flooring. Rubbing the sore spot in the center of her face and whimpering to herself in pain, she hobbled gracefully to the door and flung it open. She wore a look that promised she'd curse the dramatic door knocker and a hand cradled her injured nose. Leon was the recipient of her sweet disposition. "What?" she snapped, mentally hoping that this would finally be her excuse to fling a spell at the man.

He held up a crystal ball in her face, and she inspected it quickly, seeing nothing there but a slightly darkened orb, and then looked back to him. "Congratulations. It's an orb, Leon." What was so great about an orb with no call?

Ignoring her cranky demeanor, he spoke like the comment never left her mouth. "The Coven called me just now. They want us to come in." It didn't take long for the news to sink in. "They said they tried to call you," Leon added with a stare.

She looked behind her. "I didn't hear my crystal ball buzz. I must have…" she stopped as she remembered kicking it down the hall and the object slamming into the minotaur. The whole chain of events scrambling through her mind at top speeds before she looked back at Leon in pure horror. "Oh… Oh, imp poo," she whispered and let her shoulders slump, her head bow in defeat, and her arms dangle dejectedly.

"What?"

Her worried expression met his, and she hated every word that she spoke, "I left it in the tunnels last night…"

Leon could only stare at her blinking while he tried to remember how to speak. "You what?" She only stared back in silence. "Vanessa, tell me you didn't say that you left your crystal ball back in the tunnels." His need for clarification was masked with a forced smile and a free hand jutting a finger into his ear to clean it out.

"No…" she replied while nodding with an I'm-so-guilty cringe.

"I'm doomed," he groaned and turned to throw himself onto the wall, a clutched fist lightly banging on the surface, and he buried his face into the bend of his opposite arm. "I'm going to be demoted and—when all have forgotten my greatness—I will be killed in a horrific 'accident' and buried in the farthest reaches of an unknown graveyard," he moaned.

"What's his problem?" Bobo asked as he emerged from his room.

She leaned so Bobo could see her fully. "He thinks the Coven is going to demote him and make his death look like an accident."

"Oh, is that all?"

"Because I might have left my crystal ball in the tunnels last night, and the Coven wants us to come in today…"

That made Bobo pause and turn to face her. "Now that is an issue."

"What's an issue?" Lyx asked as she placed a cup on the breakfast bar. The movement caught Bobo's attention, and he saw the cup of cappuccino on the counter and instinctively reached for it. It was his morning ritual, after all.

Sipping the drink, he watched as a plate was then slid in front of him, next to his saucer. Blinking, Bobo looked to Lyx who beamed with joy as her tail flicked behind her in a joyful, almost spastic, dance. "Oh, I don't uhm…" he looked down as he tried to politely decline the food, but he stopped to look at the dish and was amazed at what he found. Pointing at the items on the plate, he excitedly began to list off each dish, "Is that corn beef hash? Oh, my, and that is eggs in a basket—"

Lyx added, "Only the whites. I know you've been watching your cholesterol lately."

His eyes held amazement as he looked from her to the plate

of food. "It's a perfect golden color, and the whites are pristine. You cooked it so evenly and precisely." He started to lift the egg-filled toast and inspect it from all sides. "My word," he whispered.

"Oh, I almost forgot." She spun around and grabbed a bowl from the counter and then brought it over to him, nestling it close to his plate.

Gasping, Bobo inspected the newly added dish. "Is that?" He sniffed at the bowl of assorted cut fruit and his eyes fluttered. "Honey, lemon, and mint dressing." He started to seat himself down on one of the stools.

Lyx gave a charming curve of her lips as she motioned to the circle toast cut-outs made from the eggs in a basket. "I spread a thin layer of lemon curd on these for you. Can't let good food go to waste."

"Bobo, I thought you were going to go to the Grim Bean this morning," Vanessa teased from behind Leon – who was still pounding against the wall in his silent rage.

"Honestly, it'd be a waste of coin. Besides, Lyx went through the trouble of making it, it would be a shame if I didn't eat it. The Coven shall have to wait," he declared with a fork in hand.

"I made enough for everyone," Lyx announced happily to Leon and Vanessa.

"Oh good, my last meal," Leon groaned.

"Oh, hush your griping and come eat. It's most likely just a routine check-in back at HQ," Vanessa scolded as she grabbed Leon by the arm and guided him over to the breakfast bar to eat. For that moment in time, they ignored their troubles and worries as they quietly ate the delicious meal that Lyx had prepared.

The four of them took a few moments before heading to headquarters after their breakfast. Hoping that the extra time spent before using a teleportation spell would ease their nerves and aid in settling their stomachs after the large meal. The blizzard was almost in full swing out in the streets of Tolvade. Even if they wanted to walk that day, the blistering winds and blinding blasts of fat snowflakes would make the commute on foot next to impossible.

The arrival pads had a delay due to the high volume of bodies needing to use teleportation spells because of the weather. As such, if questioned by the Coven, it was the perfect excuse for their late arrival, and none would be the wiser to the breakfast delay. While they feasted, they made sure to have their stories straight between the four of them to avoid any verbal lashing or serious repercussions.

They landed in the main entryway to the Coven. They immediately stepped out of the arrival gate, so others could port in. Almost immediately another member materialized before rushing off in a flutter of cloak and purpose toward one of the main desks. Across from them, a small group was gathered on the departure gate, and Vanessa watched as they spoke about eating at Merlin's before they *poofed* from her sight. The flow of bodies was heavily congested near the arrival and departure pads and made it hard to hear Leon when he spoke up.

"Let's check in with Ell before we head up," he advised and led the way to the main center help desk.

As they all approached the desk, Ell popped up from below the desk counter, dumping a mess of papers that she was clutching close to her chest across the surface. While she tried to sort the stack and keep a small pile in her grasp, a strand of hair fell between her eyes. Annoyed, she blew at it relentlessly as she attempted to remove it from tickling her nose. Ell was cross-eyed when they arrived at the desk, her gaze focused on the annoying lock dangling in her view.

Jumping as soon as she noticed Bobo first and then the others, she dropped the remaining papers and stared at the floor as the files fell back down. Pouting, she sighed and tucked the defiant tress behind her ear with one of her now empty hands. "Hey," Ell said before dipping down to pick up the papers again.

There were dark circles under the woman's eyes, and her mane looked messier than usual – if such a thing could be achieved. Her attire appeared worn for wear, and she seemed lethargic as she muddled about her work.

"Ell, are you all right?" Vanessa asked, clearly concerned for the poor girl.

"Hmm?" she hummed as she popped back up and tried to

sort through the paperwork. "Oh, I'm all right."

"You don't look it, darling," Lyx pointed out. "You look like you've not slept in days."

"Oh, that…" Ell sounded like it just dawned upon her that she appeared tired to them. "Things have been crazy here," she said finally. "I wound up pulling a double—" she paused to check her watch, and her eyes bulged as she realized the hour, "Make that a triple shift."

"My word, woman. That's positively absurd. Why on Raen would you do such a thing?" Bobo gasped.

She fussed with the papers again. "Dispatch stumbled onto a massive grey spell. Caused a big uproar. A few blue cloaks made a big stink about it before they called a meeting. Not long after, there was a team ordered to sweep the area that was pinged on the Great Orb. Only a few hours later there was a big scene caused at the Dark Market. Messed up a lot of future Dark Market raids and that caused even more chaos." She looked at all of them. "What are you guys doing here?"

"Coven called us in for a meeting with the High Priest Council," Leon answered.

"Oh. Let me tell them you're all here," she scrambled for a crystal ball. She mentally linked with the orb, and it floated in her hand with a dim yellow aura. One of the secretaries picked up, and Ell dropped her voice down as she informed the blue cloak's administrator that Vanessa and Leon had arrived. For some reason, the bright expression on the tired woman's face slowly left her features before it twisted into confusion. She looked upset and like she wasn't sure what to do, almost as if she were on the verge of crying.

"But—" she went very still as if she were being reprimanded. Frowning and trying to hide it, Ell nodded a bit too much while saying, "Yes, sir. I understand," over and over.

The orb went dark as it dropped back into Ell's palm. Slowly, she put the orb down, furrowed her brow, and pouted slightly. Her eyes were glued to the glass on the tiny pillow of the desktop.

"What is wrong, milady?" Bobo spoke while tilting his head at her.

"I…" she started, but she stopped as she eyed the orb over

like it wasn't real, and this was all some bad dream. Ell looked utterly baffled at whatever the blue cloak's secretary had told her. Slowly her vision rose to meet the concerned gaze of the group before her. Her voice was soft, quiet, and threaded with pain. "I've been instructed to keep you guys here until the Summoners arrive." She looked at them with a deep frown and reluctantly grabbed one of many bags of premade spells from under the desk and tossed the spell into the air.

Golden sparks erupted overhead, and the glittering string of magic grew in girth before zipping through the hustling and bustling crowed near the entryway. The magic weaved and dodged through gasping Coven members until it reached the doors where the golden light took form once again. This time, it took the shape of chain links. The front gates quickly were locked up and secured with the spellbound chains. Each large, glowing links that had appeared, crisscrossing in a dizzying path in front of the entrance to the Coven, pulsed with power and warning through the metal handles of the door. No one would get in, and no one would get out through those gates.

All the Coven members near the doors halted and spun to locate the origin of the spell and readied their weapon. Protocol for a spellbound chain spell within Coven confines. If anyone near Ell's desk moved, defensive magic was sure to fly. Spells just hit the fan.

"Was that really necessary?" Vanessa whispered.

"I'm sorry... they told me to keep you here or turn in my insignia," she whispered back.

Leon and Vanessa looked to each other, and their fear was mirrored in the other's face. All of a sudden, all eyes in Headquarters were on them, not just those at the front gates. A few nearby witches and wizards had their hands dipped in powder pouches, others had talismans in hand, and the remaining were clutching their weapons as they kept a sharp eye on the group at the front desk.

"So much for this being a routine check-in," Leon said to Vanessa through gritted teeth.

Ell looked particularly unhappy at the fact that she had to do this to her friends. The frown wasn't worn well on the sweet girl. It marred the innocent and soft features she usually portrayed. She didn't want to do this to them, but work was work. For whatever reason, the blue cloaks were hard up to make sure these four made it into their Council chambers that day.

Shortly after the embarrassing spell took place and all the active Coven members – new and old – had seen the group responsible for it being cast, the room was informed that the group was to be seen by the blue cloaks. Everyone exchanged glances before locking their sites on the four troublemakers. All the while Vanessa tried not to look as mortified as she felt.

Lyx huffed and threw her hands up on her hips. "This is not the sort of attention I like," she fussed quietly to no one in particular. Just as the demoness let out a groan of displeasure, a group of Summoners descended the spiraling staircase.

Their boots marching over the marble floors sounded like a small army stomping their way toward a battleground. The destination clearly set on reaching Vanessa and the others. She felt her crazed heartbeat attempting to keep up with the slamming of the boots against the hard, well-polished floors of Coven Headquarters. The only thing that she could think while this whole nightmare unfolded was that Leon and Lyx didn't even deserve to be there with her. Hex, Bobo shouldn't even be there.

There was no denying that they were all in trouble, Vanessa could feel it in her bones. Those three didn't need to be dragged into being disciplined simply because the Coven had paired them together for a short period of time. Any punishment that the High Priest Council would decree wouldn't be fair to anyone but her. After all, it was she who chose to delve deep into the caverns despite Coven orders, not them.

Vanessa knew that once they were behind the Council chamber's closed doors, she would beg their pardon and take full blame for everything ... depending on what the Council knew, of course. No sense in gabbing out all the gory details and getting them all in trouble if this was nothing more than a routine checkup from the blue cloaks. From the spell Ell had cast to lock them all in and the sound of the boots hammering away over the Coven floors, Vanessa doubted that was the case.

She looked at Leon, and he gave her a harsh glare. One that silently told her to say nothing about anything. That only made her worries worse. She drew her thumb to her mouth and bit the tip of it as she thought to herself, trying desperately to think of anything to get out of this whole mess. But she was coming up with nothing.

The quick, unified clicks of the Summoners' boot soles over the marbled flooring came to a sudden stop a few feet shy of Vanessa and the others. The silence that drifted in the thick tension that was rising in the air all around them, it was almost enough to send Vanessa into a panic attack. She held her hand over her heart to check the poor overworked muscle and let out a slow, calming breath. The voice that followed thereafter sent her heart rate climbing once again. Dread. Cold and hopeless dread took hold of the poor witch.

"If you would please hand over your weapons, dust pouches, talisman, and spell casting utensils," the male Summoner at the head of the group ordered politely in a warm voice. But his features betrayed that voice tenfold. He had cold, slate stained eyes and ginger-blonde hair that was shaved short and tapered off in the back. He was medium in height, but his aura poured out of him in a thick, domineering fashion. His fake smile never reached his eyes and seemed to mock the group before him. Vanessa sneered at the Summoner that was leading the group and who would escort them to the blue cloaks' Council room. It was the notorious Riker.

A man decorated in more war stories than he had badges. Singlehandedly, he had taken down a cult of blood mages when out on a routine checkup of the Borlimane district. While outnumbered, he had been hit with an arcane spike. The wound was opened further by another blood mage, causing the gash to rip from just above the eyelid to across the side of his skull and stopping at just at the back of his ear. Riker's hair being shaved made the thirteen-year-old scar visible to everyone who dared to disbelieve the tale.

He was well known for his firm belief of the Coven's laws and knew far too well how to separate personal feelings from professional ones. When he was suited up for work, you stayed on his good side. Not because he was bad… just that he was so good at his job one had to wonder if he was a golem following orders rather than a human being protecting the laws and order of Aeristria.

The Summoners stood like soldiers lined up behind a trusted general. Riker didn't seem to look as if he cared one way or another about the whole ordeal. He was simply carrying out orders. And his demands for their spelling items didn't make him bat an eyelash or give a sympathetic glance toward anyone standing within the cluster of riffraff before him.

"What?" Vanessa's voice dropped a few octaves, and her eyes narrowed at the collection of Summoners, especially at Riker. She meant to think it, but the filter between her brain and mouth apparently didn't get the memo. She half-expected Leon to pitch a fit and tell her to shut up, but he looked as flabbergasted as she did.

Leon took a few steps in front of Vanessa, and his fury was radiating from him like an out of control fire. "I demand an explanation!"

"Leon, darling, you should calm down," Lyx said softly while reaching to grab his arm.

It all happened at once. Lyx reached for Leon, Leon jerked away from the brush of her fingertips, and all those Summoners were pointing wands, staves, talisman, and dipping their hands into dust pouches, and they were all ready to blast Lyx into the next life. She went perfectly still. Bobo growled, and their attention became divided.

Swiftly realizing that they were more prepared to blast the two demons out of existence before they'd point a wand at him, Leon slowly raised his hands and relinquished his anger. "She was just trying to calm me down." Leon's voice was surprisingly less agitated. The potential threat pointed at his pet had sobered him up from his outburst. "I just want to know why we need to go through such drastic measurements," he added. Riker, who had made no movement since the initial outburst, snapped his cold and unrelenting gaze to Leon.

"The High Priest Council has instructed us to bring you before their Council unarmed and unable to perform even the most basic of spells. I'm … *we* … are just carrying out their orders." He looked the small group over and continued, "Please, don't make a scene and don't make this any more difficult than it needs to be."

Vanessa rolled her eyes. "Pfff… telling us to not make a scene when that is all that you've done since we came in on the arrival gate."

"Vanessa," Leon snapped.

"No!" she yelled back at him and then turned her seething rage to the uneasy Summoners stacked behind the coldhearted ring leader. "If I wanted to be treated like a criminal, I would have gone on the run instead of waltzing through the front doors!"

Riker smiled then, and it seemed almost sinister resting upon his lips. "Is there something that you've done that would cause you to be on the run from the Coven, Hunter Peterson?"

She opened her mouth and instantly shut it. In the moments of silence that followed, Vanessa held a staring match with Riker and, while she did, she imagined punching that stupid grin off his face. "No," she growled back, finally.

"Then I fail to see where the issue is. If you've done something wrong, I could understand your desire to run... but if you've done nothing wrong then handing over your spelling objects should be the least of your concerns." After he spoke he held out his palm and curled his fingers toward him a few times in a row, coaxing them to hand over their spelling items.

Right as Vanessa and Leon had started to remove them, two Summoners speedily came over to relieve them of their things before they had time to even contemplate reconsidering complying with them. Promptly, two more came to take Lyx's whip and Bobo's battle-ax.

"Hey, what are you doing?" Lyx snipped while swatting at a Summoner's hands that were getting too close to her hips. After realizing they were taking away her weapon, she pouted and huffed as they carried out the action. "Could have asked," she hissed while crossing her arms under her breasts and rolling her eyes aggressively.

Bobo stood still and silent as if he had expected all this all along. Vanessa felt the worst for him. He was a towering ogre that most of the Coven didn't look at fondly since the day she summoned him. Bobo was a high-class demon of the underworld, and not one revered as the usual demon that a Coven member could summon. He was supposed to be a ruthless killing machine that excelled at his job better than all other classes of demons. Once upon a time, he was the guard to imprisoned devils and other convicts of hell. Besides, when a creature his size could snarl and make the masses flee in horror, they'll point their spells at him before they'll direct a harmful spell elsewhere.

Poor Bobo was doing as he should by being a quiet and compliant giant. Vanessa spared a look over her shoulder to him, her lip jutting out in a sympathetic pout, but as soon as her eyes locked with Bobo's, he just closed his eyes slowly and gave a leisurely, almost unnoticed, nod of his head. A quiet, *it's all right* from her trusted pet… no. Her trusted partner.

"Can we get on with it?" Vanessa couldn't drop the attitude. She wanted to get out from under the condescending glares from her peers and co-workers. Even if that meant being delivered into the blue cloaks' Council room.

The head Summoner gave her a short smile and a half-nod before whirling a finger around his head. Instantly, the group of Summoners circled around her and the others. "Let's go," he said in a dark tone.

There was nothing so humiliating as the countless eyes that watched in silence, or the whispers that were passed between onlookers as they made their way to the Council's chambers.

"What did she do this time?"

"She's been a problem for the Coven since the day she walked through the front doors."

"It's no wonder she doesn't have any friends. Who'd want to be friends with a girl that will get you killed or drag you into a situation that will cost you your insignia?"

"I can't believe she got Leon in trouble!"

"What a wicked witch dragging down such a talented Spellweaver."

"How could she get Leon tangled up in her mess?"

"She should have quit ages ago. Why is she even allowed to be in the Coven?"

"I hope that they eliminate that terrible Hunter."

Each whisper that Vanessa heard made her mood sink, her pride deflate, and caused her feet to drag as she followed heartbrokenly behind Riker and his crew. It was like her soul was being sliced by tiny daggers, each slice was a word that was whispered behind her back but left a permanent mark. All the opinions that fellow Coven members thought of her were murmured as she hung her head low while escorted by the Summoners to the Council room. It hurt. It hurt so much. Her eyes blurred with the promise of tears, and a lump grew in her throat. Vanessa fought back the urge to cry by biting the side of her cheek and staring at the feet of the Summoners leading the way.

She knew ever since she came to the Coven, that people had a hard time accepting her. She never got spells right the first time. She always seemed to get into trouble. She always was in over her head... Now? Now she was dragging down the people that she cared about the most. They didn't deserve this.

Her negative thoughts shattered like a pane of thin glass over concrete flooring. Leon's fingertips brushed against the palm of her hand, breaking her of the self-loathing spiral that she was starting on. Slowly, those large digits crept over the palm of her hand and curled around until her appendage was tucked safely away in his warm hand cuddle. She looked at his hand holding hers and then up to him. A cross of wonder and confusion stretched out over her expression.

Leon whispered, "Stay with me." Then he gave her hand a light squeeze. "You're strong. The strongest witch I know." He smiled then.

Suddenly, the whispers didn't matter and the dreaded spiral up to the Council room wasn't so bad.

 *Chapter 25:*

Darker.

The hall that led to the High Priest Council Room seemed darker today, somehow. Perhaps the lighting was dimmer, or the shadows from the group of bodies swimming through the tight space made the walk seem more ominous than normal and that had made the illumination seem less vibrant than usual. Either way it went, Vanessa's poor gut was flipping about so crazily that she was sure she was one more stomach cartwheel away from losing her breakfast right there in the main hall.

The doors at the end of the hall got closer and closer, much to Vanessa's chagrin, and it was making it difficult to calm her nerves. She wondered what would happen behind those doors, but even her imagination was too frightened to entertain the nightmare that the blue cloaks could bestow upon the victim of their choosing. And what they could do didn't hold a candle next to what a Celestial could do...

They reached the end of the hall sooner than she was ready for, and she was a whirlwind of emotion. Riker turned to halt the group and then knocked on the Council room doors with a thundering fist. After a moment, the muffled voice of one of the blue cloaks told them to enter. Riker opened the door enough to slip through a crack. Vanessa couldn't see him anymore, but she heard him speak to the Council. "High Priests and Priestesses, I've brought the Coven members you asked for."

"You may let them in," one of them answered.

"As you wish." After a moment, the doors opened wide enough to let all of them enter the room. Every nerve in Vanessa's body was screaming for her to run, but she bravely lifted her head, let out a long wind of air, and took a step forward into the room.

The thirteen members were spread out in their throne-like

chairs just like before. Each of them seeming taller as they were seated with their backs completely straight, and their features and clothing looked almost regal in appearance as their hard gazes were fixed on those entering the room. Vanessa blamed the thrones they were all placed upon for their noble aura, but she knew that it was their wisdom and power that they all possessed that made them come off that way. The Celestial was the only one that didn't come off like that. The Celestial came off as divine, and rightfully so.

Although she walked proudly into the Council room, Vanessa's steps themselves were full of doubt and sluggishly slow in pace. Once all of them were fully inside the room, Riker and the other Summoners bowed respectfully to the Council members. Leon, Vanessa, and the others followed suit as well.

"You may leave us, Summoners," one of the female blue cloaks spoke, and the Summoners all lifted from their bow and started to file out of the room. It felt less stuffy in there now that they were all gone, but that peaceful image disintegrated as soon as the massive double doors slammed shut behind the leaving party. Vanessa looked back, and to her dismay, the doors were in fact closed, and as her gaze drifted back to the front of the room, she realized that she, Leon, Bobo, and Lyx were all alone before the High Priest Council. The most trusted and powerful people the Coven had to offer…

And she was scared out of her mind.

"Do you know for what you were summoned, Hunter Peterson and Spellweaver Zvěrokruh?"

They all looked to one another hoping that someone had the answer, but they both turned back to the Council and stated in unison, "Uuuh… nooo."

A few of the Council members looked unamused, a few others shifted in their seats looking like they were about to pop off at the mouth because they assumed Vanessa and Leon were joking around. "We are not sure why we were summoned," Vanessa added more seriously than her first response. Her eyes were burning with tears brought on by the blinding light that the Celestial naturally gave off. Even from under the thick fabric of the spelled blue cloak it was immensely difficult to endure.

They nodded and regained their composure. "You have been

brought before the Council because of this," Torro McTaggart spoke while stroking at his fiery red beard and staring the group down like he was judging a handful of criminals silently. He then motioned for the female blue cloak Mia to step forward and place something upon a short podium in the center of the raised flooring.

The fair Mia stepped forward and dropped a crystal ball onto a deep red, crushed velvet pillow and walked back to her seat. The moment that Vanessa saw it, she knew why they had been called before the Council. Surprisingly, the crystal ball held not a scratch on it. However, she shouldn't be concerned with such a silly detail under present circumstances. She tried to refrain from swallowing the lump of fear and regret that was ever-growing in her throat, and her eyes darted up from the ball to the thirteen members and their harsh gazes.

"Does this crystal ball belong to you, Hunter Peterson?" Torro asked, and his eyes felt like they were burrowing into her soul.

Her mouth was dry. Her skin felt clammy and all of a sudden, she felt the color drain from her face as her stomach soured. "I…" she started, but what the hex was she going to say? *It looks pretty good for being kicked into the face of a minotaur?* She bit her lip and tried to think of something that would sound reasonable and had little to no chance of getting her and the others into trouble. She wasn't coming up with anything, and the Council members were not pleased with how long it took the witch to produce an answer.

"Hunter Peterson, is this crystal ball familiar to you or not? Answer the High Priest Torro," Isolde asked as she narrowed her frightfully bright eyes at Vanessa.

All crystal balls looked the same, but that didn't mean you couldn't detect who it belongs to. For one, the magic impression retained within the orb was a dead giveaway. Magic was like a fingerprint, it was left behind in every summoning, every potion mixed, every spell cast, and every crystal ball call. Also, any spell caster knew that crystal balls held magic from the user within the orb, and that magic was like a calling device. You could find it by just reaching out magically. Just thinking about her orb made her magic reach out to the crystal ball before her. That was answer enough. There was no doubt in her mind now that the crystal ball on the podium was, indeed, her own. So, if she lied, she would get nowhere, and it would only anger the Council. She sighed and lifted her gaze to them. "It's mine," she answered honestly.

Mia pointed to the object in question and asked, "Do you know where we found your crystal ball, Hunter Peterson?"

Again, Vanessa didn't want to answer, and she nervously chewed at the inside of her bottom lip and fidgeted with her fingernails while in deep thought. She felt like the Council was making her put together and nail her own coffin with each answer she gave. But, what about everything that she—

"Hunter Peterson!" High priest Dmitri yelled so loud that it made Vanessa feel like she was about to jump out of her own skin. "The Council awaits your answer," he added in a much softer tone.

She looked at Bobo, Lyx, and Leon. She could save them from punishment if she just told the truth. She lowered her head and answered finally. "Yes, High Priest Councilmen, I know where you must have found it."

"Why were you in the tunnels after we advised you to not proceed further. It is a job for the Summoners," Mia looked pained as she asked the question.

"I… I know. I just heard word that no Summoners had been sent. The people of Tolvade know nothing of the happenings and wouldn't be prepared for an attack if one of the hellhounds had managed to escape. They would be in horrific danger, and no one would be able to answer the distress signals or calls soon enough. Especially with the encroaching yearly blizzard. There is no telling how long those tunnels are or even where they go—" she was interrupted again, this time by Isolde.

"That is not a concern for a Hunter. We have chosen to send Summoners to minimize damages to the Coven, the people of Aeristria, and to ensure that the academy isn't in any more danger."

"Then why weren't Summoners sent out yet?" Vanessa snapped.

The Council looked like she had started cracking a whip in the center of the room. "How would you know if we've dispatched Summoners or not, Hunter Peterson?" Isolde snapped back.

"I…" Banish a banshee, if she told them how it would ruin Tasgall's reputation, her business, and her father's image.

Instinctively, her eyes shifted to Torro and then dropped her gaze. She bit her lip. No, she needed that ace up her sleeve, and she needed to protect Tasgall. There was only one option for her because giving an honest answer wasn't. "Have you sent out Summoners?"

Isolde blinked her eyes and gaped her mouth, offended at the question. "How *dare* you question the Council! We've all done nothing but serve the Coven for years faithfully. You come in here and can barely adhere to a simple rule we've set in place and have the audacity, after defying our word - which is LAW - to question our means and methods?"

"I meant no disrespect," Vanessa tried to reason with them.

"You were out without speaking to your partner, I presume?" Torro asked calmly.

She swallowed whatever reply she had for Isolde and nodded to High Priest Torro. "Yes, sir."

"And your pet?" he asked, eyeing the ogre up.

Vanessa could feel Bobo tense up as soon as the Council member looked to him, and she immediately jumped to his defense. "No. He knew nothing. I snuck out."

"Surely not for long. You two are tethered. Speak, Botobolbilian, when did you meet up with your master?" Torro urged the ogre to speak for himself.

"Within the hour, sir," Bobo admitted without skipping a beat.

"Did you notify Leon of her whereabouts?"

"I ... I did not, sir."

"Did you assist her into the tunnels?"

"Yes... I did."

"Did you forget our warning? Did you dismiss our decree?" Torro tilted his head as he badgered Bobo with questions.

"I ignored it. I did wrong. Don't blame him," Vanessa shot out.

"Why should we not? Is he not just as guilty as you?" This came from Dmitri. "Not only did you defy our decree, but you put others at risk for your own selfishness. What was there to gain from you going down into those tunnels?"

"I just wanted to find out if the hellhounds were still down there. I just wanted to protect the people," she half whined her reply. She felt her chest tighten, and the world spin for a moment. She could feel herself slipping into a panic attack, and she had to focus on not hyperventilating while trying to explain her reasons to the Council while being berated with question after question.

"Hunter Peterson, how is putting the people in danger protecting them?" Isolde asked with a slight smirk on the corner of her lips.

"I... I wasn't thinking..." she stated finally and sounded so defeated as she uttered the words.

"You weren't thinking... do you *think* if anyone got harmed that those words would make the damages you brought about any better? You were reckless and risked the very people you claim you were trying to save!" Dmitri barked, and it felt like she was being slapped with words. Her vision was hazed by growing tears, and she looked to the ground to escape the Council seeing her on the brinks of weeping, and then there was a shadow blocking out the light that emitted from the Celestial. She looked up to see Leon's back as he was standing in front of her.

"She may have been wrong in acting on her own, but there is no reason to attack her verbally like this. Just—"

"Do you wish to stand alongside Hunter Peterson and have your insignia on the line as well, Spellweaver Zvěrokruh?" Isolde asked in a tone that sounded like honey-soaked venom.

Leon stumbled over finding words for a moment and that was when Vanessa lightly pushed him off to the side and slowly came to stand in front of him. "Are you ... taking my insignia away?" she whispered, and it sounded like it was laced in pain.

Dmitri sat up proudly in his chair and didn't even look at her when he stated, "Would you think someone that can barely perform their job and can't even follow standard procedure would be fit to wear the Coven insignia?"

She opened her mouth and closed it and then searched the floor. They were taking away her insignia? They were letting her go? This... no.

This wasn't happening.

"I will gladly hand over my insignia if I can have but one

question answered!" Leon had his hands at his side balled up into fists, and his chest puffed out as he boldly stared down each one of the High Priest Councilmen.

"Very well," Mia answered. "If you feel that strongly, ask your question. I implore you to remember your words well, Spellweaver Zvěrokruh."

He stepped forward again, but this time standing at Vanessa's side. He pointed to the crystal ball, "How is it that Vanessa was in the tunnels from just before dusk until almost dawn and in less time than she had been down there, the Coven was able to locate her orb, get back to headquarters, make a report, hold a meeting with the other members, and summon all of us here? Unless..." Leon scanned the Council with a mock grin, "... someone knew how to navigate the tunnels already."

There was a stunned silence over the High Priest Council. The first to speak was a very red-in-the-face Isolde. "What a presumptuous remark from a Spellweaver that didn't even contact the Coven when his partner had gone against our wishes!"

"Leave us." The voice made everyone go quiet and turn to face the source. The Celestial was standing and staring down the group at the bottom of the steps with a set of inquisitive mother-of-pearl eyes.

"High One, you can't possibly be serious?" Dmitri gawked at the Celestial.

The blinding light faded as the Celestial turned to face Dmitri. "But I am. Again," the Celestial turned to face the other six members, "I ask you to take leave into the Council chambers. I wish to speak with Leon, Vanessa, and their pets alone." Her voice was soft and sweet and far more soothing than any voice that Vanessa had heard since they walked through the doors to the High Priest Council Room or even the Coven. Though the actual gender of the Celestial was not known, Vanessa always viewed it as a feminine force and referred to her as such.

Isolde stood in a huff and was the first to storm out of the room. The rest followed to the Council chambers. The women went to the left, and the men exiting to the separate chamber room to the right. When they were all gone, the Celestial sat back down in the center throne and motioned at the group with her palm turned up. "Explain to me, Hunter Peterson, what it was that you found down in the tunnels."

Chapter 26:

Vanessa didn't know how to feel about the Celestial's request, much less about being alone in the Council room with only one member of the Council … and it wasn't just any member, it was the Celestial! THE CELESTIAL. The highest being in the Coven. Timeless, ageless, and pure power and kindness were some of the qualities that made the Celestial a most trusted member and being. The balance between genders, the voice between worlds, and it wished to speak with her. Alone.

Well, Leon, Lyx, and Bobo too. But … still.

Vanessa was so caught off guard that she stood there at the bottom of the steps transfixed on the bright ribbons of light that seeped out from behind the hood of the cloak that the Celestial wore. She recalled all that had happened and thought that if she wanted her and Leon to keep their jobs, and possibly their lives, she needed to speak up now.

"High One, I must reiterate the fact that I truly meant no harm to anyone. I was simply doing what I believed to be right. I joined the Coven to protect the people and enforce the High Priest Council's laws, not hurt the people I'm trying to serve and break those laws."

The divine one nodded once softly, silently telling Vanessa that she believed and understood where she stood on the matter. Then quietly waited for the Hunter to carry on with her tale.

Vanessa went on to explain the spells that were around the entrance of the tunnels, the fact that a minotaur was guarding them, the happening with her crystal ball, and even went on to explain the two tunnels lined in prison cells holding the ogres that were barely living … if that was what one would call it. She spoke a little slower when speaking of the gray magic she performed to give the ogres peace. When the Celestial said nothing, she continued with her story to tell her of the hellhounds and escaping the tunnels to go home and then, after only a few hours of sleep, had been summoned back to headquarters. Through it all, the divine one sat unmoving and without a sound listening to the tale.

"And… here I am…" Vanessa finished.

There was a longwinded hush that ate at the room and then moved on to eat away at Vanessa's fragile nerves. The harsh and unwavering stare of the Celestial made her want to fidget even more, but it didn't make her feel like she was in any way threatened. A good few minutes went by before they'd hear the voice of the High One again. Oddly, it brought them comfort instead of dread.

"Rest easy, little one. I believe that you speak the truth." As soon as the sentence left the Celestial's mouth, Vanessa let out a breath she didn't realize she was holding and most of the tension melted from her form. "I have had my questions on where some of the Councilmen's loyalties and priorities lie. I fear that whoever the fiend is that is hiding the truth of what is inside those tunnels is the same culprit that wishes to eliminate you and your friends as a threat to them and their plans. Not knowing who among my Council I could trust completely, I asked them all to leave to hear the truth from you, Vanessa." She stood then and dusted unseen dirt from her cloak, the action letting patches of grand, blinding white light peek through the seam of the blue cloak. "I will form a team of Summoners at once to follow you and Spellweaver Zvěrokruh down into the tunnels where you will make sure that the hellhounds are still captured as you said. If it is to be found true what you say, then the full search of the tunnels will begin immediately. If it is found that you have spoken falsely and lied to the Council and me, I will have your life in the placement of your insignia."

"Yes. Of course. Thank you!" Vanessa chirped. She didn't care that her life was just threatened because they would find the proof in the tunnels, and she would be saved from this nightmare.

"What an odd and brave little witch you are, Vanessa Peterson," the Celestial said with a smile as radiant as the light that emitted from her being.

Suddenly, before Vanessa – or anyone else – could say anything, there was a loud crash from one of the chamber rooms.

Then a yell and something that sounded like a muffled explosion from the other. Both doors that led to each of the opposing High Priest's chambers blasted off their hinges and were sent flying across the Council room. Before the divine one could react, two forms emerged from the clouds of billowing smoke and cascading debris.

The blue cloaks Isolde and Dmitri pointed their wands at the High One, and the spells shot out from the tips of the black lacquered wands before Vanessa could scream. Silver snakes with bodies like chains slithered out and swam through the air toward the divine one at lightning speeds. The mouths of the snakes opened to reveal sharp curved fangs that sank deep into the Celestial's flesh once they made contact, and it caused the being to scream out in unfathomable anguish before seizing up in place as the bodies, or chains, of the snake spell wrapped around her. Both venom hide binding spells were now in place, and the Celestial was incapacitated.

She started to fall forward down the steps, and Leon rushed forward to catch her and instantly began to drag her to a safer place in the room. Other Council members poured out from the chambers, stumbling and holding their heads. While Dmitri pointed his wand at the new threat in the room, Isolde pointed hers at Leon as he tried to find cover in an open room.

They had no spell pouches. No weapons. Nothing… nothing to save them from the deadly spells that were to be slung at them. Vanessa saw the wand being poised in their direction, and then she screamed at him, "Leon, watch out!" There was no time. She'd never make it to him before the spell did. All her body could do is stand there and scream out, "Leon!" Right as the words left her mouth, she saw Lyx dive in front of the arcane blast. The demoness hugged Leon and her succubus wings encased around the divine one and her master as she awaited the inevitable pain of the blow. Only, she felt nothing.

She started to unfurl from Leon and blinked down at those in her embrace completely bemused. Turning slowly, she looked behind her. A massive shadow had been cast over them and surrounded the three because of the large ogre that stood at her back. Just as she turned to see Bobo standing there behind her, she smiled warmly. There was a comfort that washed over her when she saw the large demon. Only, that moment of comfort would be snatched from her as she saw the rivulets of blood drop to the floor. It splattered around his feet in large, crimson pools. Her unbelieving eyes rose to see the black smoke that was spiraling up from the impact on the ogre's chest. With a grunt of pain, he hit the floor on one knee while coughing and struggling for breath. With each cough, he sputtered up more blood onto the marbled flooring. It sprayed in a cone of cherry-red droplets as he choked and strived for air. He seemed to sway in place for a moment, a short dizzy spell that spiraled out of control and the beast fell to the side, only to catch himself with a gigantic hand. As it slammed onto the hard ground below, he stifled a painful growl.

"Bobo!" Lyx's voice cracked as she frantically scrambled over to him on all fours and gently tried to pull him back to her, but the giant creature fell backward from the tug with next to no grace at all. Slamming down onto his back, all the succubus could do was watch in horror as he sprawled out limply in front of her. "No," she whispered.

Lyx's hands covered her mouth as she quickly looked him over. Her shaking hands were reaching out to his gaping wounds and stopping suddenly at the charred flesh with a stifled sob. She recoiled her fingertips from the singed edges of the wound that pulsed and quivered as blood quickly rose to fill the shallow hole in his chest. She settled with touching Bobo's face instead, and she couldn't control her urge to cry any longer as she saw nothing but pain sweeping over the strong demon's features. Uncontrollably, she wept as she spoke softly to him, "I don't know what to do. I..." she started to cry harder, "You foolish beast. Why.... Why?"

The pain on his face melted away long enough for him to produce the most charming smile. "I... I couldn't stand the thought... of... you... being hurt," Bobo wheezed and then he struggled for breath before his eyes rolled into the back of his head, the smile faded with his breath, and his body went still.

"Bobo," Lyx spoke with fear lining her voice as she called out his name, and the panic only picked up as Bobo lay speechless. "Stay with me. Please?... Bobo?" She sniffled and then heard another arcane blast. Instantly, she shielded them with her immense leathery wings as the rubble from the ceiling overhead came raining down on them.

From afar, Leon managed to get the Celestial behind a pillar and was calling to Lyx frantically, but she didn't hear it, and she didn't care about anything else at that moment. Only the ogre that lay lifeless in her cradling embrace.

As Lyx's wings lifted from Bobo, they revealed blood-red glowing eyes peering out from under the tough and massive wingspan. A snarling maw full of glistening ivory fangs followed by a line of ridged teeth peered out from a livid face bent with every blessing that Hell had to offer. Lyx's once dainty horns were now massive and twisting off to the side. Her body color had changed, and she was now painted a jet black with molten orange veins webbing all over the visible skin, and her once ebony silken strands were now a dancing uncontrollable mane of blazing fire. Her spiked tail whipped at the floor and easily broke the marble beneath it, shattering it like glass under the force of the tremendous blow.

Relinquishing her loving hold on the mammoth-sized beast, she slowly stood up, curled her dagger-like fingers, and letting an ear-splitting scream peal from her lips. Wild red eyes became fixed on her target as Lyx set her heated glare on Dmitri. Flapping her wings, the succubus hurled herself into the air and leaped into the fray like a wild beast.

Meanwhile, Vanessa dodged another blast spiraling out of a High Priests wand as Isolde controlled two blue cloaks with blood magic. Their bodies weren't as fluid as the others that fought back, and their movements were ridged as they tried to fight off the control that Isolde had on them. But, to their disgust, each time their stuttering movements ended with complying with her magic's command. She made them fling spells at their comrades as she laughed maniacally. All they could do is hopelessly beg their friends to kill them and save the city.

Arcane blasts and spells that could cripple Vanessa and the others for life were dizzily being shot through the room as she raced over to Bobo. Sliding on the floor she slammed into his massive body and lay her head on his chest to escape a blinding bolt of magic as it flew by, grazing the edge of her ear with sizzling heat. She cried out in pain and quickly snuffed out her whimpers as she tried to listen to Bobo's heartbeat. Her own heart was hammering away at her breast and it consumed her hearing. She could taste her own pulse on her tongue, and it made it difficult to make out if the ogre had life in him with all the chaos that ensued around them. She was breathing heavily as she frantically tried to find a breath or heartbeat from him.

"No. No. No," she repeated as she moved her long hair from his chest so that her bare ear could have less of a barrier between them. She felt her lip quiver as she heard nothing. She sat up and shook him lightly as if she was trying to wake him from a most inconvenient nap. "Bobo?" She sniffled and sputtered with tears that she swiftly sucked back in and tried to stay strong as she spoke to her pet. "Botobolbilian, you get up right now," her voice cracked at the end of her demand. Tears stung her eyes. Spells continued to whizz through the enclosed room. "Please. No. I can't lose you." She started to cry. "Bobo. Wake up, buddy." She eyed him over and then the space around them. Leon was in the distance, but the pillars were too far away, and she was sure to get hit before she'd lug the ogre to safety. "Wake up, Bobo!" she shouted and then lay her forehead down on his chest and bawled as she screamed into his chest obdurately, "Get up! Get up! Get up!" She wailed wordlessly and relentlessly into the beast's singed button-up shirt. Her sobbing slowed as she clutched the edges of his jacket in her fists, the final flame of her hope dimming against his unmoving body. "Please?" she whined.

This was the extent of what she had to offer. Panic and giving up. She was so worthless. All her training and studies and hard work ended with her shielding her possibly dead friend from debris with her own fragile body and hoping that the battle between the blue cloaks didn't get the rest of them all killed. "Bobo, I don't know what to do," she hiccupped as she spoke to her silent ogre.

"Vanessa!" Leon yelled, and she turned to face him with tears cascading freely down her face. "Hurry! Get to cover!" he urged her while holding the High One half in his lap.

She looked at the venom hide snake bindings and how their fangs sank in past the cloak and into the soft flesh of the ethereal being. The pain that was evident on the Celestial's face was clear as day, and she was struggling with trying to free herself. Beads of sweat forming on her brow as she mentally battled with the spells that Isolde and Dmitri had cast upon her. There was no doubt that the being could free herself but not before a higher death toll transpired. Vanessa looked at Leon as he held out a hand to her and motioned for her to come to him. But how could she leave Bobo behind?

There was a howl-like scream, and it tore Vanessa and Leon's attention from one another to the direction of the room it had been produced from. Their eyes were met with the sight of Lyx as she flew above one of the chamber doors and flung one of the banner poles at Isolde who happily made High Priest Ronan, who she was controlling with blood magic, take the blow for her. The man crumpled and fell back. Frustrated at her missed mark, Lyx screamed up into the ceiling before swiftly twisting her body and flying down in a blinding rage. Her sights set on the crazed Isolde as she laughed and played with the blue cloaks' lives that she controlled like she was the conductor and the Council members were the orchestra.

Isolde kicked Ronan out of the way with a sneer, but as she looked down to place her soled foot upon him, Lyx took the advantage and zipped behind her. Plucking the blood mage from her safe perch behind the wall of blue cloaks she was controlling, Lyx started to fly high up in the air as Isolde twisted and turned and screamed while wildly flinging spells at the succubus.

Dmitri caught a glimpse of the blood magic fading from some of the Council members and with the lack of enemies in the room, all the able High Priest Council members were coming back to the real threat and aiming their spells for him. He snarled and speedily threw a spell at Lyx, and it ripped through her right wing. Flapping awkwardly, she sputtered through the air and then took a nose dive into the elaborate highbacked chairs that lined the stage. Racing through them, they piled up as they slammed into one another until the succubus's crash came to a halt. Isolde broke some of her fall but didn't die. It did, however, knock the rebel blue cloak out.

Sounds of the broken furniture tumbling down the splintered pile of wood could be heard as Lyx emerged gasping for air and groaning in pain from a pile of snapped wooden seats and dust clouds. Dmitri flung another arcane blast at the succubus, and it broke off one of her horns and the force of the blow caused Lyx's head to thrust into the corner of a chair. Blood poured out from a gash that formed on the side of her skull, splitting open the once unblemished skin. A slow trickle of blood ran down the side of her face before it steadily dripped down onto the heap of broken chairs.

There was nothing Vanessa could do. Nothing. She watched as her friends all got hurt, while others stood on the cusp of death, and others battled fiercely for their lives, she sat weeping in the middle of the room like a little girl with a busted knee. Her hands clung to Bobo's suit, and she tried to imagine him scolding her for wrinkling the fabric, but he was so still. Just like Lyx was now.

Worthless. Leon was wrong. She wasn't strong, she was WEAK!

She was flooded with memories of being taunted and teased. They slipped in-between the sheets of her mind like cackling ghosts baring the painful moments that she had long since buried deep within her past. Hurtful words from those that didn't see her as anything but a screw-up and trouble maker invaded her thoughts. It descended upon her like a thick cruel fog.

Like it was happening all over again, she could hear whispers from peers and people that she didn't know harshly judging her. Soft mocking laughter that haunted her. Watchful and judgmental eyes following her every movement. All of them weighing down upon her like rocks tied to her body as she tried to swim to the surface of her own self-doubt. The crippling depression sunk in past blood and bone and started to make a nest inside of her heart. Deep seeded darkness rose up to snuff out the light of hope that she had slowly built over the years with hard work and devotion.

Breathe. She could just breathe if she reached the surface. But every faded fit of laughter at her own expense, every set of eyes ever cast on her with a judgmental glimmer and every derogatory remark directed at her that swelled within her memories drug her deeper into the unforgiving murky waters of insecurity.

But through the mist of doubt and self-loathing came a wind. It held perfumes of promise and hope, and she felt the fog part and give way to warmer words and fonder remembrances. *"I'm saying, I have always thought of you as a pretty tough girl. You never really relied on anyone. From the first time you set foot into the Coven, you walked with such confidence and you seemed so sure of yourself. I never looked at you and thought of you as weak."* She could see Leon's serious gaze just like she did when he admitted those words to her. Still, it wasn't enough. For all the confidence that he thought she had, Vanessa couldn't help but be hesitant of herself and her abilities again. The onyx clouds of doubt crept through her, inching its way through her being to lay claim to any morsels of happiness that she might have. "He was just being nice to me," she whispered out loud to herself.

The voices in her head had other things for her to hear...
"You're strong. The strongest witch I know."

"I'm not strong enough!" She mentally yelled at herself.

The next memory grabbed hold of her and jerked her back to her senses. *"You summoned me!"* That memory hurled her right back into reality.

She looked down at Bobo's restful face as she remembered his words. *"Not even trying or paying attention, this little witch with a whole lot of sass and one nasty temper, summoned me... you are what most envy, Vanessa. You have what others crave. Power." ... "Use it."* Sunshine broke through the daunting spiritual storm clouds. Bobo was right. Leon was right. She wiped her nose on her sleeve and looked around herself and then up to Dmitri trying to fight back the horde of blue cloaks and then at all those that were wounded and writhing on the floor.

A spell. A spell was a collection of agents combined to create... she paused as she heard a whisper in her ear, *"A spell is created by magic that flows through all things. All things have magic, daughter of Saellah. Rise up and know your glory."*

Magic.

Magic wasn't dust or weapon or artifact. Those were just amplifiers. Vanessa stared down at her hands as this realization hit her, and she felt something inside her click. Like a lock buried deep within forgotten corners of her being was finally fitted with a key, the bindings on her soul were set free.

Magic... magic was... *everywhere!*

She started to stand still looking at her hands as a pulsing heat rose under the skin, they started to glow like small light barriers were surrounding them. They glittered like gold in the sun and they throbbed, and with each beat, the surrounding light grew in size. As she rose from the ground she felt like she had opened a floodgate to her mind. It all made perfect sense now.

The power flowed like a current of warmth and prickles that traveled up her arms, over her shoulders, sliding across every inch of skin as it overtook her form until she felt this immense surge of light, electric stings covering her body. Her hands, everything, it was all glowing like she was a walking golden statue. In her gut, she felt this power like a seed that sprouted up from the ground and was now blooming like a magnificent flower under the vibrant spill of a morning's first rays of illumination. It erupted all around her in a flash of yellow light, and the warmth that engulfed her was bordering hot.

She spoke, and her voice was calm and echoed as if she were everywhere in the room all at once. "Come to me." But the words in her mind that she reached out with were different, they were older and something she had never heard before. The bodies of the injured all gravitated and floated over to her, sliding swiftly into the dome of light that surrounded her.

"Heal…" The words were so simple. But meanings were so deep. She could hear the word whispered over and over in her mind, but it wasn't the word as she knew it. It was ancient and thick with smoky accents she had not heard before. But, just hearing the word made her body tingle, and a rush of unseen air flowed throughout the dome surrounding her. Picking up in speed and momentum as she reached her hands out and thought, *Heal,* in that ancient unheard tongue. Immediately, the power erupted from her like the first spew of lava from a volcano.

Bobo's wounds sizzled as the skin remade itself anew. The singed flesh disappeared and slowly became colorful and free of blood. The pole that was sticking out of Ronan's chest gradually rose up and inch by inch sliding out until it fell with a loud metallic ping to the floor, and the blood that poured out halted in its fountain-like flow. Shortly after it stopped, the hole of the wound commenced healing at a pace your eyes could not keep up with. Then, Lyx began to slowly return to normal, her skin starting to become that lovely shade of lavender and her head wound bubbled as the injury dissipated right before everyone's eyes. Her broken horn became mended and once more were the small, dainty horns that Vanessa had always seen and known the succubus by.

The Celestial's pain-stricken features had eased in discomfort, and Vanessa reached down and grabbed one of the venom hide binding snakes, the spell-snake wriggling madly in her grasp before the form seized and instantly fell into a pile of dust in Vanessa's hand. She touched the head of the second and its mouth lifted from the Celestial, and the divine being grabbed its neck and squeezed until it blew up like a balloon and then burst becoming black liquid in the Celestial's palm.

As soon as the bindings were removed, Vanessa's golden light faded, and she slumped to the floor, but inches from her head hitting the ground, Leon was there and cradling her in his arms as he dragged her into his embrace. "What in the name of magic did you just pull off, Vanessa?" But he got no reply as Vanessa drifted off into a forced sleep.

Free of her bindings, the divine one raised her hand and shot three white orbs of power at Dmitri with an irritated yell. "Shield your eyes or be blinded!" she growled her advice before dropping her cloak and slamming three more massive white orbs into Dmitri, who was still stumbling and attempting to regain his composure from the first volley of spells the Celestial had thrown at him. Upon impact, he flew back and while in mid-air the High One sputtered out a spell, and the same snakes that he had spelled her with shot through the space between them and slithered up his body and sunk their fangs into his neck. The same was thrust at the knocked-out Isolde who, even in her unconscious state, screamed out in pain as the fangs bore deep into her shoulder.

The heavenly creature approached the fallen Dmitri and stood over his body with confusion and hurt and anger all displayed across her usual calm, kind features. Her blinding, imperious light beat down upon his incapacitated body.

"Why?" she asked in a less than comforting tone.

"Because. Filth like that has no family ties. The Coven is dwindling in numbers and the gifted are less and less each year. Yet, trash like that orphaned girl has power that some of us didn't even have at the start. It's not right. We would have made a better Coven, a better world, if you hadn't interfered."

"You risked your brothers, your seat of power, your people… for what? So, a girl that doesn't know who her family is wouldn't be part of the Coven?"

"You'll never understand. Your kind only understands logic and love and faith. But we see things differently. If she has no family, we don't have a source of where her power came from. Don't you see? The magic of this land is fading. We need stronger members to keep the flow of magic from dying."

"Why should that matter?"

"Because we fear the unknown, High One. We would rather try to recreate it to understand it than let it be."

"You disappoint me…" She turned her back to him and spoke over her shoulder to the paralyzed Dmitri, "She could have taught you so much, but you feared it because you thought her lesser than you. What a foolish man you are. You risked everything and, in turn, lost it all for ignorant reasons," she spoke lowly and when she turned she found Mia, shielding her eyes as best she could while obediently holding out the cloak for the Celestial. "Thank you, Mia," she said sweetly as she accepted the cloak.

All the blue cloaks divided in the room. Some went to the Celestial, others went to aid fallen blue cloaks, and others went to mend Lyx, Leon, Bobo, and Vanessa. But, of all of them, the only one that needed any aid was Vanessa. However, no spell could fix what her body needed. She was drained. All the spell casting took its toll on the poor girl, and her body forced itself into a deep, deep sleep.

 *Chapter 27:*

Dmitri and Isolde were thrown into the dungeons after being stripped of their title and ranks in front of the entire Coven. They were further disgraced with the tale of their betrayal being bellowed before the crowd that had collected in Tolvade's town square immediately after the incident. Their trial would be held at a later date.

Along with the tale of the fight that had broken out in the Council room, another story was being whispered. They spoke of Vanessa and her ability to cast a spell – multiple ones – without any spell casting agents, relics, or weapons. In less than forty-eight hours, Vanessa had become one of the most well-known witches in the Coven, hex, on Raen. This time, it wasn't because she muddled a spell or got into trouble that she couldn't get out of on her own, and it wasn't even because she went against the laws or wishes of the Council. It was because she had done what no other in the Coven could: cast a spell with no outside reagents.

Vanessa heard beating wings near her head, and she waved lazily around her face with a groan. "Doctor, I believe the patient is waking," the high-pitched voice of a pixie called out to the doctor in the infirmary on the main level of the Coven.

Vanessa's eyes fluttered open. She was staring at a dream catcher lightly twisting from side to side overhead. Beneath it, an incense dish hung from a hook that jutted out from the wall over her medical cot. The witch blinked, watching the warm light of the mid-afternoon sun pour through the woven string in the center of the revolving dream-catcher, and followed the streams of perfumed smoke from the hanging incense bowl as it intertwined with the object.

"How are you feeling?" The voice came from the Coven infirmary doctor, Savanna Snow. Infamous for choosing the medical field of magic and for summoning not one, not two, not even three, but *seven* red imps when she summoned her demon pet. She was kind enough to name them all: Faith, Hope, Charity, Fortitude, Justice, Prudence, and Temperance.

The red imps were smaller and more prone to mischievous acts than their tan-skinned cousins. Red imps were the shade of a ripened cherry and had patches of snowy fur on their forearms, back, and ankles (the females had patches of fur covering their chest instead of their back), and they had thin, night shaded horns curving up from their head with two black, large doe eyes peering out with a child-like curiosity. The creatures looked like tiny, lithe framed humanoids with all the proper amounts of fingers and toes and with the addition of fangs, horns, and a long, barbed tail.

Their master, Savanna, had bleach blonde hair that was a few shades shy of being white, and it fell in large, soft curls just past her shoulders. She had a set of upturned eyes that were a startling shade of marine blue. She was in her typical doctor garb: A pair of formfitting cloth pants, a sky-blue corset, and her long white doctor coat with a red Coven insignia over the breast. Her hair was in a loose side ponytail and she was looking over a few sheets of paper on her clipboard. "Vanessa Peterson," she said the witch's name, and her voice was like honey.

"Doctor Snow," Vanessa said while holding her head in a slight sleepy daze. "How long have I been out of it?"

The doctor seemed to ponder the question for a moment. Before she could reply, Vanessa felt something clawing its way up on the opposite side of the bed. "A year!" the creature bellowed. A quick-handed Doctor Snow had already pointed a wand at the thing and blasted it with a tiny bolt of magic that sent the tiny beast flying off the edge of the bed and landing into a bedpan before Vanessa could even get a glimpse of it.

Strapping the wand back in place, Doctor Snow cleared her throat and said, "About two days." After answering the witch's question, she leaned over while pulling her fingers out of a dust pouch and snapping them together. The dust on them rubbing together to create a small light spell. Controlling the orb of light, she pinched her fingers to make the ball even smaller and leaned over

Vanessa in the cot. Her cool to the touch hands pressed Vanessa's eyes as she gently peeled them open. "I am just checking your pupillary light reflexes," Doctor Snow said softly.

"Boo!" A face popped up between Vanessa and the doctor, causing Vanessa to instantly draw back and flatten herself onto the cot like she was trying to become part of it. Ebony doe eyes gazed into her own as the creature they belonged to cackled at her surprised expression.

"They work," the red imp giggled as Doctor Snow palmed the demon's face and pulled it toward her and off the side of the bed.

"Faith, how many times do I need to tell you not to get in the patients' faces?" Doctor Snow griped to the tiny creature. The woman sighed and returned her attention to Vanessa. "Now, I'm just going to check one more time," she told Vanessa, and this time expecting the procedure made Vanessa loosen up and not be so tense as she watched the ball of magical light weave from side to side. Meanwhile, the imp peered over the side of the cot, its large curious eyes visible as it watched its owner work.

Brushing her fingers off by rubbing them together, the spell faded as it fell away in a glittering cascade of dust, and Savanna stood at her full height once more. "You seem to be just fine, Vanessa." She smiled sweetly to the witch as Vanessa started to sit up in the bed, expecting to feel pings of pain throughout her body but was pleasantly shocked to find that there wasn't a sore spot or irritated limb on her. She blinked down the length of her body as she inspected her frame for anything out of place or visually wrong. Savanna seemed to pick up on the young lady's concerns and laughed lightly as a quill and notebook floated next to the doctor's shoulder, writing down a few notes.

"Oh, you are right to be double-checking over yourself. That spell you performed, or the collection of them rather, almost put you down for the count. I'd love to run some more tests to see what could have sped up your healing process, but I'd have to say your fit as a fiddle and free to go."

"I... wait. I almost died?" Vanessa asked, trying to let the information sink in.

"You look dead to me," another red imp spoke as it leaped

around Doctor Snow and hid under her jacket suddenly.

As if used to the nuisance, Savanna ignored the imp and transfixed her gaze upon Vanessa. Doctor Snow waved the quill and notebook over to her writing-table after pointing to one of the pages in the floating notepad and then motioning for the pixie to follow it to her desk. The doctor grabbed a set of tongs from a hook on the wall and used them to pick up the incense from the hanging bowl to make sure it was still burning evenly before speaking to her patient. "Yes. To put it simply, you overused your magic."

Vanessa flashed her gaze up to the doctor, and her perplexed features mirrored her tone. "Overused my magic?"

The doctor smiled again and nodded while saying, "Yes." Vanessa still looked confused and so Savanna continued to explain. "Think of it like this: everyone that has magic, has a different amount. We can use items to amplify that natural ability in them. Talisman, amulets, dust, and other reagents. But it's only amplifying what is already there. However, it can dry up…" Savanna looked at her concerned for a moment.

It hit Vanessa and she sat up, reaching for and promptly clinging to the female doctor. "Do I have Medusa's Kiss?"

She shook her head no. "Not even a trace. But the reaction would have been very similar to the disease if you had used a drop more of your magic. You are very lucky to be alive."

"Oh, by the goddess," Vanessa whispered and flung herself back onto the thin pillows to try and stop her heart from hammering so crazily against her breast.

A tiny red face was hovering over hers as the imp craned its head from side to side. "Kiss?" It puckered up its lips and made kissing sounds as its wet lips slowly descended close to her own. Vanessa shielded the oncoming kiss as best she could, but her salvation came from a tiny whispered spell from Doctor Snow.

"Force push," she flicked her wrist, and the small spell flashed across the bed and slammed into the side of the imp's face, sending it flipping up into the air and then slapping against the floor with a grunt of pain. Sitting up from its landing spot, the imp shook its head and whirled for a moment before falling backward and lying still on the ground.

Straightening her jacket and pushing her bangs out of her view, she spoke to Vanessa like the incident never took place. "I need you to be more careful over the next few days. Let yourself heal up and rejuvenate. You are powerful, no one can ever say that you're not – at least, not under the Coven's roof – but you have your limits too… keep that in mind in the future, okay?"

Vanessa swallowed hard, and it felt like it was a mouthful of hot sand painfully burning down her throat. All of a sudden it felt like her mouth had become dryer than humanly possible. "Yes, I will," she managed to croak out right before her throat threatened to squeeze shut completely.

"I'll get you some water and your release forms and then I believe that you have some very concerned friends wanting to see you," Savanna stated softly as she patted the young witch's shoulder before departing to do as she informed.

As she stepped away, Vanessa turned her attention to the other end of the room where two imps were attempting to make their way for the main door. One was riding on the other's shoulders and yipping with glee as the other tried to stay upright and walk to the door. "Whoa. Whoa," the one on the bottom called out as its stride strayed dramatically from one side to the next. The rider just giggled loudly as they almost toppled over quite a few times. Eventually, together, the imps managed to finally stagger their way to the door. The giggling rider clamped both hands down onto the doorknob and turned it as the other stumbled backward to aid in pulling it open.

The first thing Vanessa saw on the other side of the door was Leon and how his eyes lit up when he saw her awake in the hospital bed. However, the poor Spellweaver was almost run over as Bobo pushed past him in his haste to get over to Vanessa, carelessly shoving the door open the rest of the way and causing the two imps still struggling with opening it to be smooshed behind the large, wooden object.

"Give it to me straight, Doctor, is there anything wrong with her?" Bobo looked utterly afraid of anything the doctor would say.

Laughing and handing the cup of water to the imp at her side to give to Vanessa, she answered while tapping the bar that made up the foot of her patience bed. "She's fine. Nothing different than before."

"I knew it. She's incurable. Vanessa, darling, she said you're just fine. Just like you used to be," he announced, yet sounded saddened by the news.

"That's a good thing, Bobo," Vanessa stated irately and took the cup of water from the imp.

"Clearly you've never had to deal with you on a daily basis. This is bad. You'll never be cured of your stubbornness," he threw his forearm over the front of his forehead and turned his face to the ceiling.

"You'll live, big guy." Leon pat the ogre's back a few times as he passed by to stand closer to Vanessa at the side of her bed. "Don't let that lug fool you. He was worried sick about you."

"I was worried rent wouldn't be paid if she were crippled by her own stupidity…" Bobo snipped back, dropping the dramatic act instantly.

"You were worried. Don't even try to fake it," Lyx's seductive voice rolled through the room as she sashayed in and winked at Vanessa. "Looking pretty good for almost dying on us, darling."

"Thanks," Vanessa replied nervously and sipped at her water. The crisp, cool contents soothing her sore throat and unbearably dry mouth. "I don't feel like it. But everyone says I almost did," she admitted.

"We can fix that." An imp leaped up to perch at the end of her bed but was instantly met with a clipboard to the face and fell off with a wail of dread before it was met with the glossy floors below.

Doctor Snow then held out the weapon … clipboard…to Vanessa. "Fill this out and you're free to go. I will want a thorough check-up with you in two weeks."

The witch nodded, took the clipboard, and started to read over the paperwork as Doctor Snow spoke with Lyx, Leon, and Bobo. "She's to take it easy. I am well aware of her troublesome behavior, so I'm letting you guys know to double down on her and make sure she gets plenty of rest."

The trio nodded just as they heard pills fall and scatter all over the floor across the room. They turned to see an imp jumping up and down while yelling at two others over the mess. Before they knew it, the three imps started to slap each other repeatedly while a fourth imp snuck over to the pile. "Caaandyyy…" it said in a mesmerized sing-song tone as it started to pick up the pills and shove them into his mouth.

"I have to go. Remember. Rest," Savanna ordered sternly, pointing firmly at Vanessa. She turned and rushed off to break up the fight between the imps and ran while yelling, "Charity, those are pills. Spit that out this instance! They are for patients, not you."

"There for *me!*" An imp bellowed and slapped the back of Chastity's head with a food tray it was carrying after serving another patient their afternoon meal.

"No, Temperance. They are for the patients!"

One of the imps leaped up into the air and yipped with joy, "Yay. It's for meeeee!"

"No, Patience! For the sick people, not you!" Doctor Snow corrected exasperated. "They are pills, not candy. No one is to eat them."

"Aw, man…" All the imps hung their heads and pouted after hearing their master's final word on the matter.

After finishing up the paperwork, Vanessa got dressed in her old outfit and met Bobo and the others outside the Coven hospital doors. They walked through the main halls on their way to the front desk in the main entrance of Coven headquarters. Leon had to pick up a case number and check on their filed reports. Ell had also asked if she could see Vanessa when she got out. Two birds, one stone, as Leon explained.

They poured into the main room from the dark hall. Any chatter or noise coming from within the lobby died down. Conversations dropped in tone, laughter swiftly ebbed, mummers slowly came to a halt until there was silence and every set of eyes seemed to watch Vanessa as they passed. Unusually so. "Uh… Leon?" she whispered.

"Yeah?"

"Why is everyone looking at me like I'm the hottest item on Merlin's menu?"

He stopped and turned to face her fully as he whispered back, "Because you just did something no witch has done that we know of, Vanessa. You performed, not one, but three big-time area spells as well as a tremendous amount of healing to multiple targets and brought back comrades that were on death's doorstep in a short amount of time with NO magical enhancers." He leaned in toward her even more for theatrical purposes and whispered to her even lower than before, "You're kind of a big deal."

That made her blush as she watched people gawk at her and start to murmur amongst themselves once more. This time, the whispers? She didn't mind them so much.

"That's her. That's the witch."

"She has to be super powerful."

"I heard she saved four of the High Priests all on her own."

"She's so lucky to be partnered with Leon. They are, like, the best team in the Coven now."

With a new perk in her step, they made it over to the service desk in record time, and Ell waved at her frantically as she saw them approach. "Vanessa! I'm... oh, my goddess... I'm so glad you are all right." The enthusiastic girl lunged over the counter space and hugged Vanessa around the waist.

Giggling, Vanessa patted Ell's head a few times and tried not to turn red as a cherry. "I'm fine. The doctor just wants me to take it easy."

Ell squeaked and released Vanessa thinking she might have hurt the Hunter with her quick embrace. She slid back down onto her feet. Hearing that Vanessa was fine made her smile. "It's just... so... so..."

"Amazing," Riker finished for Ell as he and a handful of Summoners approached. "You'll have to teach us how you did that one of these days, Hunter Peterson."

Vanessa turned her amazed expression to the scarred man and nodded, not sure how to respond right away. Casually, she leaned on the service desk as she melted into a cool and collected pose and pointed at Riker with her index finger. "You got it, buddy."

Riker grinned and chuckled. "I hear you need to rest up for now. Perhaps you can teach us another time. Take it easy, Vanessa." He nodded over his shoulder to his men and he and the others marched on toward the third floor saying something about the Dark Market buckling down on security and needing to check in on leads for new portal keepers once they were done checking up on the hellhounds in the containment area.

Bobo leaned on the desk next to Vanessa, cleared his throat into his massive balled-up fist, and turned to Vanessa to mumble, "You have no idea how you performed that magic, do you?"

She spoke through a fixed smile and ground her teeth at having to admit her lack of knowledge to the one creature that would never let her live it down, "Not. A. Clue."

Leon and Lyx overheard them and burst out into laughter while Ell rummaged through the paperwork Leon had requested. "So, they retrieved the hellhounds already?" Vanessa asked.

"Oh, darling, yes," Lyx started. "They have them locked away in Zaraltrac for now, and a team of researchers trying to figure out how to de-summon a demon."

"Good luck with that. No one's known how to do that since the last pack of hellhounds were de-summoned two hundred years ago," Leon scoffed.

Lyx inspected her nails and hummed, "Mhmmm. Not to mention tons of spells and information that was lost in the fires."

Bobo started to lift his finger, stopped in deep thought, and then raised the digit fully as he spoke to the group, "I found something mentioning a possible lead on that, actually..." Everyone turned to him and got ready to listen to his idea.

Just then, the main doors to the Coven flew open, letting in a blast of freezing air and soon to be melted snowflakes. They blurred the image of a Hunter racing inside the main entrance. A sloppily slung spell slammed the massive doors shut behind him, gaining more attention as the sound it produced echoed through the hollow space and side halls.

The Hunter was huffing and puffing while carrying a stack of manila folders and paper-clipped papers that was almost as tall as him. A few stray pieces of parchment became caught in the wind as he rushed right for Vanessa and the others at the main desk. The man clearly looked like he had been running for a while with the sheets of snow that fell off his ashen cape and slapped onto the floor with a thick, wet *plop*. The monumental stack of records most likely wasn't light either, and it showed on his reddened face and with his labored breathing.

The records were slammed onto the open space near Leon and everyone backed away as half of the pile toppled over into a wide-spread mess around them. Ell immediately started to gather the folders that had fallen over onto her side of the service desk. As the files were collected so they could restack them, the poor guy tried to stabilize his breathing. He didn't seem to care one bit about the mess he had just made or about trying to clean it up.

"Whoa there, buddy. You all right? That's a lot of files to carry all at once," Leon said.

"Honestly, you should pace yourself, lad. That's a good way to get your ticker to explode," Bobo stated while trying to help organize the untidiness.

Vanessa grabbed a folder after it fell on the floor in front of her. She held it out for the young Coven member to take. It was then she noticed that despite the man fighting to inhale at a steadier pace. She shook the folder to gain his attention, and he blenched as if he had not noticed her there. His worried expression made it seem like he had just received the worst news of his life. Her brow pinched in worry as she put the folder down onto the service desk.

"Hey, are you… all right?" she asked while giving his attire a quick once over to be sure he wasn't injured or singed from a harmful spell.

The man shook his head no and stabbed the pile of folders and papers with a single-digit plowing into the remaining mass. He was still wheezing loudly as he attempted to catch his breath, his face twisted in pain as he struggled to swallow between gulps of air.

"This…" he swallowed again and coughed before continuing, "This is all the demon sightings in Aeristria." He paused and slowly looked up to them and waited for all their attention to be fully on him and his wide-with-fear gaze. "In the past twenty-four hours."

To be continued…

Made in the USA
Coppell, TX
08 December 2020

43574807R00125